Peggy's house was across the street and down from mine, and when I saw one with the door open I figured that was it. I had two bottles of wine in my arms and a taut leash, thus not afforded the freedom to look up the address on my phone.

"Hellooo," I said, walking in. "I come bearing wine and a lovable beast."

I let Bardot loose and headed inside. It was awfully quiet. There were supposed to be something like six women in this club, but I couldn't hear any voices. The drapes were closed and I was so busy trying to catch up to Bardot at the dark end of the hall that I didn't see the telephone table until my waist hit it, forcing me to slump across the top. When I reached the end, Bardot was scratching at the back door. It was locked from the inside with a deadbolt. I should know, every apartment door in NYC has at least three of them.

Strange. Did they all come in through the driveway? Then why is the front door open?

I turned the key and Bardot bolted out. When my eyes adjusted from the dark to the sunlight, I saw that she was anxiously circling a woman laying facedown on the grass . . .

Full Bodied Murder

CHRISTINE E. BLUM

KENSINGTON PUBLISHING CORP.
www.kensingtonbooks.com

KENSINGTON BOOKS are published by

Kensington Publishing Corp.
119 West 40th Street
New York, NY 10018

All Kensington titles, imprints, and distributed lines are available at special quantity discounts for bulk purchases for sales promotion, premiums, fund-raising, educational, or institutional use. Special book excerpts or customized printings can also be created to fit specific needs. For details, write or phone the office of the Kensington Sales Manager: Kensington Publishing Corp., 119 West 40th Street, New York, NY 10018. Attn. Sales Department. Phone: 1-800-221-2647.

Kensington and the K logo Reg. U.S. Pat. & TM Off.

eISBN-13: 978-1-4967-1211-0
eISBN-10: 1-4967-1211-0
Kensington Electronic Edition: December 2017

ISBN-13: 978-1-4967-1210-3
ISBN-10: 1-4967-1210-2
First Kensington Mass Market Edition: December 2017

10 9 8 7 6 5 4 3 2 1

Printed in the United States of America

To Mom and Dad for believing unconditionally

Chapter 1

You're a long way from home, Dorothy.

I finally had time to think about what I had just done. As I passed the Santa Monica Airport, my car loaded down with the few belongings too precious to trust to any mover, I was overcome with a stomach sinking anxiety. Which was hilarious because I had pretty much landed in paradise. My nine-month-old yellow Lab, Bardot, (think Brigitte), was taking it all in with unchecked wonderment. I was taking deep breaths and trying not to dry heave.

New lives don't happen overnight. I needed to give myself some slack. Heck, I'd already bought the house on Rose Avenue. So it was clear across the country. No biggie.

The neighborhood I'd moved to was just south of the Santa Monica Airport. It is located about two miles from the Pacific Ocean in Southern California and has a rich history.

It was originally called "Clover Field," named

after Greayer "Grubby" Clover, a First World War aviator.

"Greayer" or "Grubby"? It's an embarrassment of riches.

The airport blossomed in 1926, when it became the home of the Douglas Aircraft Company, known for developing the air travel innovation the DC-3. In its heyday the company employed some forty-four thousand people, and to keep them productive, built housing on the undeveloped grasslands of the airport's perimeter. Today, the airport hosts hangars for small planes, a dog park, sports fields and, much to the locals' chagrin, private jets owned by celebrities and business CEOs who would otherwise be taking off over the hill in the dreaded Valley.

Just south of the airport sits Rose Avenue. This suburban cocoon, with its homey California bungalows built up as the original owners made way for a younger, more affluent clientele, was now my new permanent address. Rose Avenue begins at the top of a hill and rolls down as it makes its way to the ocean. The closer you are to the top, the more of a sea breeze you'll enjoy. Mine was one of the lucky "upper berth" houses. I was promised that I would never be too hot living there, and rarely too cold.

My alter ego "Dorothy's" real name is Annie Elizabeth Hall. I am the only child of lovely parents who innocently gave me a perfectly fine name, unaware that Woody Allen had already claimed it as his own. Luckily people had started nicknaming me Halsey early on, so apart from events like jury duty, I am saved the bad Diane Keaton impressions.

I think of myself as average. I'm five foot eight, not fat, not thin, have brown hair that I highlight when I have the time and funds, and a pleasant but unremarkable face. I'd be hard to pick out of a police lineup except for one feature. I have Kelly green eyes. And they tend to turn to sea foam from the salt when I cry. Believe me, I know.

There had been too many tears recently, and I was done with that. At thirty-six I was starting over. And the wounds were fresh, so I'll quickly summarize. I left behind a failed marriage in New York City to a self-absorbed, meagerly talented writer whose most seductively crafted line to me was, "I love you like shit."

I've been told that I am "smarter than the average bear," and I am certainly no pushover. How could I have forgotten this the minute I saw his tight jeans and dimpled smile? I missed every sign, distracted with creating the perfect romantic life in my mind rather than in real life. Maybe it was because of my lack of training being an only child and all. Or, maybe I just don't play well with others. Or probably, he was a better liar than I'd realized when we first met.

The day he came home from work and passed up playing with a soft, wiggly puppy whose head was stuck in a shoe and stifled the aromas of my coq au vin with his fetid bong, I knew I was done.

Equally so, I had had my fill of my business partner of the last three years. Starting a software apps company after the bubble was a Sisyphean enough task without having to play "mommy" to the person who was supposed to be sharing the burden. Questions like, "Can we get paid today?" or "Is it okay if I go home?" were not going to contribute to building the next high tech empire. Since I could technically work from anywhere, I took my toys, my puppy, and my intellectual property and followed the sun to the left coast.

I pulled into the driveway and took a deep breath. The smell of jasmine and freshly mowed grass had a calming effect.

Was it too early for a glass of wine? A nice, crisp Sancerre?

Before I hopped out, I shut the engine and sat and stared at my home. Who would have guessed that I'd be moving to a quiet, Chinese elm-lined street, and living in a dream California Craftsman? It was so suburban. It made me think of running barefoot, listening to the "sssssssh-chk-chk-chk" of the sprinklers, and waiting on a tire swing for the ice cream truck. I looked down at my navy Talbot's shift dress and matching striped espadrilles and felt like the one chocolate in the box that nobody wants to eat. I couldn't wait to change, this time I was going to fit in, damn it.

Next door, of course, Marisol was outside and pretending not to prowl. I'd been warned about her when I'd come out to finalize the purchase. At the time I wondered why Vincent, the previous owner, had listed Marisol in the disclosures statement of the property sale. Typically, my realtor explained, a seller steers clear of disclosures, unless forced to by extreme conditions such as when a murder had occurred in the house, it sat upon sacred Indian burial grounds, or there was a clear image of the Virgin Mary in the wallpaper and the Vatican had been called. Vincent was a bit of a character, so I chalked this up to some real estate tomfoolery.

To look at her she seemed harmless enough, watering her lawn in a denim housedress while eyeing the neighborhood. She kept her head down pretending not to notice me. Thin and a bit frail, she had chin length hair that she kept out of the way with small combs. It was blue black but betrayed by a band of gray at the crown.

Time for Clairol #124, Marisol.

I pictured her standing at the sink, an old towel around her shoulders, applying a wand of purple touch up goo to her roots. All the while using the vanity mirror to check on the backyard next door.

My car was bouncing like a monster truck because Bardot was impatient and excited to get out and start exploring. The two of us stepped onto the front lawn and were suddenly face-to-face with Marisol.

How did she make her way over here so fast?

"My name is Mrs. Marisol Ysabel Rosario Priscila Cordoba," she announced without extending her hand. "I hope there is not going to be any trouble like the last people," she added, laying down the residential gauntlet.

Does she know I own this house now?

Bardot cocked her head at Marisol and then stuck her nose up the woman's housedress. Today's exploring had begun. I'd have to ask Bardot later what she'd learned.

I was about to apologize and reply when I realized that Marisol was gone.

How does she do that?

A flash of light hit my face as her metal-screened outer door opened and closed, blinding me for a minute. I made a mental note to recheck my disclosure statements.

I glanced past her property to the next fenced-in yard. A man I hadn't seen before was dressed all in black and sat crouched atop an equally black motorcycle. His tall, sinewy frame formed a perfect "s" shape with the bike. The sleek, mirrored helmet revealed nothing of his face, but I could tell that he was staring at me.

Darth Vader called and he wants his suit back. "Attitude, Halsey," I heard my mother admonish in my head.

I felt a chill in spite of the seventy-five-degree weather. With barely a move he started his bike and it gave off a thunderous roar. I jumped and gasped with surprise. Without looking anywhere but at me, he drove off down Rose Avenue.

All at once Bardot and I were alone, standing on our new front lawn, far away from home and, seemingly, civilization as we knew it.

Was all of this a mistake? I wasn't expecting the Emerald City, but a little bit of a yellow brick road would've been nice.

Then Bardot proudly squatted in front of the entire street and laid claim to our new home. As we headed in, I saw a slat shift slightly from the blinds in one of Marisol's side windows. I stopped myself from picking up Bardot's deposit, something I would never do, and grinned in Marisol's direction as we walked into my house.

A little civil disobedience was always good for the soul.

Chapter 2

The modest house I had first seen on the Internet, I later discovered looked pretty much like its photos. The best two features were:

1. It had a completely separate guesthouse for my office and, because it was a corner lot, you could enter from the side street, thereby affording me a separation of work and life.
2. There was a beautiful swimming pool in the backyard.

The closest that I had ever come to that kind of luxury before was if during a blisteringly hot day in the City someone had popped a fire hydrant. I was hoping that once Bardot got used to it, the pool would become her aquatic doggie day care while I worked.

The neighborhood was about as different from my last one as Randy is from Dennis Quaid. I had left a third-floor walk-up in the Village where you could hear parties, fights, and lovemaking all night long for a life in suburbia with neat lawns and the nightly aroma of outdoor grilling. I had hoped that I would spot a pink flamingo or garden gnome so that I could join in the fun, but alas, saw none. People do not appreciate kitsch enough.

A few minutes after I entered the house, I changed and mentally tried to cleanse from Marisol's less than heartfelt welcome and the mystery man-in-black. My iPhone reminded me that I had an important appointment at four today, my introduction to the Rose Avenue Wine Club.

On my last trip out here, I'd been advised by my realtor to get a feel for the neighborhood before sealing the deal. I suspect that the fact that I was from New York City, dressed all in black like a mime, and held my purse tightly over my stomach, may have had him wondering if something on Melrose might be more to my liking.

I took a walk and about halfway down Rose Avenue encountered a striking, statuesque African American woman trimming her roses.

"Hi, I'm Sally," she proclaimed with a smile.

"I'm Halsey and I think I'm about to become your neighbor."

"Welcome to Rose Avenue, although you said 'I think,' having second thoughts?"

I shook my head although I was. When I lived in the City everything and everybody annoyed me at one time or another, but I learned to brush it off because we were all dealing with the same issues. But here, a nosy, mean neighbor and a creepy guy aren't as easily forgotten. Kind of like if you go snorkeling along a reef and see so many tropical fish that you don't really remember any in particular, but if you come across a rock with just two fish they'll more likely leave an imprint in your mind.

If you saw Sally, the first word you would think of is "patrician." She is a tall, lean, golden brown woman in her early sixties, with angular features and elegant long fingers that look like they should be holding a paintbrush in front of an easel overlooking a scenic panorama. She's let her hair go white and that serves to add a halo around her long neck and jaw line. Her lovely oval face and broad smile exude a warm and nurturing aura.

"SLOW DOWN YOU SHITBALL DINGLEBERRY!" Sally screamed at a speeding motorist. "They all think they can race through Rose," she explained to me, regaining her composure.

Pretty sure "shitball dingleberry" is redundant. . . .

Sally is patrician, but with balls, one of my favorite combinations.

"Will you be available Wednesdays about four o'clock? Some of the girls on the block like to get together, we rotate houses."

"Oh, gee, I work during the—"

"We usually open a couple bottles of wine," she continued.

"Then I'll make sure that I move in on a Wednesday," I said without skipping a beat.

I was told that we were meeting at Peggy's house today so Bardot and I headed out. The months of clicker training (you look like such a fool doing that) had vanished like the results of Oprah's diets, and my once heeling dog was trying to pull me down the block.

I should explain a little about Bardot. She is not the big, boxy kind of Lab who, for even a scintilla of a treat, will lie contented while the kids dress her up and try to get milk from each of her eight nipples. Bardot is an American Field Lab; they tend to be smaller, much leaner, and built with a Ferrari engine. She is hardwired to run through caustically thorny brambles and crash into pond ice to retrieve whatever form of fowl you have shot out of the sky.

It was a treat to be able to walk down the street at our own pace and smell the flowers instead of the urine of New York City sidewalks. The blue sky glistened from the sun, but that sea breeze kept the air pleasantly cool. The sounds of all kinds of birds punctuated the air in a symphony. This was sweet music, and absent was the grunting and throaty coo of the Manhattan pigeons (rats with wings) that I'd hated on sight.

Gardeners at the house across the street were working on trimming a giant palm tree. The oldest and smallest man was perched close to the peak, held up by one strap looped around the trunk and his waist. He maneuvered using what looked like two planks of wood tied to the bottom of his boots, each had nails sticking out of them.

Next time I'm home I will snag Dad's old golf shoes and sell them at freeway exits. . . .

He was wielding a large chainsaw, and I was torn

between going back in for a lawn chair to watch the disaster unfold or moving on to spare me the task of having to interview new therapists right away. I opted for the latter.

We passed Marisol's house quickly; I was done with her for the time being. I noticed something in my peripheral vision, looked back and saw that she had dropped bread for the birds on her lawn.

So somewhere in that Clairol-infused body there was a heart?

Not so much. The bread was all scattered close to the opposite side of her yard, next to the motorcycle man's driveway. I had learned from Vincent on my last visit that he was Italian, and did something with cars, but that's about it. Walking Bardot gave me the perfect foil for spying on the guy, and she complied by going in for an extended sniff. There was a slipshod faux redwood fence around the outer perimeter, surrounding what was otherwise a very nice place with a highly manicured yard. The bike was gone and there was no sign of life coming from inside the house. In the driveway were two luxury model cars and several others were parked at the curb. I was starting to suspect that this was Marisol's way of showing her discontent when I saw the bird crap splayed all over a new, plateless Mercedes. I wondered what he had done to deserve her wrath, and if I was in for similar treatment. A whirring sound distracted me and I looked up in the direction of the source. I no-

ticed that a surveillance camera tucked into the
eave of the roof was pointed directly at me. Bardot
pulled me toward the base of a tree in front of his
yard and the camera followed us. In fact, so did
the cameras that were mounted all around the
roof of the house. I had checked the crime reports
before buying my house, and this was a really safe
area.

So what's with the intense security? I assumed
that the images they recorded were being posted
somewhere for remote access. Was he maneuver-
ing the cameras or were they doing this automatically? In either case, ew.

I quickly moved on, feeling his stare once again,
even through cyberspace. Deep inside of me a
barely healed wound was giving way. Scrutiny was
creeping in, and I was feeling like I was being controlled. I'd been at the intersection of "Aiming to
Please" and "Losing my Identity" too many times
with my ex-husband. In the end nothing I did was
right to him and everything I did felt wrong and
detached to me. I decided to ignore the cameras
and the intrusion but do some further investigating on the neighborhood later for safety's sake.

Continuing on our walk, the view changed to
something out of a bucolic Disney movie. A neighbor waved while picking grapefruit from a front
yard tree, another loaded the kids into the family van
and gave me a welcome smile. At a third doorstep I
saw that someone had left a basket of garden fresh-
looking squash and tomatoes on the threshold. Now
this was more like it. Bardot was sniffing every-

thing in sight and peeing like a camel that had just returned from the desert. She was in snout heaven.

Peggy's house was across the street and down from mine, and when I saw one with the door open I figured that was it. I had two bottles of wine in my arms and a taut leash, thus not afforded the freedom to look up the address on my phone.

"Hellooo," I said, walking in. "I come bearing wine and a lovable beast."

I let Bardot loose and headed inside. It was awfully quiet, there were supposed to be something like six winos, I mean women in this club, but I couldn't hear any voices. The drapes were closed and I was so busy trying to catch up to Bardot at the dark end of the hall that I didn't see the telephone table until my waist hit it, forcing me to slump across the top. When I reached the end, Bardot was scratching at the back door. It was locked from the inside with a deadbolt. I should know, every apartment door in NYC has at least three of them.

Strange. Did they all come in through the driveway? Then why is the front door open?

I turned the key and Bardot bolted out. When my eyes adjusted from the dark to the sunlight, I saw that she was anxiously circling a woman laying face-down on the grass. A large, professional-looking chef's knife had been plunged into her back.

Bardot let out a cry that I'd never heard before and I did a quick scan to make sure that we were alone in the yard. I ran to the woman to see how I could help. Of all the crazy things that I'd witnessed in New York City, I'd never seen this and I dropped to my knees in panic. My mind became a bowl of cotton balls and I couldn't focus on what I should be doing. I looked at the knife and wondered if I should pull it, there was very little blood around the wound, maybe it was just superficial. Bardot stood over me and kept scanning the yard, ready for any intruder. It was starting to get dark and I would need to rely on her nose and ears.

I decided that I should first check and see if she was breathing. I knelt down by her face, thinking that if I put my head down I would be able to hear her take a breath. But by just touching her cold cheek I could tell that she was dead.

It was time to call 9-1-1.

When I stood I felt something sticky on my hands and looked at them and then down to the body. That was when I registered the viscous, dark spreading circle. She had bled out through her nose and mouth.

Definitely not in Kansas anymore. . . .

Chapter 3

I must have gotten an hour's sleep last night, if I was lucky. Just one day into my new life, it had been gruesomely tainted, and I didn't know how I was going to rebound. Even Bardot was a little less exuberant this morning.

I'd withstood three hours of questioning on site after the police arrived, and lost count of how many officers had asked me to "start at the beginning." They sat me on a wooden chair in the middle of the front room so as not to contaminate any part of the crime scene. They told me that her name had been Rosa. I kept fighting with the mental image of the dead woman's sweet family photos and mementos on the living room mantel versus her knifed body lying crumpled out back.

Each time I retold the story, a group of officers would gather and watch me with blank expressions. It was clear that no one was on my side. Except maybe this one guy they called Augie. I noticed him carrying a bowl with water from the kitchen to his squad car where they had sequestered Bardot. I guess they figured that without opposable thumbs she really couldn't wield a knife. Silly them, I'd seen her do the unimaginable with those paws.

When they were satisfied that everyone had gotten their turn at trying to break me, I was taken to the station to be fingerprinted.

They paraded me in front of the entire neighborhood into a police car, and I clearly felt the prying eyes of a group of ladies with travel cups. Not only had I undershot the Wine Club by two houses, but I would probably be the shortest-term member they'd ever had.

How can they see me as a suspect? I've just moved here damn it!

As I sat sipping my morning tea that was doing little to revive me, I heard the hum of a car's engine stopping outside. It sounded like a van, but the movers had deposited their last box days ago. I looked out the window and saw what was indeed the largest Suburban truck they must make. Out stepped a beefy man about six foot four, with a shaved head and nicely trimmed beard.

This guy likes his razor.

I watched with fascination as he opened the passenger side door and the largest black terrier-like dog I had ever seen hopped out and immediately sat, looking intently at his master for further instructions. Bardot, seeing this, started vertically scaling my picture window like a tree frog.

It took me a moment to make the connection

that I had been at Whole Foods to get some staples and had seen cards tacked on the community bulletin board advertising "The Well-Behaved Dog." Well, Mother had always put manners next to godliness, so I grabbed one. What I was really looking for was someone to help me teach Bardot to swim and be safe in the pool.

"Hi, I'm Jack," said this amber-eyed redwood. "And this is my giant Schnauzer, Clarence."

The dog-statue sat rock still at my doorstep.

"Um, hi." I was not ready for this.

"If you don't mind, I want to leave the truck running; I have dogs in the back and they'll need the air-conditioning. I understand you have a pup who needs a little guidance?"

Bardot jumped off the window and peed.

I was about to suggest that we reschedule but then thought, if I explain that "discovering a dead body really puts a damper on my week," I may send him away for good. Plus, the distraction might be just what I needed.

Jack stripped down to his swim trunks and was now in my pool. Clarence sat sphinx-like on the lawn. I explained to Jack that I had worked hard with Bardot on basic obedience, which needed explaining since she had clearly suffered amnesia while driving cross-country. He suggested a refresher course, but thought I was right for safety's sake, to start with the pool.

"She's a Lab, so a natural swimmer, but she needs to learn where the steps are, and to not freak out the first few times she gets in water. Bardot, do you want to go swimming?" he asked in a higher tone that must be his "dog" voice.

On cue, Bardot took a running leap, jumped on and skidded off Jack's bald head, and belly flopped into the water. She popped up like a cork and propelled herself in circles, making jerky waves like a whisk in a bowl of scrambled eggs. Jack and I kept yelling and pointing to the steps, instructions she heard, but completely ignored. When she was finally ready to get out, she put her front paws on the side and kicked with her little back legs until she could shimmy out. She then did the customary shake, giving Clarence, who was still sitting rock still, a cool shower. His expression didn't change but something in his eyes said that he was intrigued.

Satisfied that my dog was not going to drown anytime soon, Jack and I had a chance to talk; I sat in my shorts, dangling my legs in the pool and trying to remember if I'd shaved that morning. He stood bare-chested and waist deep in the water, displaying an impressive six-pack that I didn't think he got from housetraining a Pomeranian. And for a guy who spent his days speaking in one-syllable words to a variety of canines, he was astonishingly interesting and well spoken. And cute.

Oh well.

It was a hot day, and I wished I'd had the nerve to change into a suit and share the cool water with my first California friend.

"No, Halsey," I admonished myself.

My mind slipped back to Rosa for a moment and I felt a bit ashamed that I was having such a good time just one day later.

After an awkward silence when I was sure he was trying to figure out what I was thinking, he's an animal behaviorist after all, he asked, "Mind if I do some laps? I have training sessions up until about ten tonight and could use a little stretch."

"Sure," I said.

"Catch my watch, it's too heavy to swim with," he said, and took off this monstrosity and tossed it to me.

I was still staring at his nice abs and missed it completely. It sank down into the deep end of the pool and I turned redder than a German tourist after her first day at the beach.

SPLASH! I saw a flash of yellow and realized that Bardot had dived in for it. I screamed and told Jack to go down after her. At the same time, I was pulling off my top, ready to dive in to help. Jack disappeared underwater, and for a terrifying moment I could see nothing but flat water.

Then Bardot emerged, the watch in her mouth, and shimmied out. She took her find to a corner of the lawn for disembowelment. Jack emerged next, took a breath and quick look at me in my bra, and went back under. I didn't have the heart to give him the good news/bad news about Bardot and his watch until about the fourth time up.

I walked Jack to his truck/ground zeppelin, and despite my repeated offers, he refused to let me pay for his watch. Bardot had indeed adopted the ways of her new laid-back home, and no longer had any use for time. When we were finally able to coax the watch out of her mouth with handfuls of treats, it looked more like something Salvador Dalí would wear.

If I had been hoping to slip into Rose Avenue inconspicuously, then standing at the curb, talking to a giant man and his giant dog next to his giant truck was probably not the best approach. But I guess that ship had already sailed. No one was going to forget that I'd discovered a murder any-time soon.

I tried to give Jack my undivided attention as he talked, but from behind my dark sunglasses, I was stealing glances at the neighbors and cars passing by. A few times I heard the light "tap-tap" of a car horn as someone waved "hello" to someone else. Not once did I hear, "Outta my way, I'm driving here!" Ah, tranquility. I tuned back to Jack. That was also when I spied a police car parked up at the corner but in direct view of my house. My stomach sank.

"You've got quite a talented dog there, I know you don't think so now but you do. Clarence and I are a certified dog search and rescue team with CARA, Canine Rescue Association. We're on call 24/7, and so far we have assisted in eight success-ful rescues, people in all kinds of bad situations. I'm not suggesting you go out for this, but Bardot does have special skills."

I looked at him with the expression of dyed-in-the-wool skeptic. Eyelids at half-mast, head tilted to one side.

"Regardless," he ignored me and continued, "with a little bit of structure, she'll be great, and you will have a lot of fun with her."

When he loaded Clarence into the truck, I noticed a ragged piece of paper stuck under his windshield wiper.

"Is this some funky kind of California traffic ticket?" I asked, trying to sound casual, while a bit suspect and nervous.

The questioning look on his face told me not. He grabbed it and read out loud:

> People live here, and they need peace and
> quiet, this thing does not belong here. We
> had problems before and don't want them
> again.

A quick flash of light hit my face as I turned to look at the houses on my side of the street. This was the second time that had happened to me in as many days.

"I wonder who wrote this," he said, actually looking hurt. "I want to apologize and explain. Maybe I should start knocking on doors until I find the person."

I had a good inkling of who the windshield wiper menace was, and I could just picture Marisol, if she even opened her door, sneering at this bald hulk and making him cry.

"No, no, I am so sorry," I said. "Let me check

this out and make amends, I'm sure this is just a misunderstanding."

And I was going to make *Miss* understand. Jack really didn't want to leave without making his own atonement to the neighbors, but I insisted. This was only my first week living on Rose Avenue and I'd already discovered a dead body, was probably a suspect, and had a neighbor who was poised to cite me with whichever malfeasance she deemed was a break in the code.

As Bardot and I walked back to my house, I glanced over at Marisol's neat bungalow. All was still but I knew that she was watching. Maybe I should have questioned the seller Vincent more about her as she was starting to give me the creeps. I was pretty sure that she was the author of that harsh note, but then again I didn't know Jack, or anyone on this street at all.

I needed a glass of wine and a plan for how to protect myself from the Matron of Rose Avenue and the cops. I wonder what pairs best with finding a murderer?

A nice Chianti, perhaps?

Chapter 4

I was surprised, no make that shocked, when I was invited to an emergency Wine Club that afternoon. I figured that I had immediately become "ING," imbiber non grata, what with discovering the first murder on Rose Avenue and all.

I knew very little about the poor victim. Her name had been Rosa Sobel and she had lived here since childhood. There had been a battle between Rosa and her brother Ray for ownership of the house after her parents passed, but she prevailed. She had been married and divorced and was struggling to make ends meet on her own. All of which would more likely lead to a suicide than a murder.

When I walked in, this time at the correct house, the voices of jocularity went silent for a moment until Sally said, "The cops let you go on good behavior? I bet you could use a glass of wine. Come meet the girls."

We were again convening at Peggy's house. Peggy

looks like everybody's favorite Grandma. White-haired and fleeced, the eighty-seven-year-old who putters around her pristinely clean house with rosy cheeks and a loving nature. If I hadn't seen the two cases at the curb brimming with empty wine bottles, I would have thought she spent her days baking cookies and knitting booties for her grand-babies. I soon discovered that she liked to "taste wines." She had white wooden shutters on her win-dows, which I noticed were strategically positioned so that she could see out, but we couldn't see in. The house smelled of freshly baked banana bread and I decided right then that if I ever needed to borrow a cup of sugar, I would hit up Peggy.

Sally had told me that the night Peggy became a widow, some twelve years ago, she and her hus-band were throwing a dinner party. Thankfully, he slumped over peacefully at the table and went to heaven. Everyone stayed while the coroner came and after, slowly started to leave.

"Where's everyone going?" Peggy asked. "Vern would never want to break up a party!"

They drank until dawn telling story after story about him. A flag flies at Peggy's house every day and comes inside at dusk, homage to Vern's Air Force career.

I remember at the time thinking that Peggy must have a strong constitution for death, especially after losing a loved one so suddenly in front of her. Me? Not so much.

Peggy has four kids and ten grandkids, if the

framed collage of photos on her wall is accurate and up-to-date. (I learned later that two more had joined the clan.) She still lives in the house she got married in on Rose Avenue.

"You're late," she yelled out the window to the gardeners who had just pulled up. "And don't use that damn blower, we're havin' an important meeting!"

That split second, I stopped being concerned about Peggy living alone. She was a tough, take charge granny. I wasn't sure what she meant by "damn blower," but I promised to familiarize myself with all things in the landscaping trade later.

She pulled her head back in and placed a dish of Jordon almonds on the coffee table next to me. I hadn't seen those since my college roommate's baby shower, which for me, had been the high point of the day. There was deliberateness to Peggy's movements that surprised me for someone her age.

"I guess I'll leave the bottles out for our recycle bin poacher, Inez, now that Rosa's gone. They are starting to pile up out there and I don't want folks to get the wrong idea," she said, leaving me wondering how many meanings there could be for lots of empty wine bottles left at the curb.

With the mention of Rosa's name everybody got silent and I started thinking that I should leave. Even if they believed I had nothing to do with her death, I had poisoned the street by discovering it.

"I think maybe this was too soon, I'd better go," I said, heading for the door.

"You'll do no such thing, my dear, we all need to stick together, don't we girls?" Peggy took head-nodding roll call and didn't continue talking until she was satisfied that everyone was on the same page.

"Good, now let's not have anything spoil Halsey's first Wine Club."

I felt a little better; I could curl up in that fleece-covered bosom and feel very safe. But I'll admit, not knowing her, I was a bit leery of how quickly Peggy had gotten over the brutal violence that had occurred just a few doors from her. Maybe that was just Peggy, or maybe she had a reason for wanting to change the subject.

Sally, who was a retired nurse, gave me a soothing pat on the back and then introduced me to Cassie, "sassy Cassie," she whispered. Cassie looked about my age, seemed to be a fun dresser, today sporting over the knee riding boots, black leggings, and a belted white blouse open one more button than most would. I guessed that she was a fashion experimenter. Sally had told me that Cassie is Carl's new, younger wife, a good catch as he is the owner of a handful of hardware stores that affords them a really nice, if nouveau riche life: a house in the mountains, a boat in the Marina, and cars that get upgraded every year.

"I brought bacon-wrapped dates stuffed with Marcona almonds and Saga Bleu," she happily said, proud of her French pronunciation of "bleu." "Have one, or two, hell eat a bunch, you probably need it after the mu-, er everything, they're yummy," she said, thrusting the tray at me. I thought that I detected a hint of "Valley Girl" in her slightly loud voice, but my only source was Moon Unit Zappa and that was a long time ago.

Cassie looked at me with a glint in her eye, and her dimpled smile told me that she loves feeding people and making them happy. And she didn't mind being noticed for doing so. Attention was her drug of choice.

With bacon-ensconced date in hand, I next met Aimee. Dressed in a pink Polo shirt with the words "Chill Out" embroidered on it, Aimee was around thirty and had cherubic cheeks that changed color like a mood ring. Sally had briefed me on her beforehand too. Unlike Cassie's French-manicured nails, Aimee's red knuckles and short nails gave away her daily food service labors at the frozen yogurt shop she owned in a nearby strip mall. She worked increasingly longer hours recently, as she was also helping her boyfriend Tom through medical school. Tom had put his career on hold when his mom was diagnosed with pancreatic cancer, getting on-the-job training tending to her while picking up odd mechanic gigs to get by. Now that she had succumbed, he was even more resolute to get back to his calling.

With all the tough living going on around her, Aimee still had the wide-eyed innocence of a child, and a knack for asking the questions everybody else wanted to, but didn't.

"You must be in shock after seeing Rosa with a knife in her back, and all that blood, did the cops have any ideas on who did this horrible thing?" she asked in a voice that was high enough to be that of a ten-year-old girl's. In a strange contrast she gave me a motherly kind of hug.

I heard some gasps in the room, a reaction to

Aimee's outright bodacious question, although I also noticed that the group had circled the wagons closer around me and the Jordan almonds.

"Aimee, this isn't the right time," Cassie said, surveying the group. "Is it?"

"As Peggy said, let's get back to wine and unfettered high jinx," Sally declared.

Sally sure has an interesting lexicon.

"No, it's fine, I've certainly told the story enough times to the cops." I settled down into a soft club chair and began.

"The front door of Rosa's house was half open, so believing that I was at Peggy's, I figured that it was okay if I just walked in."

"Sounds logical to me," Cassie said. The others looked at me with serious faces, which didn't inspire confidence in me.

"Go on," Peggy urged, the most serious of all of them.

"It was dark inside, all the shades were drawn, I let Bardot loose and heard her bounding to the back of the house. I figured that you all were in the backyard, so I chased after her to make sure that she didn't bolt out of the house and jump on all of you.

"I remember running into a narrow table and there were some letters under an opener and I was just about to read the address when I heard Bardot give off a pained whimper. So I quickly raced to her."

"So you touched things?" Peggy asked.

I nodded and swallowed. I was getting clammy and scared all over again.

"If only I'd taken another second and seen Rosa's name on the envelopes. I would have turned tail and gotten out of there, and not be in this mess."

"That would have been worse, the cops would still have found out that you'd been in the house, it would look really bad for you, honey," Peggy informed me.

I visibly recoiled and gasped.

"And Rosa might still be lying there facedown with a knife in her back. You did a good thing finding her, Halsey," Sally soothed.

"Are the cops satisfied with your recount of events, are they done with you now, Halsey?" Peggy asked.

I could see her wheels turning and I couldn't tell if she was with me or against me.

"I don't think so, they haven't said much but there's a patrol car watching my house 24/7," I said. "God, how could they think that I did it?"

"Of course you didn't, honey, they'll come to their senses," Peggy replied, not just to me but also to the room. They all took a cue from her and nodded.

Aimee decided to try and lighten the mood.

"So, is your husband or boyfriend joining you?"

The other ladies mimed shock but sidled even closer again to me so as not to miss a word of my response. This apparently was the real good stuff to them.

"I pack light so I divorced the husband before I moved," I flippantly explained. "And I haven't had time to get a boyfriend yet." I saw Cassie's whispering men's names to Sally and I quickly admired a decoupage Jesus Peggy had on her wall to divert attention.

No such luck. Now that this was out in the open, they barraged me with questions. Cassie was fixing me up with her brother, cousin, manager at the hardware store, etc.

"What happened, sweetie," Peggy said proffering the dish of Jordan almonds to me.

"I think I need a glass of wine if I'm to tell the whole sad tale." I sighed. To which at least three of the girls opened bottles.

I was told that a couple of Peggy's girls live in the Pacific Northwest and she has become partial to Oregon wines. I can't remember ever trying one. She had decanted a peachy Viognier with a complex aroma. In other words, delicious. I could have stuck with that the entire time, but those bottles were soon drained and we were on to a fresh, spicy Pinot Noir.

It seemed that before I'd moved in, Sally had told them about my computer skills, and they had elected me archivist of the wines we tasted at each club. I'd decided to handle this with a photo album of wine labels taken with my iPhone.

These girls knew their wines. With me, up until recently I either liked the wine or I drank it quickly.

We spent the next three hours sharing, commiserating, laughing, showing off, and even bickering a bit. I was too new to the group to understand the "oil and water" dynamics yet.

With the clunk of the fourth wine bottle into the trash, I had enough liquid courage to ask, "Uh, who was Rosa, and was she also part of this wonderful group?"

"In a way, honey," Peggy answered. "See, here we separate our trash into three bins: waste, grass and plants, and recyclables. The bottles we throw away are worth five cents a pop, it is charged at point of purchase and is a way for the city to make some money and encourage recycling."

"It is also a great way for needy people to put food on the table. They get to the bins first, collect the bottles, and exchange them for cash at a recycle center," Aimee said.

"Like Inez," Cassie added. "She's a hard worker, I see her sometimes go up and down Rose several times in a night. And she's good for information, she's how I knew that the Bergers were getting a divorce."

I was having trouble keeping all this straight in my mind.

"Rosa was a sweet woman who unfortunately was hit with some tough breaks," Sally said to me while trying to diffuse the situation.

"She had lousy luck with men, one was her brother, a junkie and overall stinker, and the husband she stupidly chose, who was a friend of her brother's. What is it they say about 'fruit from the poisonous tree'?" Peggy harumphed. "Don't get me wrong, Rosa was a lovely woman, so giving. I tried many times to convince her to stop giving her brother money, for Ray's own good. And, I'll admit it, I was tired of seeing all the riffraff on our street."

"PEGGY," they all shouted.

"Anyway, we got together and decided that Rosa would be our charity." Aimee proudly beamed.

"What Aimee means is that we all separated our recyclables and gave them to Rosa before anyone else could get them, not that we have anything against Inez," Sally explained and the others smiled at me.

I'm starting to think that you could retire after a deal like that from this group.

"So why . . ." I trailed off, utterly confused and saddened.

"That's the big mystery," Cassie said and the others nodded. "If it were up to me, I'd point the spotlight on the shitty men in her life. Poor honey."

"And Rosa had those two cute little, tiny dogs, what is going to happen to them?" Aimee added wide-eyed, and a bit teary.

"I didn't see any dogs when I was there," I said, looking around the room.

"Got to go make dinner for Carl," Cassie abruptly announced, popping up out of her chair like a Whack-A-Mole contestant. She lifted up her white blouse and gave her leggings a tug, which I couldn't help thinking was also an excuse to show off her impressively flat tummy. She was quickly out the door.

I wondered if "dogs" was some kind of safe word. It seemed to me that Cassie would be one of the last to leave an audience, um party.

The rest of the group got up and quickly dispersed as well. I guess it was dinnertime and they all had responsibilities. I for once didn't, so why was I feeling like the circus had just left town. A Jordan almond or two might make me feel better. . . .

"How about we two single gals have one more drink?" Peggy asked, bringing the elusive banana bread out from the kitchen.

She was back in grandmother mode and my mouth started watering at the aroma. But then I remembered her husband's last meal, cooked by Peggy, and I asked if I could take a slice home instead. Just in case.

So began my initiation into The Rose Avenue Wine Club. I staggered home proudly clutching an engraved tiny silver flask, my new member gift.

Chapter 5

The next morning I stepped out, a little bleary-eyed from Wine Club, to get the paper and heard yelling coming from Marisol's direction. *Now what?*

I hopped off my stoop to investigate, not really thinking that my ex-husband's boxers and a wifebeater, albeit a pink one, might not be appropriate Rose Avenue attire. Marisol was yelling, more like a high cackle, at two people in the driveway of the house with all the surveillance cameras. There was that guy again, he was way over six feet, lean, and dressed in tight tailored pants, a pleated shirt also tight, and pointed brown leather shoes. I could finally see part of his face, and while on paper you might say that he was handsome, there was also something disturbing about his looks that I couldn't pinpoint.

He wasn't saying much, but his girlfriend was giving Marisol the business punctuated with a heavy Eastern European accent. My guess is that someone had been caught spreading breadcrumbs too close to the Lamborghini. I didn't want to draw attention to myself but I was desperate to get a better look at this guy. He held his head down, and his long straight hair covered most of his face.

Imagine Fabio's evil twin.

I suspect that the obscurity was intentional. Then, slowly, he brushed his hair back and stared straight at me.

I could hear a siren in the distance, and wifebeater be damned, I wasn't missing this. He was making me feel self-conscious, and when I followed his eyes down, I realized that my nipples were standing at full attention from the cool morning. I draped one arm across my chest and looked back at him defiantly.

At that point, the screaming woman picked up the garden hose and aimed it at Marisol. Well, that was all I needed to see, she may be a witch or something, but this was not going to turn into a WWE Smackdown. I ran in and grabbed Bardot, put her on a long leash, and explained the situation in Lab language.

"Get 'em!"

I let out the line and Bardot went straight for the offending sprayer. I purposefully pulled her up just before contact, but it was enough to make the point. The Ukrainian lurched back and the running hose went wayward, spraying several neighbors' cars as they drove by. She then dropped the hose and it convulsed across their lawn dousing each of his luxury cars. The Italian turned off the water and pulled the screaming woman into the house just as a squad car pulled up. At this point the only one who was dry and seemingly self-possessed was Marisol.

Wouldn't you know it, one of the officers to arrive was Augie, now catching me at the scene of another potential crime. At least he had seemed to be the nicest of the lot at Rosa's.

"Auntie Marisol," he said with open arms.

Auntie? His bloodline is connected to the devil in a blue housedress? Maybe kindness is just his subterfuge. . . .

There were hugs and introductions all around. When his wallet came out with baby pictures, I ran in and quickly threw on some sweats to avoid another trip downtown.

It seems that the Italian's girlfriend was the one who had called for police assistance, claiming that Marisol had been trespassing and defacing their vehicles. While the cops went up to their door to get a report, Marisol dashed into her house and returned with cold waters for them.

Oh, she's good.

We could hear her yelling and his deep, slow Italian accented voice coming from the doorway. A few minutes later Marisol's nephew came back to us and explained that the woman, her name was Tala, had called the police in haste, there was nothing wrong and she was sorry to have wasted their time.

"He made her say that," Marisol summed up.

Ironically, the cops then gave Marisol the option of filing a report, which she reluctantly declined.

Before Augie left he told Marisol that he might be sending someone over to ask her some more detailed questions about this neighbor. Something about them didn't seem right, he told her. Marisol gleamed at the prospect and, I must admit, my curiosity was piqued. She then whispered something back to Augie that I didn't catch, but clearly saw her looking at me a few times during the conversation. I didn't think that she was praising Bardot's hose wrangling skills.

Before heading to his car, he turned to me and put his hand on my shoulder.

"How're you doing? Remember anything else about the afternoon at Rosa's house?"

While his tone was that of a caring friend, I noticed that he didn't say "the afternoon you *discovered* Rosa's murder," my walls were going up.

"You'll be the first to know," I said, shaking my head.

Right after I tell the Wine Club, the best criminal defense attorney in Los Angeles, and Perez Hilton. Seems like everyone tells him everything.

The other cops had watched this exchange intently, and it took all my will not to give them a defiant finger as they drove off.

"Well that was fun," I said to Marisol and got no reply.

Her pleasant "cop face" was gone and her eyes half closed as she glared at me.

Et tu, nosy neighbor?

As I headed back in for breakfast and to give Bardot a bone, I swear I heard a faint "thank you" from Marisol. When I turned to look, she was gone. I was beginning to think that on Rose Avenue, nothing is quite what it seems.

Chapter 6

A little further east of Rose Avenue, I pulled to the curb beside a suburban strip mall that seemed to be all about drop off or pick up commerce. I saw a take-out restaurant, a vacuum repair shop, a laundry that specialized in oversized loads, a check-cashing facility, and a liquor store. Cars pulled in and out of the cramped parking lot constantly, no one wanted to stay there a minute longer than necessary.

When Aimee had invited me to have breakfast with her and see her shop, I was thrilled. Anyone who "tells it like it is," becomes an instant a friend of mine.

I rolled down my window to get some air and watched as the two men who ran the vacuum place exited their storefront and ambled over to the Chill Out. They didn't look like they knew the first thing about domestic science. One of them, trying to be cute I guess, walked up on the hood of an old El Camino parked in front, kept going over the roof and the flatbed part of the truck before hopping off and joining his buddy on the walk. The other guy shook his head, not happy with the performance.

"Morning, beautiful," one of them said while plopping down on a seat at one of the precious few tables on Aimee's patio. They acted like they owned the place.

I didn't like their brazen familiarity with her, something wasn't right. I jumped out of my car and speed-walked to her shop.

"Halsey, hi," she said while handing out coffees to her guests. "These are my friends, Ali Baba and Zeke. Guys, meet my sweet new neighbor Halsey."

One of them nodded and the other tried to kiss my hand. I quickly pulled it away and looked for Ashton Kutcher. Clearly I was being punked.

Aimee linked my arm and we headed into her shop.

"Okay, what are their real names? Cheech and Chong?"

"Those are their real names, Halsey, I swear."

"Show me their birth certificates! Wow, this is really cute," I said, looking around.

"Welcome to my humble café. I'm sorry if it isn't in shipshape, we were just getting ready to do a major clean. Halsey, meet Kimberly my assistant. She's the best."

"Pleased to meet you, Kimberly. And I don't know what you are talking about—the place looks fantastic."

And it did. Bright neon-colored chairs and tables gave a whimsical, fun mood to the place. Too bad people had to go through the scary outside mall first. And it smelled delicious. They say that you eat with your eyes, but in the case of Chill Out, it is the organ between them that does all the work.

"What would you like, Halsey?"

"I want a cup of every flavor you have."

"Aw hell, Kimberly, sounds like she needs you to make her the Special, Special."

We sat down at a window table and in the dawn light, I was able to get a good look at Aimee. She has such a pretty, fresh face. And her chameleon cheeks are fun to watch. When she speaks her eyes animate, although she is often looking into neutral space rather than right at you. I knew little of her life except that she put everyone else before herself. That takes a toll.

"This is such a treat, thank you both," I said, as Kimberly set a boat of delicious yogurt scoops and toppings in front of me. "What have we here?"

"This is cinnamon bun, that's blood orange, maple bacon donut, and apple pie."

"Did you say 'bacon'? I may need some privacy here," I said, making Aimee laugh.

"Delicious, you must love your job," I said, letting a little taste of heaven melt in my mouth.

"I do, but sometimes it's tough." Aimee sighed. "I work my tail off to survive understaffed and on a meager budget. Luckily, every day at noon, the teens from the school behind us swarm the place like Black Friday shoppers to a Walmart. For an hour or so, Kimberly and I dole out enough fat free soft serve and toppings to keep us going. Barely."

There was the flat out honesty I'd come to expect from Aimee, followed by the signature tears.

I glanced out the window at the two guys on the patio. The one who tried to kiss my hand was holding a wildly animated conversation with the other one. He just sat there kind of stoically.

The shop's phone rang.

"Sorry, Halsey," Aimee said, seeing Kimberly wave the receiver at her.

"No problem, take your time."

Kimberly opened the front door for business and I was seated close enough to it to pick up the guys' conversation.

"That some good shit we got in," said the one I think was Ali Baba. He was nodding his head and bouncing one knee up and down rapidly. As he took out his wallet to check his cash situation, his body rocked back and forth to imaginary music. Ali Baba seemed to be a perpetual motion machine.

"Keep it down, you fool," spat Zeke, looking over both shoulders. I quickly pretended to study the menu but saw that he had no concern for me. He bit nervously at an already chewed-down fingernail, I'll bet this one's the worrier. Unlike his partner, Zeke's five foot ten frame was dressed in muted grays and blacks, his hair was short, he wore no jewelry, making him totally forgettable.

"I'm just sayin', should bring in some nice scratch. Pops is not gettin' any younger and I need to go see him one more time," Ali Baba said, clutching an oversized gold cross that hung from his neck.

He walked into the shop and placed ten dollars into the tip jar on the counter. Aimee waved, still on the phone and he blew her a kiss as he left. He nodded at me warily. When he returned to the table, Zeke stood and they headed back to their store.

She's awfully chummy with the resident drug dealers.

I overheard Aimee saying into the phone something about "payments next week," and I decided to give her some privacy and stepped outside to take in the start of the day at the mall. I watched as the shopkeepers were getting ready to ply whichever trade kept them in strip mall business. The check-cashing store remained shut; I'm guessing that the owners were inside, putting the cash they had withdrawn from the bank into a safe.

Ingredients for breakfast burritos had started frying on the flat top grill of the Taquería next door. I smelled bell peppers, onions, and diced potatoes sizzling in bacon grease and margarine, and figured a large bowl of eggs was being whisked. The exhaust kicked in, causing the Mexican flag pennant banner overhead to flutter. The spicy odors spilled out onto the sidewalk and transported me to a white sand beach south of the border.

The only place open for business at this hour besides Aimee's was the liquor store on the corner. If it was like the ones in New York, it provided the three essentials for living: booze, cigarettes, and lottery tickets. A post office and a drug store com-

pleted the strip mall biosphere that could sustain
life if necessary.

A black Escalade pulled into a space near the
vacuum store. It had that just-detailed look and
the must-have custom rims that are in Chapter 1 of
the Cool Escalade Owners' handbook.

The man who stepped down from the glorified
pickup truck also filled the bill: tall, dark hair slicked
back and tied in a man-bun, headphones tuning
everyone out, and dressed all in denim. A Benicio
del Toro wannabe riding in on three miles per gal-
lon of chrome and muscle.

"Here comes Ray," said Zeke as they stood outside their door. "You keep your mouth shut. You
want money to go see your daddy? We gonna need
to make this guy happy."

You could almost hear the dark, wistful western
music as the lanky, strip mall outlaw approached.
When he reached them, he slung the headphones
down around his neck and just stood there, looking around slowly.

"Goooood morning, Ray," said Zeke, extending
his hand, which was ignored. In an awkward move
he quickly ran it over the back of his scalp to try
and save face. His tone of voice had changed to a
respectful singsong. "Wonderful day." He smiled,
and with a side-glance saw Ali Baba do the same,
and raise his hands to the heavens.

Ray was still silent, forcing Zeke to bear the burden of having to entertain or report something of
great value.

Before he could, Ali Baba chimed in, "Got some

really high quality product in last night, Raymundo."
His head bounced up and down and he grinned
like he'd tapped an underground platinum vein.

Zeke closed his eyes and cringed.

"What have I told you about talking about business in public?" sneered Ray, looking in my direction. "If you want to see another day, get inside."
His face was less than an inch from Ali Baba's.

That was my cue to head back inside. I'd probably eavesdropped for ten seconds too long, this guy
Ray had definitely caught me in the act. I didn't
think that I wanted to get on his bad side.

Aimee had gotten off the phone and was giving
Kimberly instructions for picking up the supplies
at Costco, crossing some items off the list saying
that they could "make do."

*Hmm, is this because of the budget problems she'd re-
ferred to?*

Aimee refilled her coffee cup and joined me at
the table.

"Sorry about that." She turned red and shook
her head.

"So, how's Tom doing with med school?" I
asked, thinking that we were moving onto a much
cheerier topic.

"He's working so hard, Halsey. It's easy for him
to get discouraged, everyone else is ten years
younger or more. If his mom hadn't gotten sick,
he'd be practicing by now. It is tough on the both
of us," she said, looking away and getting misty-
eyed.

"That's not good, Aimee, and you are here all
the time."

"I have to be, we don't sell enough for me to bring on another person unless it is part time for a catering gig."

"You make a better margin on catering?"

"Absolutely, but it's offset by the fact that I have to close the shop when we are onsite."

"Sounds like you need to get the word out," I said, considering licking my bowl again. "You need a web presence, some social media. I mean this is incredible and healthy for you. Right? It is diet?" I asked, praying for a nod.

Aimee complied and I let out my breath.

"So let me help. I can build you a simple site, get you a fan page, and start spreading the news about Chill Out. We can deliver samples to radio stations for the deejays to talk up, and pass out coupons and free yogurt to the office buildings around here. You'll be expanding your staff in no time."

"That all sounds great, Halsey, but my marketing budget is very small," she said, looking nervous.

"Honey, you just gave me a down payment," I said, waving my hand over the empty, clean yogurt bowl. "And Tom can pay the balance when he becomes my doctor."

"I'm not sure about this. You need to be paid for your time."

"This is what friends do for one another."

We hugged and she sent me home with a pint of yogurt for Bardot.

When I'd arrived I'd thought that some of the freedom of Aimee's fresh honesty would rub off on me and I could forget for a moment about my troubles. But there was a lot going on in this tiny mall a few miles from home. I thought about Aimee's struggles with work and home life and her drug-dealing friends. They made for strange bed-fellows.

Chapter 7

If I don't buckle down to work soon, I thought, I'm going to have to consider selling a kidney to keep up with my mortgage payments. But when you have frozen yogurt for breakfast I reasoned, bacon-flavored no less, then the natural progression is to move onto wine in the afternoon. Even if you do have a murder hanging over your head.

Everyone was seated out back on Sally's patio when I joined them. She has a cozy set of wicker chairs and sofas with soft cushions protected by a pastel palette of sun umbrellas. A Koi pond with a fountain is nestled in one corner and the soft sounds of running water complete the pastoral picture. An African brass *Nsoromma* star hangs on the back wall, reminding us that we are all "children of the heavens."

"There she is!" said Sally. "Those cuckoo-rama-mama cops finally leaving you alone?"

This was the perfect segue so I recounted my Italian neighbor story for the Wine Club, which was a Spanish themed event with a nice Rioja and tapas. When I finished, a cacophony of noise erupted as they all started talking over each other with stories about the car dealer of Rose Avenue. It seems that both Sally's husband and Cassie's husband Carl had been drive-by victims of the spraying hose.

"I've seen them loading cars onto a flatbed truck at two a.m.," said Peggy, breaking through the clutter. "I couldn't sleep and wondered what the commotion outside was all about. Strange goings on for Rose Avenue in the middle of the night."

"There must be a simple explanation," I baited them, hoping for clues to nail him.

"He's been here for quite a few years," Sally supplied. "Didn't have that horrible girlfriend then. He seemed nice enough, I used to see Rosa and him talking together quite often at her fence."

Aimee passed around a beautifully laid out tray of manchego served with sobrasada, quince paste, and little toasts, brought courtesy of Cassie. The sweet of the paste offset the strong cheese giving each bite a heavenly umami taste. Cassie also had Serrano ham wrapped around figs, some amazing looking mixed olives, and empanadas stuffed with goat cheese and chorizo. And a beautiful set of serving knives for each item.

Cassie has quite a collection of knives. I wonder if there is an empty slot in her wood block where a chef's knife once rested.

The first wine we tasted was a Vina Bujanda Crianza, a perfect pairing with the appetizers as it is fairly low in acidity, and with age contains flavors of rich cherry and spice. It is made 100 percent from Spain's native grapes, Tempranillo. I quickly snapped a photo of the label for our wine album. I gave my glass a deep inhale and took a sip. I swallowed slowly, letting the crisp fruit flavors transition to something like mom's cherry pie and then finish with a slightly earthy descent. I closed my eyes and dreamt of Pamplona.

"Last week Carl and I were walking after dinner," said Cassie, making an intended spectacle of herself, sucking every last bit of olive meat off its pit, "and some guys were carrying wooden boxes off a truck and into his house. Of course Carl had to snap their picture, seems he doesn't leave the house without that camera anymore."

I would love to get my hands on those photos. . . .

Today Cassie was in one of those built-in bra maxi dresses and her hair was in a loose bun. Very Anna Nicole Smith.

"I know him, that's Mussolini," Aimee announced. Her cheeks were vermillion. "Never says much, but has come in the shop on several occasions."

"Who names their kid Mussolini?" I asked.

"I don't think that's his real name," suggested Sally.

Ya think?

"It is, everyone calls him that, or Musso," explained naive Aimee. "He's never bothered me, he always orders strawberry shortcake. Leaves a nice tip, unlike the majority of people."

Oops.

"You seem to hang out with some questionable characters, Aimee, including those creepy guys who own the store a few doors down." Peggy said this with a concerned frown. "You should be more careful since you're all by yourself."

"If you mean Zeke and Ali Baba, they are decent guys too. A lot of times when I lock up at night Ali Baba waits and makes sure I get to my car safely."

A considerate druggie, that's what I look for in a friend.

"C'mon, anyone can see that they are dealing." Peggy was disgusted.

"I'm still waiting on those birth certificates, Aimee," I said only half joking. "I've sipped a tad of wine, but for the life of me, I can't figure out why Musso would come into a yogurt shop. No offense."

Sally shrugged her shoulders and refilled my glass.

"And I don't believe it's for your strawberry shortcake," I added, taking a sip, "not after being weaned on gelato."

"It's true, I swear, he comes at a quiet time and pours over some spreadsheets and a big calendar," said Aimee, placing her hand over her heart.

"Maybe he just needs some time away from his annoying girlfriend. I'm guessing he doesn't have an office anywhere?" I asked.

"She may be a be-atch, but she did something good for him. Since she's arrived on the scene the house got repainted, the used cars were replaced with luxury ones, and he is MUCH better dressed. He'd be kind of fun to dress. . . ." Cassie trailed off, imagining.

"Musso and Marisol get into it a lot," added

Sally. "Well more his girlfriend than him. She's very protective of Musso and does not cotton to Marisol's snooping."

"Who does?" I asked.

"Maybe she's being protective because he's got something to hide," Peggy mused.

I made a mental note to do some computer research on Peggy as well. She's got an awfully calculating mind for a fleeced granny.

We had moved on to a slightly chilled Lustau Dry Amontillado Los Arcos Solera Sherry Reserva that brought out the nutty, smoky taste of the cheeses and ham. This golden honeyed pour tossed my fuddy-duddy preconceptions of sherry straight out the window. And God love Sally for serving it in a grown up-sized copita glass.

"This car business has got Carl and me suspicious. He tells me to stay out of it, but I don't like this happening on Rose Avenue." Cassie was now expertly wielding a knife, slicing the ham-wrapped figs into more manageable bites.

"Then that is where I start. I've got to see what he is up to at night and bring some real evidence to the cops." I said this while watching Cassie work.

"What's up with all those security cameras around Musso's house?" I asked, remembering.

"I have no idea," replied Cassie. "Never saw them being put up. Lance, our security guy, says they are top of the line."

The girls all looked at her.

"With everything that is going on we're having a major security system installed," Cassie explained.

"Well, I'll bet those cameras are all networked

and uploading whatever they capture to a server so that Mussolini can watch his house from anywhere," I explained.

God I feel stupid saying "Mussolini."

"And if he's not using traffic encryption, then I should be able to monitor his ISP gateway and intercept his data packet."

Yes, I was showing off, but hell, I was the only one among them still paying a mortgage, except for poor Aimee. I needed something.

"Wait, what again do you do?" asked Sally, utterly confused.

I tried to explain in simpler terms.

"You lost me at 'traffic,' " Peggy said, looking bewildered. I wondered if that was true. I'd seen quite the computer setup at her house, including a camera and speaker system. She'd said that it was to talk to her grandkids, but she'd still need to know how to operate everything. I tucked the thought into the back of my mind.

"Sounds dirty." Cassie giggled, pulling up the bodice of her dress and creating quite the cleavage.

"Godspeed," Sally said, putting her hand on my shoulder.

Chapter 8

I hung up the phone and thought seriously about putting the house back on the market.

Thank you, Detective Marquez.

I guess that wouldn't do much good, what I really needed to do was think about getting a lawyer. The detective had said that they'd found my fingerprints all over Rosa's house *and* on the knife in her back. I explained why my prints were found in the hallway and pointed out that they would not find them anywhere else. As for the knife, I was pretty sure that I'd never touched it, although much of that period is a fog to me. Detective Marquez conceded that my prints were only found in that one section of the house, but didn't budge on the knife. He said they were doing more testing. He also said that no one else's prints besides Rosa's were found.

Not good.

Then he asked me about something in my past

that, up until now, I had been very proud to mention.

"When you were living in New York City, Ms. Hall, did you have occasion to work at Panzavecchia & Sons?"

"Yes, the roosters had finally decided to let a hen into the house. What's this about?" I asked warily.

"What did you do for them?" he asked, ignoring my question.

"Well, one of the sons, Frank, was a guest speaker at a cooking seminar I attended one summer. He really admired my knife skills and offered me an apprenticeship at his butcher shop—I see where this is going!"

He explained that this was just routine, in order to rule me out, blah, blah, blah. He also told me not to leave town.

Problem was I didn't see them making any effort to rule someone else *in*. Had they even talked to this elusive ex-husband? Or the brother? Maybe focus on someone who actually had a motive? Ray is clearly dealing drugs, no doubt assisted by his band of contraband brothers, Ali Baba and Zeke. With Rosa out of the picture, he can sell the house and use the proceeds to expand his operation deeper into the Westside. And he'd need someone to help manage his growing company. A person nobody would suspect and who might need a short-term infusion of cash. It pained me to think about Aimee but desperation does inhuman things to the mind. If there was a connection, hopefully it was just that she sees those two dealers at work, and anything they do away from there is their own business.

Even though I didn't trust him either, Augie was the closest thing I had to an open-minded ally. I had his card and would check in with him, but first I needed some fresh air, my mind was about to self-combust.

Sally and I went to the Farmers' Market. She had said that the produce was great and we liked spending time getting to know one another. She and her husband Joe were both from the East Coast originally, so we had an innate affinity for certain ways of doing things. We wrote thank-you notes, we always brought gifts to each other's houses when invited, and we loved finding something like an old wooden milking stool at a yard sale. She was like an older, wiser big sister. With balls.

Which is why I felt comfortable confiding in her about the police accusations.

"That's ridiculous, who in the ham-fat would think that you had a reason to kill Rosa? Until you walked into her house by mistake, you didn't even know she existed."

Who in the what?

"I know, but they're digging up my past to try and make a case. They don't seem to have anyone else to blame this on," I said, exasperated.

"Well then the Rose Avenue Wine Club will just have to find them some guilty people!"

As silly as this sounded—what does a group of

cork-popping ladies know about solving a murder—it still relaxed me a bit. Although not enough to share with Sally my thoughts on Aimee's ties to Ray and his minions and Peggy's seemingly being at ease with death. Those are nefarious thoughts to have about a couple of sweet ladies. No, I needed to drive this bus, after all I had the most to lose.

"Oh look, squash blossoms," Sally cooed. "Joe loves those," she said about her husband. Our baskets were already brimming with early summer bounty.

I had to smile, thinking back to when I first moved to New York City after college. There was a Korean green grocery on the corner from my apartment, owned by an enterprising young woman named Bong Cha.

On my meager entry-level salary, writing code at the only start-up to fail in the boom, my money went on rent, clothes, and clubbing. So for sustenance, I discovered that mixing Jell-O with Bong Cha's fruit did the trick. And if I went just before closing, she would give me the produce that hadn't sold and wouldn't be good the next day. In return I helped her network her computer and set up email.

Cut to the present with Sally and I strolling under the morning sunshine, tasting the first peaches of the season and testing avocados for their ripeness. True, my life was now much tamer, with the exception of the murder, but gone was the constant human interaction day and night, something I never thought I would miss. Oh well, you can't have everything and I was learning to be happy alone. Hell, people can be overrated.

Just at the right moment, a farmer with a tray of blueberry juice in little cups came over and brightened our morning. I downed mine in one gulp. Hey, I know what to do when presented with a shot glass. . . .

"What's the deal with Rosa's brother?" I asked.

"Ray? I actually think that deep down he's a good egg. I watched he and Rosa grow up, they lived right across the street. Saw him learn to ride his first bike. It's those damn drugs. Ray is amiable and wears his emotions on his sleeve. But unfortunately when he's high that emotion often turns to anger."

"You think that he could have killed Rosa?"

"I pray to God no, he tries to act all tough, but with Ray it's all 'big hat, no cattle.' "

We were now perusing a baked goods stand with warm boules of sourdough, crusty whole grain loaves, fruit tarts, and the most delicious looking nut bread that I just couldn't pass up. I had to act fast as I could feel a crowd behind me poised to pounce if I showed even the least bit of indecision. Sally had swooped in like a pro and was now standing at the side with her gluten goodies.

"All the same, if the cops aren't going to investigate him then I must," I said while paying the baker. "Hey, isn't that Musso's girlfriend over there?"

Sally followed my eyes and, sure enough, we spotted Tala, the woman with the fondness for the garden hose. She was negotiating with the mushroom man like she was buying a used car.

"Time to do a little sleuthing," Sally suggested and we headed in her direction.

Hanging behind enough to avoid being noticed, we could now see and hear her clearly.

"How much for these shiitakes? They don't look so fresh," she told the mushroom monger.

"Check out her bag, that's a huge Louis Vuitton," whispered Sally.

"I'm trying, but the glare from that rock on her finger keeps blinding me. I guess she really is good with hoses."

For that comment, Sally elbowed me in the side. "Is that watch Chanel?"

"Seriously. She is walking around this market with about two hundred and fifty thousand dollars of accessories on her. Musso must be selling a lot of cars curbside each night," I said.

"Something to definitely throw into the mix." Sally nodded.

Chapter 9

A loud, rumbling noise coming from outside brought me out of the food coma I'd slipped into after gorging on a Farmer's Market dinner

Tomorrow's trash day.

I ran out and as I pulled my cans to the curb, I thought about the morning after trash day. It is always a bit of a letdown for the people of Rose Avenue because it marks the end of the once-a-week neighborhood "show and tell" into each other's private lives. And there are those who work hard to glean as much information as possible.

Which is partly why I decided to take Bardot for a late postprandial walk on trash day eve. I didn't know what, but I was hoping to see something that would swing the executioner's spotlight in another direction.

Who else would be out at this time of night?

Marisol.

We caught her handing over a large paper bag

to Inez, our Rose Avenue recycle bin poacher. In return for whatever was in the bag, I have no doubt that Marisol got a rundown of what was in the trash of select neighbors she's keeping tabs on. A tossed credit card bill or a take-home container from a restaurant fill in pieces of her puzzle and give her a week's worth of profiling.

Inez had introduced herself when I moved in, and was a big help when she offered to take the used boxes off my hands. Everyone in the neighborhood seemed to like her, except for Bardot. I don't know why, maybe she thought that Inez didn't like dogs, but whenever she'd come around, Bardot would go crazy at the window. She rarely did this and usually only when she sensed someone was a threat to me.

I'd have to ask Jack.

As predicted, Bardot stopped in her tracks and started growling at Inez. She has a deep belly growl that would have made Godzilla proud, although most often it is accompanied by tail wagging.

This time it wasn't. I knew this wasn't directed at Marisol, she and Bardot were becoming great pals, much to my dismay.

"Sorry," I said sheepishly, "she must smell a raccoon or an aardvark or something."

What did I know of the animals of the suburban jungle?

They both looked at me like deer caught in headlights, so we started moving on.

I wonder what they're up to. . . .

I'd found out that another surefire way to learn more about the people who share this quaint street is to take note of the extra items that they lay out on the tree lawn. People assume that "somebody will take it."

The random castoffs on the tree lawn of Marisol's home was a good example. This week she was showcasing a portable hood hair dryer that probably helped finish the girls' home perms when they were teens. I'd seen their photos hanging in the hallway one rare time that Marisol let me step over the threshold, and they were both sporting ringlets. There was also a *Fantasy Island* Christmas snow globe the size of a bowling ball. Lastly, I saw a collection of old faucets, which must have had everyone scratching their heads. When Bardot tried to fit the snow globe into her mouth, I quickly pulled her away and we kept walking.

Moving along and in front of Cassie and Carl's two-story Tudor house were items that deserved a sit down and a bit of a think. This week's treasures included neon pink skis, a gravity inversion table, a book of carpet samples, and a five-tray food dehydrator. Knock yourselves out.

From inside the house, we heard the high-pitched yips I'd known to come from those little lap dogs.

Before I knew what was happening, Bardot had pulled me clear across their lawn and up to the front door. A chorus of barks and yips ensued from the three that sounded remarkably like counting out the steps in a waltz. "Bark-yip-yip, bark-yip-yip." Then I heard Cassie on the other side of the door, which she opened a tiny bit, trying to shoo them away.

"I didn't know you had dogs, Cassie," I said through the crack in the door. I'm pretty sure that I saw little fur butts and tails skitter away.

I heard some whispering that I couldn't decipher, and then the door slowly opened all the way.

"Oh, hi, Halsey. What are you doing out so late?"

"Just enjoying the evening air. Were those Chihuahuas I saw?"

"What? No. Listen I'd love to invite you in for a glass of wine but Carl is upstairs waiting for me, if you know what I mean." She winked at me.

For once Cassie was dressed like anybody else relaxing at home, sweats and a T-shirt. Somehow I doubted that this attire turned Carl into a rabid Casanova.

Before I could respond, she blew me a kiss and shut the front door.

I looked at Bardot, and she returned the favor with an expression that said, "What the hell have you gotten me into??"

Those were clearly dogs, and Bardot agreed. So why was she lying? I remembered the girls saying that Rosa's Chihuahuas had been missing since the murder. Were those them? If Cassie had rescued the dogs, why wouldn't she just say so?

Course every second person seems to have a Chihuahua in California, and frankly they all look alike to me. Maybe I'm overthinking this, Cassie is impulsive and needs instant gratification, so she could have bought the dogs. And she may be hiding them from Carl so she doesn't have to bargain with him for anything.

I saw that by now Inez had made her way down this side of the street and was doing her poaching across the avenue.

We watched as she approached Peggy's house, which I guessed looked as pristine outside as it did when it was built in the 1950s. It is always so clean that you can eat off the front porch, and it's quite possible that the neighborhood cat asleep on the doormat wiped his feet before tucking in. At the curb the trash bins also look like new. And just as neatly sat her two cases of empty wine and liquor bottles.

Inez made fast work of gathering up the recyclables and then stopped for quite a while, fumbling with them in her cart. When Bardot followed my gaze and saw Inez, a slow growl started to rumble in her belly.

I had to sit on the curb and let her lick my face and ears in order to distract her.

Finally finished with her trash machinations, Inez passed poor Rosa's house and stopped at the next one. I had no idea who lived there and decided it was time to head home.

I needed to think through what we'd seen tonight:

Marisol handing a mysterious bag to Inez, both of them looking guilty of something, and Cassie clearly lying about having those dogs.

I looked across one last time and was mystified to see that at this particular house Inez was actually putting bottles *into* the trash cans. All the while trying to be very stealth.

What the hell?

Chapter 10

Miraculously, I found that my newspaper was now being placed in my mailbox right outside my door in the morning, and it wasn't because the delivery guy who tossed it from a slow moving truck had the arm of a pro baller. It also wasn't to stop me from parading out in my wifebeater. It was the beginning of my acceptance by Marisol. And I suspected that once you were in the Marisol Club, you were in for life. Like it or not.

My only question was, why the change of heart? Did I pass some kind of Marisol good neighbor test? Or was she lulling me into trusting her while there was an active murder case to be solved? Maybe she and Augie were trying a new angle to break me.

As I was coming back from a trip to the store, I heard my name being called. I didn't see anyone and was about to go in when I heard it again. The sound was coming from Marisol's house, and I could faintly make out her shadow behind the black, metal security screen door.

So this was how she did her spying. She must have seen something the day of the murder. Time for me to make nice and ask her about it.

I approached but she remained behind the screen.

"A guy came to see me, a detective, he had a book," she said.

I felt a bit like I was back in Catholic school, talking to a priest in a confessional.

"What kind of book?"

"It had pictures of people in it; he wanted me to look through, see if I'd seen any of them around here visiting Musso."

She got right up to the screen and I could see that she was definitely proud of her sudden importance.

"So he showed you a mug shot book?"

I'm pretty sure I saw Marisol nod on the other side of the screen. The gray roots were showing when she tipped her head.

"Wow, well did you recognize any of them?" She was going to drag this out for all it was worth.

"Some I seen around, they'd come and look at the cars during the day, do a lot of talking and then leave with nothing. You can't make a living doing that."

"Why were they in the book of criminals, did he tell you what they'd done?" I was getting tired of talking to a door.

"I asked but the detective didn't say much. Something about taxes. I'll get the scoop from Augie."

Finally she opened the screen door and stepped out.

At that moment Musso came out of his house and headed to a Mercedes that was parked at the curb. Halfway down the driveway, he stopped and looked at us with a blank face. If that was his death stare, then he needed more time in front of the bathroom mirror.

"I used to babysit them kids, Rosa and Ray," Marisol said, watching Musso drive off. "If he had anything to do with her death, I'll kill him myself!"

Why is she yelling at me??

"What exactly do you think Musso is doing with those cars at night? You must see things."

"I seen him moving cars in and out during the week. Taking up all the goddamn street parking when he can't park any more in the back of his house. Then Thursday nights they get loaded onto trucks and shipped out. Don't know where they go from here."

"Then I'm going to have to follow them one Thursday night."

"I'm going with you."

"What? No." I didn't like where this was heading.

"I'm going, you'll see. Now, don't you have one of them stupid wine club thingies to go to?"

She may be off her meds. . . .

"No you won't, but thanks for bringing my paper up to the door every morning."

I still needed information from her so I decided to make nice.

"I don't know what you're talking about," I heard from a muffled voice as the screen door slammed.

Monday mornings I make my weekly foray to Trader Joe's, usually around ten to avoid any sort of crowd, something I abhor now that I don't have to put up with it. I'd been to one in New York, but it was nothing compared to the wide aisles and interesting and unique items that filled the shelves in my local store.

Trader Joe's is like the IKEA of food purveyors. They often set the style for the latest gastronomy while having the buying power to price everything affordably. They've also made liars out of a good many patrons, myself included, in at least two scenarios:

1. Before you can stop yourself, you proudly take credit for a particularly delicious creation of theirs, whether an appetizer, dessert, or cheese tray combination.
2. You discover a new, tasty treat they just got in, and when your guests ask where you got it you reply, "Just a little shop downtown, but I think I got the last one."

I am at least thirty years younger than any of the other patrons shopping at that time. I'm spared the moms with babies and toddlers who give me a peek into the challenge of herding cats, and also make me want to get my tubes tied. I also avoid the folks who just got out of yoga class, just finished three sets of tennis, or made TJ's the destination after a five-mile jog. I hate everything about those people.

I've found my place with the octogenarians. I don't mind listening to them talk about their ailments with anyone who will listen. And it appears that to this group, Trader Joe's is also a spectator sport. I've had to learn how to navigate around the old men who walk about with their hands clasped behind their backs and peruse the shelves like they are visiting a wing of the Louvre. If you see someone with no list, no bags, and no cart, go hit another aisle.

I get my fish and meat for the week, explore the cheeses they have gotten in, there is a certain Camembert from Petaluma that is stinky and delicious either sucked off a cheese knife, which Bardot and I have been known to do in private, or spread over a slice of Granny Smith apple. And let's not forget the wines, if you give yourself the time, you are bound to find some reasonably priced gems. Look for the Pancake Cellars Big Day White Wine, the Hogue Riesling, only slightly sweet with peach, apricot and tangerine flavors. And the Laurent Dublanc Cotes du Rhone is a steal and doesn't disappoint.

I wheeled my cart back to my car, satisfied with my haul and happy that I would be back at work by eleven a.m. at the latest. I noticed a van parked facing me with two people in it, and thought, "Yes!" They are pulling out so I can drive straight ahead and not even have to deal with backing out. That is the one drawback to shopping when the seniors do, you have to deal with them being behind the wheel. Avoidance is the best policy.

My phone rang and I saw that it was Augie.

"Hey, thanks for calling me back. Any news on the list of suspects I texted you?"

"I'm not a magician, I can't pull murderers out of a hat." He chuckled.

"Why not?" I laughed back. Jocularity breeds allegiance, I hoped.

"That was a long list of names which was very short on evidence. But, before you start yelling, let me tell you where we're at."

"Since when do I yell?" I was about to say that he was confusing me with his aunt, but caught myself just in time.

"You're right, I've never heard you, but I could sense the frustration over the phone. We're still working on tracking down the ex-husband. I seem to remember that he is doing time, but that's not confirmed. The brother, Ray, is around but we have nothing to pin on him. Yet."

"I didn't ask you to make me look like a stronger suspect, Augie, tell me you've got *something*."

"A few things, this clown Musso, he sure lives lean and clean. Very little paper on him, no mortgage, no car payments, claims a very modest income."

"But what about all the bling his girfriend's sporting?"

"That's what we are looking into. If we can tie him to any kind of crime, then we can go to town on him."

"Well, he's not going to call you before he commits one, what's your plan for catching him?"

Augie ignored me and continued.

"The two guys at the strip mall, who you think are dealing drugs, probably are. Vice is watching them, they'll need to find something bigger than a bag of dope. But we're not looking at them for the murder, really no motive."

The van facing me started up. The glare of the sun made it difficult to make out the people in the front seats, but this boded well for my car getting out of the lot unscathed.

"Also—you're not going to like this—one of guys in our division turned up a report on you from a couple of years ago. Did you really throw a Römertopf oven at your husband? An oven?"

"It's actually just a clay pot, he's my EX-husband, and it didn't even come close to him. With a coq au vin inside, it was too heavy to get up any kind of velocity!" I shouted.

"Okay, okay, I'm just telling you that this gives Marquez one more reason to keep you as a suspect."

"And not look for the real killer! How about Musso's girlfriend, Tala? She has a hot temper."

"She's on an extended visitor's visa, she's going to have to return to the Ukraine and reapply unless someone pulls some strings."

"So Musso has a clock running on him, huh?"

The sun had moved slightly and I could see the driver of the van put it in gear. I started my car ready to pounce. Just before backing out, the passenger door opened and out stepped a tall guy dressed all in black.

Musso!

"Augie, I'll call you back." I disconnected and fumbled with the camera on my phone; I needed to get a shot and hopefully capture the license plate of the van.

Musso looked in my direction through mirrored aviators. If he recognized me, he didn't show it. By the time I had the camera app up the van had pulled out. All I caught was the sign on the side:

NIGHTHAWK FILM PRODUCTION CO.

Chapter 11

I spent the next few days hidden in my house
and not answering the phone. If the cops needed
to get to me, then they'd have to knock on my door.
It depressed me to think that I might very well have
to put my life on hold to fight for my freedom.

Each time I sat at my computer to work, I found
myself instead doing online research and developing an elaborate matrix of possible suspects in
Rosa's murder. I had started an archive of search
results for Musso, this Nighthawk Film Company,
Ray, and out of curiosity, Tala.

It was slow going and I reminded myself that I
also had to get out and do "actual police work" if I
had any hope of success. I also decided to enlist
the help of the Wine Club.

The first part of my plan was hatched "off cam-
pus" at Aimee's birthday lunch. She was on a total
health kick, she told us that she'd gained ten
pounds since January. I figured that it was all

stress, although a thought about binge eating after smoking pot did enter my mind. . . .

She chose an organic sandwich shop named Fennel, which we reluctantly agreed to go to when we found out that they had a wine and beer license. Cassie was in charge of ordering the wine; on her unlimited budget she offered to treat because she "wanted something good."

Cassie and Sally arranged for tables to be pulled together to accommodate all of us. This was no small feat since the place was very popular among the yoga and protein shake crowd. We were tucked toward the back, but I could still feel cold eyes on us, resenting the fact that they would have to enjoy their fat free, gluten free, meat free, taste free food in their cars.

Everyone was on a lazy afternoon time schedule but me. We didn't start until after one p.m., and with two bottles ordered from the start, and the insistence that there must be cake for the birthday girl, I had already conceded that I would have to go home, take a nap, and work through the night. Not to mention that Cassie had chosen an excellent Grüner Veltliner.

When everyone was settled, I threw down the challenge to the group.

"Someone needs to follow Musso for a day, see where he goes and who he deals with," I said, knowing that I was going to take the night shift. "How about you, Peggy, you have the most inconspicuous car."

"I'm game, but someone needs to come with me

so I can keep my eye on the road," said Peggy, ever cautious at eighty-seven.

"I'll go with you and take pictures, we'll be a regular Cagney and Lacey," said Cassie, miming a two-handed pistol hold.

She clearly hadn't watched TV in a while.

"Carl has a great camera I'll use. I'll have to sneak it out, he doesn't like me touching his photography equipment, but I'll put it back before he even knows it's gone."

I am going to work on getting a look at that SD card.

"That's a good start, you guys comfortable doing this? You'd better have an excuse prepared if he catches you."

"We're pretty good at making up stories on the fly and carrying them out to get what we want," Peggy said, and they all giggled.

"Like we did with Freddy," said the birthday girl who was sporting a glittery tiara that we'd given her for the occasion.

"And Freddy is?"

"He's my cutie nephew, he helped us when we needed to get rid of those squatters who had taken over the house behind me, they were growing pot in back of the garage," Cassie explained. "Like they didn't think we'd notice when they put up this really ugly chimney on the roof that doesn't go at all with reclaimed wood siding?" Cassie laughed at the ridiculousness of this.

"Is Freddy a cop?" I asked warily.

"Hell no," said Peggy. "Young Freddie is a brave,

good sport and we had him pose as a building inspector and we went along with him to that house."

My mouth dropped open wide enough for planes to land.

"Bastards wouldn't let us into the property, but sometime in the middle of the night they bugged out. That was a good plan I thought of," Peggy reminisced.

"*What?*" They were all talking at once, claiming ownership of the ruse and bickering back and forth.

I had no idea the Rose Avenue Wine Club was a cover for a group of oenophile vigilantes.

"Okay, so Musso is the prime suspect?" I asked, hoping mostly to shut them up.

They paused and I could see the wheels turning.

"He's the prime suspect to *us*. I know whom the cops like," I said, pointing to myself.

That got a unanimous nod. It was time to tell them about Musso and the film company van, it could only help them in their investigation.

"Well, you've just knocked me naked," Sally declared. "I never would have pegged Musso as a Trader Joe's guy, he's much more Whole Foods to me."

"Uh-uh," said Peggy, "Costco. He's got to save money so he can afford that girlfriend."

I was afraid that the wine was getting the better of them.

I made some notes on my pad. "With each connection we are getting closer to the truth, but we better get digging because I am running out of time.

"Let operation 'Nab Musso' begin," Cassie proclaimed with a toast.

"You all, I don't know about this," Aimee pleaded. "I'm afraid, sometimes he talks with the vacuum repair guys when he leaves my shop, and I don't want to get them in any trouble. They're good kids."

"Why are you protecting those bums, Aimee? And if they're so clean, then why would you worry about getting heat on them?" Peggy got right to her point.

"I'm not saying they would; sure, they can be a pain sitting at my tables all day, but they love the yogurt and they actually pay for it. They also give me a hand from time to time if I need some heavy lifting." Aimee was now getting teary as she often did when the least bit of emotion was involved. Her cheeks were growing purple.

"Are you crying?" asked Cassie, wiping away a tear from Aimee's face with a recycled Fennel paper napkin.

"But we'd be following Musso, not your guys, child," reasoned Sally. "So stop looking as nervous as a pig in a bacon factory."

"We need to find out what they are up to and go to the police. For Halsey's sake," said Cassie.

"I can keep tabs on Rosa's brother, Ray, since I live right across the street. I've already seen him nosing around the house, but I'm pretty sure he's harmless."

There Sally goes again, protecting him.

"What about her ex, was he with him?" I asked, and Sally shook her head.

"He's up in Tehachapi, serving out an assault and battery charge, according to Siri," Cassie said, holding up her latest iPhone.

"One less to worry about," I said.

"With Musso, all we're going to do is stir the pot a bit, see what comes out of it, and pass the info along to the authorities," Peggy soothed Aimee.

"Sure, piece of cake," said Sally gently patting Aimee's hand.

Speaking of, from behind them, I saw a glowing cake being brought to our table.

"Okay, we've got a plan in motion," I announced while squeezing the last drop of wine out of bottle number two, "anything to get those detectives off my back. I can keep tabs on Marisol, as wily as she is. With all her shenanigans, we could discover that she's running a billion-dollar online casino out of her garage." I wasn't kidding.

I'll also keep an eye on Peggy and Aimee, but I'll keep that to myself.

Chapter 12

A general search for Nighthawk Film Production Company, returned lots of variations:

Moonrise Nighthawk Films

Shanghai Nighthawk Movies (a porn site)

Nighthawk Birds Productions

And lots and lots of Nighthawk companies peddling everything from shipping to energy to bird watching blinds.

But I found nothing local and nothing with those exact words. I started realizing that anybody could have a sign made and stick it on a van, and knew that I would have to enter a deeper level of search parameters.

I started with the Los Angeles County Registrar and found the search engine for Fictitious Business Names of DBAs. It came up with "Name Not

Found." Rats. This means that I am going to have to broaden my geographic base.

I tried another few counties and got the same results, or lack thereof.

The office door opened and Bardot, who had been humping her doggie pillow since she realized my attention was solidly on my computer screen, suddenly sat politely, like a show dog.

"Gooood girl," cooed Jack, commanding my dog with his focus and then with a slight nod, getting her to drop down on all fours. "Hi." He grinned at me. "I was in the neighborhood and thought I'd check in on Bardot."

Lame but cute excuse . . .

"Hi," I responded, a little too high-pitched. "Just finishing with a program," I explained, and then winced with guilt at the lie. White as it was.

I decided to wait on the business name search, I could write a simple program to automatically search the entire United States and archive the positive results.

Jack quickly and politely gave me my space, and sat at the small conference table in the center of the room for rare client meetings. He busied himself with absolutely nothing, sitting straight-backed. I was starting to appreciate that California Zen.

I moved on to Musso's security system. I really wasn't going to be happy unless I found something to move the ball forward today.

My first step was to confirm that his security cameras were wired to the Internet, as I suspected. I entered the make and model numbers I'd gotten by sneaking a shot on my phone while picking up

Bardot's poop. I was in luck his was a basic WiFi-enabled system from a box store. These cameras run on nondefault ports that are well documented and fairly easy to find on the Internet. I was going to have to look for those ports to find Musso's cameras, and believe it or not I could do this with Google. But since this was technically hacking (for a good cause!), I figured I'd better wait until I was alone.

I looked over at Jack in his sleep state and wished that I could shut the world out and just Zen like that. Instead I roused him and asked, "You hungry? Since you wouldn't let me replace your watch, least I can do is buy you dinner."

Smooth or what?

Typhoon is a Pacific Rim restaurant that sits right on the runway at the Santa Monica airport. I had read about it and kept promising myself to walk over for lunch, but somehow always ended up having boxed miso soup at my desk instead. It was now close to sunset, which meant catching the last flights that were landing for the day, and it meant it was time for those two delightful words, "Happy Hour."

The restaurant looks like it is modeled after an air traffic control tower. It is sort of a half moon shape with windows all along the runway side. Across is an open kitchen where pots steam dumplings, chefs concoct with speedy hands, and whole catfish sit perched in a glass case, waiting to be fried. And it has a real bar, something I take for granted coming from New York, but I've learned is more of a rarity here.

We decided to start with martinis and later have hot sake with our meal. Once that plan was hatched, there was no doubt how the rest of the evening was going to play out. Jack had visited Viet Nam so was happy to order from the eclectic pan-Asian menu. I was game for most of it, but when the fried crickets arrived, I drew the line. Instead, I dined on sumptuous Chinese crispy duck and pineapple fried rice.

I decided that it was time to bring Jack into the fold—better to hear it from me—so I roughly outlined Rosa's murder, glossing over the fact that I was the cops' prime suspect.

"Whoa," he said, shaking his head, "who would do such a thing?"

I returned the head shaking.

"Want me to have some people check it out?" he asked. "I do work training a number of private detectives and their animals."

Good to know.

"Wait a minute, they don't think you had anything to—"

"They kind of do, just because they haven't been searching properly for any other suspects."

"I'm going to talk to my detective friend; he's a narc but there's always all kinds of crossover. That's crazy that they've stopped looking."

"I meant to ask," I quickly interrupted, tired of the subject. "Why'd you come by today, not that I'm sorry you did." I watched him pick up the last bug between his chopsticks.

"The truth, or the *truth*," he asked, saying the second "truth" in a dragged out, playful way.

"Okay, gimme both truths," I said, having fun with the word myself.

"Well, I keep thinking about Bardot and her underwater diving skills, and I wanted to see if I could persuade you to take her to a CARA training demo, just to see what it is all about."

"Sounds like fun, although I told you before there's no way I'll have the time to devote to really doing this."

"Understood," Jack replied.

"And the other truth?"

"Let's head back to your pool, and I'll show you."

This time Bardot wasn't the only one skinny-dipping. She couldn't believe her luck that her two favorite people were sharing her pool. We discovered that we could keep her occupied by just throwing a sinkable toy down to the bottom. But when she cut her retrieve time down to less than ten seconds, we decided that it was time to head out for dry land.

We were surprised by how much cooler the air was than the heated pool. I gave Jack an extra-long bath towel to dry off and while he was freshening up in the bathroom his cell phone rang. Of course, he had a puppy yip ring tone.

"Can you answer that? It might be CARA calling with an emergency."

The bat signal, at least it waited for us to get our business done.

"Jack's phone." Ugh, that sounded dumb.

"Who the hell is this?" a woman's angry voice came back at me, never a good sign.

"It's Halsey, Jack will be right with you."

At this point even *I* wanted to punch me in the face.

"Sounds like he's been with *you,* slut. And what kind of dumb name is Halsey?"

Thank God I didn't say "Annie Hall."

My whole body sank.

"Put him on the damn phone!"

I felt a hand grab the phone from me, and Jack went out through the French doors to talk to her in private.

Not sure why, except that I needed to calm down, I decided that this was as good a time as any to do laundry. I could feel my face burn. How could I have been so stupid? This is what I get for opening myself up to someone again. Of course he had somebody and I was just a convenient new diversion. Had I not learned my lesson from the last time? You can't trust people, they all lie.

"Hey, sorry about that. Ex-girlfriend," he said with a hangdog look as he followed me to the laundry room.

"Ex-girlfriend, really? Since when do ex-girlfriends still have your cell phone number and feel they can call you any time of night? Damn it, Jack, she talked to me like I was the hooker who stole her trick."

"I've been meaning to change my number. . . ."

"Jack, when you want someone out of your life, you do it, immediately. Heck, I put three thousand miles between me and my ex."

". . . I have to let all my clients know." Amazing how Jack could suddenly look so small.

"Jack, you're an adult and you make your own decisions."

"Look, let me explain about Kat."

"No need, I think you should go," I responded. "This was a mistake."

I can be really cold if I want to be.

"But this isn't—"

"No it's not. You need to go and tend to your 'ex' girlfriend and I need to separate my whites from my colors."

Chapter 13

It took a good week for me to get over Jack. I'll admit that for the first two days I didn't get out of bed, preferring to binge on *Real Housewives* and Flamin' Hot Cheetos.

What? Don't knock 'em if you haven't tried 'em.

This thing with Jack was wrong on so many levels. Clearly I don't know him and it seems that he's got secrets. This is my first time living alone since college, and if I am going to learn to stop compromising myself for other people, then I am going to have to establish my own lifestyle boundaries. I didn't move across the country to become a remora fish on another male shark.

I needed to jump full force into work, the best medicine no doubt. I had some ongoing clients from New York, but I could definitely use a big, fat app-building project. Preferably one where I could repurpose some code I'd already developed for another paradigm.

Before moving out here, I had joined several

tech newsgroups where people share job opportu-
nities, ask for advice when they are having trouble
with a sticky piece of code, and let everyone know
when Krispy Kreme is giving away free donuts. I set
my email preferences to save these posts to a separate folder because when people get on a jag about
something your inbox can get inundated. God for-
bid somebody starts a post entitled, "Friday Fun." It
will include a link to an online game or video, and
immediately others will reply with their sugges-
tions. The majority are ridiculous time wasters, but
like watching a high-speed car chase on the news,
you have to see it through.

It was time to weed through them and see if there
were any good leads. I quickly bypassed a number of
unopened messages from Jack. Too soon, if ever.

A lot of the project listings were past their deadline, but a few were still open. I really couldn't
bring myself to sign on to create an accounting
and customer portal for one of the largest com-
mercial sanitation companies in LA. Just not *moi*.

Another for developing an online appointment
system for a chain of hair salons could have been
fun, but their budget was hilariously low.

I was about to delete a government job just because of all the red tape when the words "life-saving
service" popped out at me. This was an RFP (Re-
quest for Proposal) from the US Coast Guard in
Marina del Rey. The job was to build an online secured extranet for internal communications during
search and rescue missions. The data needed to
also be encrypted and sent to Homeland Security's
internal system. This one I was going for.

For the rest of the week, I filled out unending pages of questions like, "Do you or any of your employees have a criminal record? If so, please list the personnel and their respective criminal history."

Shouldn't "yes" to the first question basically end it right there?

I realized that I should be more sympathetic to anyone with a criminal past, given that I was headed down that same road unless I tracked down the real Rose Avenue murderer.

"Hi honey," Aimee said, coming in the side door of my office. "I was wondering if you have a minute?"

"Sure, I'll always find an excuse for a break, and in your case this is a pleasant surprise."

Bardot sniffed all Aimee's body parts in search of frozen yogurt.

"I wanted to ask you about Inez, have you had a chance to get to know her at all?"

Bardot growled.

"No, not really, want a water? A glass of Cab?" I asked with a mischievous grin.

"What? Oh, no thank you, I have to go to work soon. This chair looks comfy."

"Take it for a test drive. So did something happen with Inez?"

"Well sort of, not really. I came home late last night dog tired from work, and there was Inez busying herself with the recyclables. I really admire anyone who is that industrious, and I'd been hatching this plan for a while."

"Involving Inez?"

"Yes, I can't imagine that she does this digging in the trash all day, every day; if she is, then it just shows how much she needs the money. So I told her that I could probably afford some part-time help at my yogurt shop, was she interested? I said that I can't pay much, what with Tom in school and me helping out my uncle in Iowa, but for a few hours each day she could be inside, and have all the free yogurt she wants."

"I'm guessing that she didn't take this in the spirit it was meant?"

Aimee exhaled. "I'd been rehearsing this for days, rewriting it in my mind so that she'd understood that I cared about her and wanted to help."

"What did she say?"

"She said she was too busy and closed into herself like a clam. Brought her cart up next to her and held onto it. That's when I really messed it up."

"You know, there are some people who have a hard time accepting help, they want to do everything themselves. I speak from experience."

"Yeah well, I was stupid enough to continue making my case. I told her she'd make a lot more money, picked up one of her bottles and said 'you get what, five cents a bottle? How much can you make a night, even if you do start with an empty cart for each run? I'm worried about you making ends meet.' Inez quickly grabbed for the bottle and it slipped out of my hand, shattering in the street."

I thought back to that night when Bardot and I watched Inez do some sort of bottle swapping between the bins and her cart. I would need to expend some additional brain cells on this.

"My guess is that you hurt her pride. I know you were just trying to help, but before you save the world, Aimee, you need to pay all your attention to yourself. Did Inez say anything else?"

"Pretty much what you just said, she told me that she minds her own business and suggested that I do the same."

I spent the next few days mapping out the website for the Coast Guard. Sometimes called wire frames, this exercise would become the blueprint for the project.

I heard a ping emanate from my computer, and tried to stay focused on my task at hand. I was pretty sure that this alert was another time waster from my newsgroup. It pinged again and this time it had me.

I was glad that I did, this was notification that my search program on the film company Musso was involved in was complete.

After deciphering the results and doing a bit more research, I discovered that the Nighthawk Film Production Company was a dummy corporation registered out of Nevada. This lead was both good and bad. Good because I'd confirmed that it exists and was clearly intended to be kept off the books. It was bad because, by definition, a dummy company's true owners usually hide behind an attorney or bagman. Connecting all this to Musso just became a herculean task.

I remembered what Marisol has said about Thursday night being the time Musso loaded the cars onto a truck and drove them somewhere. I wondered if Rosa had been up one of those nights and had confronted him. Or helped him? Tomorrow was Thursday, and I needed to find out and get something on Musso.

I had no idea how long I'd be gone, so I packed the car with waters, a Thermos of tea, some snacks, and a laptop.

Never leave home without one.

I'd decided to bring Bardot, for company, safety, and comic relief. And for good measure, I texted Sally, letting her know what I was doing, and sent it in the last minute so she couldn't stop me.

It was about eleven thirty at night and the loading of the cars had begun. This time there were only four so the truck was a bit smaller. I loaded Bardot into the back and as I started closing the door, I felt some resistance. I let up for a second and Marisol appeared from behind and slithered into my car.

"Oh no you don't!" I yell-whispered.

She grinned at me and Bardot, delighted to have a back seat mate, barked with joy.

"Get out!"

"No, I'm helping you, Halsey."

Bardot thought that this was a game and barked louder. I needed to quickly diffuse the noise. The truck had started up; there was no time to argue.

As I got into the driver's seat, I said, "I'm letting you out at the first light, and you can walk home. This is a one woman job."

Marisol fastened her seat belt and Bardot curled up in her denim dress lap. I knew that I was stuck with her.

"How much wine did you drink today at that club, you safe to drive?"

I followed at a safe distance although the driver seemed to have come with the truck, so I doubt he'd be concerned about a tail. Musso was in the passenger seat but he'd have to have been tipped off to want to reposition the long side mirror to see past the truck to what was behind. We were heading northeast and with little to no traffic, we were cruising.

"So are you and Inez friends, Marisol?"

"Not really, but I help her out, give her the girls' old clothes, shoes I no longer wear, cookies I get on sale."

"So that's what was in the paper bag you handed her the other night?'

"Maybe."

She looked over at me surprised and a little nervous by my observation.

It doesn't feel so good when the shoe's on the other foot, does it Marisol?

"And in return she tells you what's going on in the 'hood based on her trash bin forays?"

"She volunteers, I don't ask for it," Marisol said, raising her chin up in a display of dignity.

"And?" I asked, suspecting that she'd clam up.

"Nothing worth repeating, yet."

Marisol the mysterious. But not a murderer, I decided.

"You got any new information to contribute to our little field trip, Marisol?" I looked into the rearview mirror and saw her sitting comfortably and looking at the scenery. A nice night for a drive in her mind.

"I know you didn't kill Rosa," she replied.

"What? How?" I almost veered off the road. "Has Augie found evidence on Musso?"

"Not yet, but you weren't the first one to go into Rosa's house that day."

Why was this only now coming out?

I tried to remain calm. "Who else went in?"

"I can't remember."

I slowed the car, seriously considering throwing her out.

"What do you mean you can't remember?" My voice was rising and I woke Bardot up.

"I seen the front door open and somebody was coming out; there was shade on the front stoop so I couldn't see who it was. I'd have to wait until they reached the sidewalk."

"So who'd you see when they got to the street?"

"I didn't see nobody. You and Bardot came out of your house, and I was more interested in seeing what you were up to."

"Arrrgh!" Tossing her out was too soft, I started thinking about tying her to the rear fender and making her run.

"Think, you sure you didn't see who came out of that house?"

"I been trying, ever since Augie and me-" She stopped herself.

"Ever since what? You like torturing me, don't you?"

"Since we decided you could stay and we'd help you prove someone else did the murder."

There it was, straight out of the horse's mouth, I had indeed been accepted into Marisol's coven.

Chapter 14

About forty minutes into the trip, we exited the freeway and made our way on a smaller route. We had left most of the vestiges of civilization behind, and even in the dark, the beauty of the hilly terrain and forestry did not go unnoticed.

My ears were popping from the altitude as we passed the ENTERING ANGELES NATIONAL FOREST sign and then began ringing as Bardot got a nose full of critters and started yelping excitedly. It was risky but I decided to turn my headlights off so that I could follow closer to the truck. I didn't want to get lost in here in the middle of the night.

"They're turning, Halsey!"

"I see it; don't back seat drive."

With that, Marisol slithered her way into the passenger seat.

"How old are you again?"

She just grinned.

The truck was starting to slow, and I wondered what we were going to be faced with next. Some sort

of rendezvous? God, I hoped we were not going to
see another murder.

The truck stopped and I had to hang my upper
body out the window to see what was happening. I
watched a guard unlock a large chain anchored on
each side of the dirt road by concrete posts so that
the truck could pass. As soon as it did, the man re-
locked it.

"What's happening?" Marisol asked, squeezing
her body into my window as well.

"Ow! Get back in your seat! What's happened is
we're screwed, that's what's happened."

With the truck gone and clear moonlight, we
could now see that a fence went around on both
sides of the road into the forest, there was no way
we could bypass it.

"I'm going to take a look, maybe there's a way,"
Marisol said, hopping out.

"Don't let the dog—"

It was too late; Bardot took off like a flash.

"AARGH!"

I grabbed the emergency backpack my dad had
put together and insisted I take for the trip across
county. Inside I found a flashlight which I quickly
made use of. The bag also had water, some tools, a
flare, and some dehydrated food. Dear ole Dad.

"I don't suppose that if I told you to wait in the
car you'd do so?" I asked Marisol, who was already
heading up the path.

"Come on, she can't have gotten too far."

I found Bardot's leash in the back and off we
went.

It was so quiet away from city noise that our footsteps echoed. We whispered Bardot's name as softly as we could.

There was a sudden rustle emanating from the brush and I swung the light, hoping to see yellow Lab ears. Instead, the golden fur of a mountain lion came into view.

We both screamed. I was sure that if this cat didn't kill us Musso would.

I signaled for Marisol to stay still, and the animal disappeared.

I caught my breath and we continued on, even more quietly.

A second noise, this time running toward us, sent me into a cold sweat.

Did the lion go and get reinforcements? Did my dad pack any pepper spray in the backpack? I closed my eyes and braced for the worst.

I felt the weight of an animal hit my chest and then the wetness of a tongue on my face.

"Bardot!" Marisol said, petting her. That triggered a lick on her face.

Bardot jumped down and took off again, this time stopping up ahead and looking back. I grabbed her leash and approached gently.

"Where'd they go, Bardot?" Marisol asked and Bardot went running.

"I'm trying to get a leash on her so we can get out of here, thanks a lot!"

"We've got to follow her, she wants to lead us to Musso."

Did Marisol speak dog now?

"Look, there's a bunch of lights up there by that waterfall," Marisol said.

Bardot wagged her tail and smiled as we caught up to her.

"Good girl," I said and gave her some dehydrated peas.

What wasn't in my pack were binoculars, but I had a souped-up camera app with a great zoom feature. Marisol crouched next to me and we scanned all the activity. Musso was directing the off-loading of the cars. We watched big lights being positioned, as well as cameras. I saw several trucks with *Nighthawk Film Production Company* signs on them, and some people waiting at the side in director's chairs.

"This is a film shoot," I said, doing a camera pan from one end to the other. "Musso is supplying cars for movies."

"Why does he have to be so secretive about that?" Marisol asked, standing up.

"Because he's working off the books with a sham company. He probably gets paid in cash and certainly doesn't pay any taxes on the income."

"He doesn't have it long enough, that bitch makes him buy her things every week. I hear her whining all the time, 'Musso, I need jewelry, buy me some diamonds,' makes me sick."

"You do an awfully good impression of her," I said, looking at her suspiciously. "How do you hear all these things?"

She looked at me and shrugged.

"Never mind."

I took some photos of the scene and then we headed back to the car.

Finally I had something. If only I could tie it to Rosa.

Chapter 15

The next Wine Club happened to fall on the day of the autumnal equinox. My exhausted body was magically lifted when I arrived at Cassie's and was handed a candied apple martini.

Wine Club can be about real booze? Unless I win the lottery, I'm never moving. Unless I go to jail.

You've gotta love Cassie's quirky sense of occasion, this was all about fall; she served baked brie with raspberry preserves, homemade pretzels with mustard and gherkins, maple-spiced nuts, and hallowed out mini pumpkins filled with turkey chili. But I must say that I was a little stumped by a bowl of small rectangular-shaped candies.

"Get it? Squirrel Nut Zippers." She giggled.

The Chihuahuas were out of sight and I decided not to ask, for now.

This was my first real visit to Cassie and Carl's house. It was really kind of fun to see the blending of both personalities. I knew Cassie was much younger than Carl, and I suspected that he had become pretty set in his ways before she met him. I'll break it down the way she told me:

Pre-Cassie Furnishings & Accoutrements
- Barroom fully stocked with mini fridge, dartboard, and pinball machine
- Living room recliner chair, albeit a leather one
- Wall-mounted collection of framed *Rolling Stones* covers

Post-Cassie Furnishings & Accoutrements
- Custom color painted walls and carved moldings
- An antique, full-size women's mannequin also in the living room and currently dressed in a kimono
- A bedazzled yoga mat sprawled in front of a TV as large as my garage door

And you know what? It all worked perfectly together.

"You should tell Augie," Aimee urged after I told them all about my trip with Marisol to the Angeles Forest and what Musso was doing with those cars each week.

"But this doesn't put him any closer to Rosa," I said. "Sally, did I hear you say earlier that Musso and Rosa had a thing going at some point?"

"I said that I'd see them talking together, it looked like a sweet romance. You know, when you see a couple and they laugh at every imbecilic thing each of them says? Even if it is as dumb as a sack of wet mice?"

A sack of what?

"So maybe we should be looking at his nasty ass girlfriend Tala instead," Cassie added.

"Just what I was thinking, does anyone know her last name?"

"Seems like Augie would have that," proffered Sally.

"You'd better add my sleuthing report when you call Augie," Peggy teased, waiting for us to press her for details.

"What did you do?" Aimee asked, frightened for her.

"Well," Peggy replied, and then paused for effect. "I got up early this morning and decided to take care of the damn weeds growing in with my rose bushes."

"*And?*" we all shouted.

"I saw Ray carrying bags full of stuff out of Rosa's house. Probably going to pawn the family heirlooms, such that they are, for cash to buy drugs."

"I imagine that he's allowed to go in there now, the cops have finished with the crime scene and he has to be the next of kin," I said, wincing at the reminder of that day.

"That's it?" Cassie asked, disappointed.

"You didn't confront him, did you?" Aimee asked.

"That's what I intended to do, Momma didn't raise no dumbass."

"So what did he say?" I was getting impatient.

"Nothing, he was heading back into the house when I got up there. And that's when I saw her."

"*Who?*" We were all ready to tear our hair out.

"Inez, she came out of Rosa's house and gave him a big smooch."

"Oh my God," chimed Sally, Cassie, and Aimee.

"They have a thing? Did you all know about this?"

They all shook their heads at me. This was getting more and more complicated. Sure we were gathering pieces to the puzzle, but each one only seemed to be opening the case up for more suspects.

"Peggy, did either of them see you?" Aimee asked, a tear forming in the corner of her eye.

"Not Ray, but Inez did. Maybe she'll keep her mouth shut, Ray is the one I'd worry about."

"I'd worry about Inez too," Cassie said.

"Oh, Peggy, no." Aimee stood.

"Worrying about what's done is like watering a dead plant, Aimee," Sally remarked and got a blank look.

"I'll do some checking on both of them when I research Tala. You'd think with all these possible murderers that I'd finally be knocked off the list."

"Even more important that you fill in Augie," Sally said, nodding to my phone.

"Right," I said, bringing it to life. "Hey, I have a voice mail from Augie, I wonder how I missed that?"

"Put it on speaker," Cassie demanded, trying to take over the phone operation. I pulled it away from her and tapped "play."

"Hi, Halsey, a couple of updates: First off, it seems that Rosa had recently changed her will to leave her estate to the Mar Vista Boys and Girls Club. That cuts Ray out, but we are confirming that this was actually filed or is just a draft."

"Wait until I tell him about Ray cleaning out her house." I noticed that the girls had formed a circle around my phone and had linked arms.

"Second, like I warned you, it seems that your ex did file a police report on you but didn't press charges and everybody here has seen it. It doesn't prove motive but it does show a history of violence. Marquez wants you to come down and make a statement about this. I would do it sooner rather than later. I know it's nothing but you have to convince them."

They all gasped.

Looks like I got some splainin to do. . . .

"Lastly, we got an anonymous tip from one of your neighbors living across the street from Rosa. They emailed us a recording from the security camera mounted over their front porch. From the day she was stabbed. It's really grainy and needs to be enhanced; our IT guys are working on it. I'll keep you posted, and let me know if you have anything more to report."

Wow, I wonder who sent it. . . .

That was the end of the message but we all kept looking at the phone for another minute in silence. Like Siri was suddenly going to wrap this all up for us.

Chapter 16

As requested, I summarized the Wine Club's sleuthing results in an email and sent it off to Augie. He once again warned us about sticking our noses where they don't belong, and said he hoped that we would just move on. Like I could do that knowing that the deck was stacked against me.

At this point the Wine Club was hooked and not about to give up until the real killer was found. I started to close my email so I could get down to researching Tala and Ray. I paused when I saw the list of unopened emails.

Curiosity got the better of me and I figured that it was about time I took a look at the messages Jack had sent me. After all, just because he was conflicted about his last relationship didn't make him a bad person. But it did make him a bad person for *me* and my new drama-free life.

Halsey, I read from the first email. *I can't tell you how sorry I am that you had to deal with my ex. And she*

IS my ex. We used to work together and she has referred clients to me over the years, so I didn't want to totally cut off the lines of communication. I know I messed up and I've told her only to contact me if there is an emergency and to do so by text.

Turns out this was an emergency, friends of hers were holed up in their bedroom with their infant because the family Rottweiler suddenly turned aggressive toward the baby. Classic jealousy behavior, so I went over and calmed him down and am now working with them to resolve this.

I miss you so much and want to start over, take you out for a nice dinner, take it slow and get to know each other.

BTW: I got some info on Rosa's brother from a detective friend. His K-9 unit was brought out for a drug bust a few months ago.

Well, he did sound sincere and he clearly had a big heart. And something that might help with the case . . .

I dashed off a quick reply explaining that I was really busy with work but would call him once I got this project out, and yes, dinner and getting know him sounded nice.

But that was it, I thought to myself.

The office phone rang and I saw from the caller ID that it was the prospective Coast Guard client. I picked up and tried to sound as professional as possible. It turned out that he just needed some corporate info on my company and wanted to know how many people I was bringing to the presentation. Security needed to have their names. Pretty standard, but it's amazing how differently you take things when the police are watching your every move. I have got to get this murder figured out.

We were having a pleasant conversation that was moving off the agenda for the call and more into the getting-to-know-you business relationship. Bardot suddenly started barking fiercely by the window facing the side street. No tail wagging this time, she meant business. I tried tossing jellybeans for her, hoping the chewy confections would occupy her mouth otherwise, while I held my hand over the mouthpiece of the phone. No such luck, her fur on her back had gone up and her anger had intensified. I quickly ended the call, apologizing and claiming that FedEx had sent the neighbor's dog into a frenzy.

I took a breath and got up to look out and see what all the fuss was about. Bardot had finally stopped barking and was getting colorful food dye all over her fur from rolling on the candy. I had a headache that became exacerbated by the deep roar of a car starting up. By the time I got to the window, I could just make out the back end of a Mercedes as it turned the corner and was out of sight. I'd seen that car in Musso's driveway.

I really hadn't spent any time in Marina del Rey since I'd moved here, and I needed to experience it if I had any hope of winning this pitch for the Coast Guard website. I decided to go there and I invited Cassie to come along, I knew she used to sail and figured she could help. She also offered to bring Carl's camera so I could get shots for my presentation. She told me that Carl was down in the desert for a week at a golf tournament, so I'd have plenty of time to download all the photos before his return.

Perfect all around.

Marina del Rey serves multiple audiences. It is a safe harbor for any vessel in distress, it is home to the yachts of the rich and famous and to the early houseboat settlers who would be hard pressed to make it out past the jetty.

It offers practice waters for both the UCLA and Loyola Marymount crew teams, teaches kids to captain sailfish boats in the summer, and launches larger craft carrying hopeful fishermen daily. Add to that waterside restaurants, a park for concerts, and condos with fabulous views, and you have a lovely place to visit.

It also provides access for boats large and small entering from anywhere off the Pacific. It is not unusual to see a 250-foot yacht belonging to a pro golfer or tech wizard resting in the channel. Los Angeles County manages the large harbor along with harbor patrol, the fire and sheriff departments, the Army Corps of Engineers and the Coast Guard, and Homeland Security.

"So you taught sailing here?" I asked Cassie as we drove out the south side of the Marina to Fisherman's Village.

Since I was living in the film capitol of the world, it should have come as no surprise to me that the waterfront looked like a typical New England port. It has been used as a backdrop in numerous movies

and TV shows. Brightly colored cottage style buildings of various heights line the boardwalk, fooling
you into thinking that you just disembarked from
the ferry to Nantucket. There is even a blue and
white decorative lighthouse, with a burger stand at
the base.

"Only for a summer, when I got back from Greece.
I wasn't sure what I was going to do next and didn't
want to give up the water just yet," she replied, leaving me with so many questions.

She saw my look and laughed.

"Don't worry, honey, I'll explain it all over
lunch."

We parked near the Coast Guard station and
started our tour. I let Cassie handle the picture taking so that I could observe and really get a sense of
the place.

Cassie, in her full-length geometric print halter
dress, walked the boardwalk like she was about to
board a yacht and go for a nice long luncheon
cruise.

The large channel was rife with activity. It was still
morning and the last of the rowing crews were finishing up their workouts before the traffic got heavy
and the water got choppy. I watched a women's
eight sweep boat glide smoothly with each send of
its oars. Their blades dropped perfectly in unison,
this UCLA collegiate team was going to go far.

Cassie and I walked and photographed for a little
over an hour. When I saw that she had moved on to
shooting tourists with their phones and restyling
their outfits, I figured it was time to break and get
some lunch.

Of course, Cassie had an opinion on that as well.

"There is this little café over here, way less touristy and pretty decent food."

She was walking ahead of me now, so I guess we were not going to be discussing dining alternatives.

"Their wine is crap though; I've tried before to sneak my own in, but I swear those guys can smell it. They're like those pigs in France that find those mushrooms. I suggest we stick with the Prosecco, can't go wrong with that."

I wasn't thinking of drinking anything but iced tea. This was lunch after all, and I would have to get back to work in a couple of hours.

You placed your order up front and they brought your food to your table when it was ready. Seemed simple enough, unless you are Cassie.

"I'm thinking about the Windjammer Salad but I'm not a big fan of chickpeas, can you do edamame instead?

The woman behind the counter stopped punching the order into the computer. "I'm not sure we have edamame—"

"Ooh, the Greek Chicken Wrap sounds really good. Lemon brined free-range chicken? I don't think I've ever had that. Hmmm."

The line was backing up and I tried to pretend that I wasn't with Cassie and was equally annoyed.

"What are you going to get, Halsey?"

Busted.

Before I could reply, she said, "I think I'll go with the Mediterranean Platter. Wait, what is the Feta marinated in?"

After tasting all the wines, she decided on a bottle of Prosecco. I knew I'd only drink one glass, but if I'd argued, I would have probably been left swinging lifeless from a brass harbor lantern.

"How's your pizza?" she asked after we had finally sat down and got our food. I'd ordered the daily special because it seemed simple and fast.

"Good—would you like some?"

"Are those capers?"

I knew we were headed back down a slippery slope, so I quickly moved the conversation to one of Cassie's favorite subjects.

"Here's to our first lunch, just the two of us. I believe you teased me about some stories, Cassie."

We clinked glasses, she beamed, and off she went.

As I suspected, Cassie is not exactly what you would think. Sure, she's got the playful minx act down pat, but there is always method to her minxness. Here's a synopsis of her hour-plus dissertation:

She has five brothers and she's the oldest. She calls them her "army of minions," and you can just imagine how she commanded her troops. With such a large family they had to live very simple lives. From the get-go, Cassie worked hard to rise above doing babysitting gigs, working in the summer at a luggage store, even a short-lived stint as an all-around assistant to a Hollywood stunt man.

Cassie's a college graduate, "poli-sci." Although that's not really what she majored in. She also conceded that she finished in five years, the last being done some time later.

"When I was a junior, I got bored. See you had

to take a lot of history courses with a poli-sci major and I just hated it until I discovered ancient Greece."

Wait, what now?

"You familiar with Plato's dialogues, his descriptions of a peaceful utopia called Atlantis?"

"I remember the Bermuda Triangle stories, which were mostly debunked, and of course the Disney movie on the lost city, which left me with an odd craving for spanakopita."

"No," said Cassie, helping herself to a slice of my pizza and picking out the capers. She then grabbed some sun-dried tomatoes from another slice and doubled up.

"Those stories are all BS. You've got to look at the Greek island of Santorini. Sometime in 1600 BC a volcano erupted and sent the middle of it down to the bottom of the sea. The prevailing theory back then was that this was the location of the lost city of Atlantis."

Who are you and what have you done with Cassie?

"Ah, it's coming back to me. Wasn't it also thought to be in the Azores, and Cyprus, even off the coast of Cuba?"

"Yeah, well, I went on an archaeological vacation one Christmas and ended up staying on Santorini for a year."

"Wow!"

"Yes, it was a lot of dusting and cleaning of objets d'art, which is why I told Carl that we have to have the maid come three times a week. But there is nothing like the blue of the Aegean, and Giorgo taught me so much about the Minoan civilization. And other things."

She was smiling and lost in her own reverie.

"And did you know that Santorini produces some of the best wines in Greece? We'd go around on his motor scooter from place to place tasting wines and yummy cheeses."

"Isn't Santorini built along cliffs, with cobblestone roads?"

I was scared for her even now despite knowing that she had lived to tell about it.

"Oh, I wasn't scared. I just held on tight to my handsome Greek man, closed my eyes, and thought about all the different ways that I could wear my 'worry beads.' I once got them so caught in my hair that I had to cut them out!"

I was glad to hear that "College Cassie" wasn't a total stranger from the one I know and love.

"I have to ask you about those dogs, Cassie. I'm afraid you can't fool Bardot's nose, it goes up in the air each time we walk by your house," I said, changing the subject. I figured that thoughts of Giorgo might lull her into being more forthcoming.

"Okay, okay, I have adopted two cute Chihuahuas. They're really fun to dress up and we all paint our nails the same color."

She held out her hands and I shuddered, thinking of those dogs' paws sporting "Jungle Red."

"Were they Rosa's?"

"I don't know, they came to my door and didn't tell me where they came from. They were shivering so I let them in, what else was I supposed to do? You know how I love animals of all kinds."

Of course. They were Rosa's.

"Did they have anything on them, scratches? Blood?"

"No nothing. Then all hell broke loose with the murder and I figured that they had been through enough, so I kept it quiet. I was going to make my debut with them in time."

"I was thinking that you should tell someone, the cops maybe? But if there was any evidence, it is long gone by now. It's not like they are going to tell us what they saw."

"Oh, but they will. Carl and I found this medium that can talk to dogs. He's coming by next week. This will crack the case wide open!"

The next thing I knew, the Prosecco was gone and Cassie was on a quest for a coffee with Ouzo. I wasn't sure if she'd taken those dogs from Rosa or found them just like she described. Either way it was a tad suspicious, especially since she was keeping it a secret. Cassie was the kind of girl Facebook status updates were created for, she tells you every little thing.

Before we parted on Rose Avenue, she handed me the SD card from Carl's camera. I promised to offload the photos in a few days and return it before Carl got back.

Needless to say I did not make it back to work during that day and had to spend the night playing catch up. I couldn't help myself, I wasn't comfortable being in the office alone this late despite having Bardot to guard me. I couldn't count on her nose sending an alarm to the rest of her deep sleeping body which was so sprawled out that she looked like a passed out snow angel.

So I set the alarm in the house and worked from bed on my laptop. When I could no longer coherently write code, I switched to an e-book and a glass of Croft's Fine Ruby Port wine.

Chapter 17

"Good morning, Manny," Aimee singsonged while unlocking the door to Chill Out. I'd dropped her off as her car was being serviced and she'd promised me a cup of sumptin' sumptin'.

"Morning," returned Manny as he hosed off the front patio before setting up the little café tables and chairs for today's guests.

We were the only ones in the strip mall working at such an early hour. Aimee had told me that this was the favorite part of her day. With only the sounds of waking birds expanding their little lungs with enthusiastic chirps, Aimee had time to think about the rosy future she hoped she and Tom were working toward. Oh, she said that she planned to keep working even once Tom got his practice, but hopefully doing something that allowed her to be home and have days off the same time Tom did. Right now, she relayed that if they managed to have even one dinner together it was a good week.

Manny finished rinsing the patio and went around

back to the shed to get out the tables. At that same time Aimee had the door unlocked and flipped on the lights.

"ARGHHHH!" Aimee screamed.

"Jesus, Mary, Joseph, and the Easter Bunny," I yelled, not sure where the hell that came from.

The yogurt shop looked like it had been ransacked by a band of marauding pirates. Serving cups were strewn all over the floor, shredded into tiny pieces. Some of the cute neon-colored chairs lay on their sides amid plastic shavings from gnawed legs. Framed photos from a shelf displaying "Chill Out's Biggest Fans" had toppled and lay broken where they fell. Nonperishable toppings while in canisters had been opened and gotten at. And forget about the napkin dispensers. Manny ran in and contributed another scream.

"I thought we'd been robbed," Aimee said, hyperventilating. "We never keep more than a hundred dollars in the register overnight, so that would have been okay." She was now also crying which made it really hard for her to catch her breath. "This is much, much worse," she said in a whisper, fearfully scanning the restaurant.

"Who or what did this?" Manny was now whispering out of deference as well.

"Looks like rats on 'roids," I said, gagging a little.

I looked around and couldn't believe my eyes. In addition to the destruction of goods and furniture, the floor was littered with rat droppings about the size of Tootsie Rolls. I shuddered when I thought about the size of the animal that did this.

"You think somebody did this to us? How? Why?"

"I don't know," Manny replied. "But these are no ordinary rats, they're not from around here. I know the rats around here and they are fat and slow. This was a feeding frenzy."

"OH GOD," Aimee shrieked as a rat the size of Shaq's shoe leapt from the counter and disappeared under the cabinets. When a second varmint joined chase, Manny, Aimee, and I raced to the door and had a Three Stooges moment trying to all fit through at the same time.

"I don't understand, we have a rat control service. I have never so much as seen one dropping! How could we have an infestation all of a sudden?"

She was getting close to a pitch that only dogs could hear.

"I may know how," Manny said, heading toward the shed at the back. Aimee and I slowly followed, she resting her hand on her forehead.

"What exactly did the police say?" asked Sally.

She and Cassie were plying giant brooms and disinfectant all over Chill Out. Cassie, always one to rise to the occasion with fashion, was dressed accordingly in a "Rosie the Riveter" denim shirt and red bandana loosely holding her hair back. A man's wide brown leather belt over white jeans completed the picture, but never one to sacrifice fashion, her wedge open-toed sandals seemed a little off.

"They said since there was no forced entry, that I should look at the people who have keys to the place. That would be Tom, Manny, and Kimberly, and I trust them like the back of my hand," Aimee explained, actually looking at the back of her hand.

"Of course you do, there has to be another explanation." I'd seen rats in New York eating egg rolls with chopsticks, so I was not quite as horrified as my friends.

"What about the broken shed and the roof, did they check that? Seems obvious that's how the rats were put in here," Sally said conclusively.

"They kinda checked it, but I don't even think they actually went up on the roof," answered Aimee. "Manny's going to help me get up there tonight and check it out. Although I don't know if I'm ready to face the possibility that this was done to me on purpose."

"Whaaa? Can't you hire people to do that? Should I call Augie?"

Cassie seemed to think that now that she'd heard his voice mail Augie was hers for all police matters.

"Completely different division, Cassie," Aimee clarified.

"Why wait, let's go up there now and check it out," I decided and headed out the back door. Sally, Cassie, and Aimee went into the back to look for the stepladder.

"What are these crazy girls doin'?" I heard Ali Baba say. I'd noticed that he and Zeke were sitting out front of their shop, having a smoke as I headed out back. Now was a good time to listen in and maybe get something on Ray.

"Don't say nothin', Ray wants us to stay clear away from them," whispered Zeke.

"The yogurt lady always been nice to us, let us set there and feeds us. . . ." whined Ali Baba. "She let me try every flavor, angel food, German chocolate, pecan praline, watermelon grape, red velvet, key lime-"

"She so nice, why she gonna go climbing on the roof, snooping all around? You go up there? They gonna find anything?" I heard Zeke's urgent voice say.

"I ain't been up there, I swear, Zeke."

"And how come you can remember all those yogurt flavors, but you forget to tell me that our supplier missed a shipment?"

I inched as close as I could to them without being noticed.

"I didn't forget, he tol' me that the storm in Mexico made them a day late," said Ali Baba, with his hand on his heart.

"Well, you didn't tell me that and now we have to play catch-up. Work even harder."

"I can do dat Zeke, I can do dat, anything you need me to do I do. You know dat, right?"

Ali Baba's blind ignorance and dog-like willingness to please gnawed at me.

"I know that, Ali Baba, we just got to tighten up our act a little bit. We are getting close to a big payday, as long as we keep Ray and his partner happy."

"Woo, 'I need mon-ey, that's what I want, I need mon-ey,' " Ali Baba sang while slapping out a beat on his thighs.

* * *

"What was that," said Cassie, taking her steadying hands off the stool we were using to climb from the shed up to the roof. Aimee started to teeter as she was reaching for Sally's hand to hoist her up.

"CASSIE," we all shouted. Cassie went back to her duties and Sally pulled Aimee up onto the roof.

I'd been the first up, pretty easily scaling the side, thanks in part to the rock wall classes I'd taken during a snowstorm one winter.

"Okay, let's look around, but don't touch anything," said Sally, channeling her best TV crime detective.

"Wow, look at the view up here, I should do rooftop seating," said Aimee, desperately looking for a silver lining to this dire situation.

The building wasn't tall enough for them to see all the way to the ocean, but it did offer a nice bird's-eye view of the neatly kept residential neighborhood just south of the mall. The Jacaranda trees were just starting to bear their lavender flowers.

"Rat poop," observed Sally. "Someone must have dropped them down this vent. And is this a cigarette or"—she sniffed—"mary-wanna!"

"And not just the lone doobie, check out this stash." I'd kicked over an orange Home Depot bucket because it looked so out of place. A quart baggie was lying there fully expanded. Inside, the dried leaves and broken branches looked like a swollen, used scouring pad.

"That is not chia seed," Sally said upon closer inspection.

"Are you saying that someone deliberately brought a bunch of rats up here and had a pot party while dropping them into my shop?"

"This isn't yours, Aimee?" I asked.

"Oh my God no! I have never—"

Aimee was too shocked even to cry.

"I want to see," said Cassie, pulling herself up to the roof. "It is sorta nice up here, and look there are your shop neighbors out front. Hieee." She waved.

Zeke and Ali Baba quickly got into the El Camino and drove off.

"I think I'm going to be sick," said Aimee.

I think I can cross Aimee off my list of suspects, I said to myself. She's never smoked pot so I doubt she'd help sell it, and it seems to me that this shot over the bow was a warning sign of things to come if she and we didn't stop poking around.

Chapter 18

I was excited at the prospect of spending the day in fresh air after dealing with all the rat detritus at Aimee's. I'd finally acquiesced to Jack's offer of taking me on a CARA training session.

I know, resuming anything with Jack was trouble with a capital *T*, but since when do I listen to the "good Halsey"? Plus, I was dying to know what he'd found out about Ray. This was our first date since our "time out" period, and I figured that it was a good way to start getting to know each other. Jack delicately suggested that maybe Bardot should sit this first one out so that I could focus on what it all entailed.

Translation: it is highly possible that Bardot's exuberance could result in us all needing to be rescued.

I thought hard about what to wear. I certainly didn't want to show up as "Carrie Bradshaw goes hiking." I was determined to keep up and show

Jack my athletic prowess. I also didn't want to dress too butch and send him running back to his old girlfriend.

I settled on a "G.I. Jane meets Jane Rizzoli" look. Need more of a mental image? From the bottom up: hiking boots, neon yellow socks, fatigue skinny jeans, white wifebeater (I tried on but decided against a black bra), a beige cotton bolero sweater, and hair in a sexy, loose bun. Bardot watched me examine the finished product in the mirror, and I swear I saw her mouth the words, "keep trying."

Jack had said that we would be working in the Santa Monica Mountains, but that was about all I knew. When the time for him to pick me up had passed, I decided to wait outside so we could get going as soon as he arrived. That was when I saw Jack sitting on Marisol's stoop, showing her photos on his Smartphone. *What the*—?

"Hey," he said, waving at me. "You ready?"

I looked from him to Marisol who seemed disappointed at my arrival.

"Are those flowers for me?" I asked, spying a bouquet on her stoop.

"Nope, he brought them for me, on account of last time and his noisy truck," she said, gloating at me.

"You look hot," he whispered as he put his arm around me and we headed to his truck.

If I'm jealous, I'm an idiot.

I assumed we were headed for the freeway but Jack turned into the Santa Monica airport. I looked at him questioningly and he just grinned. We pulled up to a gate and Jack punched in a code. Next thing I knew we were driving onto the runway.

"Cool." I beamed.

Jack raised his eyebrows and gently nodded. He was enjoying this.

"Here we are," he said, parking by a helicopter fired up and ready to go.

Jack was wearing his official CARA attire, which made him look like a paratrooper or, with his shaved head, a lost member of the Village People. He grabbed a gear bag and his dog Clarence who hopped out and as usual, stood at attention.

"The first thing Bardot would have to learn is how to be calm and comfortable getting on and off a copter," he shouted over the noise of the rotor blades. "Clarence, come."

Fat chance, I thought.

We boarded, sat, belted up, and put on headsets to hear each other.

"Say hello to our pilot, Sydney," Jack introduced.

Sydney was a woman, an attractive woman, and I suddenly regretted nixing the black bra.

"And this is Neil, he's in charge of running the rescue lines," Jack informed me.

I suddenly had a bad feeling about what was coming.

We took off vertically and headed up the coastline.

"Approaching Malibu Colony," Sydney said in my headphones. "Special fly-by tour just for you, Halsey," she added.

It seemed that Jack had orchestrated some preferential treatment for this date. We flew over one mansion after another. You had dreaded faux Mediterranean style monstrosities, super modern boxes that I named "Walmart by the Shore," and thankfully some white and blue Cape Cod homes that seemed just right. Note to self, when I win the lottery I'll take my realtor on a plane ride and point out the ones I would consider.

"See anything you like?" Jack asked me, grinning.

"I need to see some of these close up," I replied. "Think they'd mind if we dropped in?"

We took a turn and headed inland to the mountains. I knew this was going to be work and I tried to imagine having beachside cocktails with Cher instead. We coasted up a mountainside and at the top, I saw a clearing and some people and their dogs.

"This is where we'll set down for the moment," informed Sydney.

Neil started to pull out ropes and other gear I did not recognize and got busy preparing.

"These teams are all getting ready to take their Wilderness Trailing test for certification. They've been training for over two years," Jack explained as we disembarked from the helicopter.

This was hardcore. The handlers were dressed similar to Jack and had backpacks stuffed with gear, first aid supplies and plenty of water. And I did not see one dog sniff another's butt or randomly pee. The dogs were all wearing red vests with a white cross on them. The bigger ones were also carrying supplies. I decided I'd just tell Bardot that her beauty and talents would be wasted with CARA. . . .

Jack outlined how this was going to go.

"There are three participants in this test, the CARA evaluator, the K-9 team, and the subject needing rescue. In this case the subject's gone on ahead and left 'evidence' at four locations along the way. In this bag is a scent pad that was rubbed across his arms, neck, and hair. That's what the rescue team has to go on. They must find at least three of the clues and then the subject within ninety minutes."

"And this is all volunteer?" I asked incredulously.

"Pretty much—we rely on donations for training materials, transportation expenses, and other supplies," Jack told me while heading back toward the helicopter. "We usually average about three hundred rescues a year."

I followed Jack back into the helicopter, took my same seat and belted up. Over the headphones, I heard him say to the group, "K-9 team is off and running, let's follow them."

We lifted off and hovered low over the trees and terrain. Jack had an aerial map of the wilderness, showing the sites where evidence had been left. In the team below were a German shepherd and her female handler. They were moving at quite a clip using mostly nonverbal communication.

"This is all about scent tracking," said Jack. "We chose this course because of its natural obstacles. The heavy brush we are over now, up ahead is a creek, and toward the end there is a rock quarry. Jodi has her dog Macy on a long lead so that they can work together as a team. Jodi told us up front that when Macy finds scented evidence she barks once and lies down a few feet away from it. We'll be able to see that from up here."

Hovering just above the treetops, we could easily follow their progress, and peering out of open windows, we were treated to some of the scents and smells of the woods. I picked up pine, sage, and lots of woody scents and salty air.

"This is amazing," I said, watching a sort of canine *Hunger Games* play out below me. "And what part of this do you think Bardot has an innate aptitude for, exactly?"

Jack chuckled. "I know she is all over the place right now, but she will not let anything get in the way of her retrieving. Not water, not distractions I'll bet, and certainly with her energy, she won't give up until she has gotten her prize. From what you told me she comes from a long line of field Labs and as a result these characteristics are in her DNA."

I wanted to prove him right and divulge our Angeles Forest adventure, but would have to wait until we were off the headphones and mics. I watched the team go to work. A couple of times they veered off course according to the map, but Jodi seemed to recognize when Macy lost the scent and they'd backtrack and pick it up again.

"Neil, why don't you tell Halsey what you and Sydney know about Ray?"

"Sure, we were called out about two a.m. the other night to track some suspected drug activity being conducted in the Marina, just south of the channel.

DEA on the ground didn't want to show themselves just yet, said they were waiting for a bigger bust."

"I kept us far enough away," Sydney added, "but we used night vision to see exactly what they were doing."

"Turns out that it was just a run-through, the boat was a local fishing vessel. The DEA identified the guy as Ray Sobel, but they didn't know who the woman was," Neil said. He had unbelted, gotten up, and was now securing ropes to some sort of pulley.

"I know exactly who she is," I said to them. "Her name is Inez. She may be his girlfriend."

"We'll let the DEA know as soon as we get back, Halsey. Let's move ahead, Sydney," Jack instructed. "Ready?" he asked, grinning at me.

My eyes opened wide and I froze. "Ready for what?"

"We're going to complicate things a little bit for our K-9 team. Throw in some unrelated scents from a couple of people and an animal," said Jack, putting on some sort of harness.

I noticed that his dog Clarence was also getting harnessed and breathed a sigh of relief. They were going to be lowered down while I watched safely from my seat. Wait. Did he say "a couple of people"?

Next thing I knew, Jack was strapping something over my shoulders and across my chest. He had that glint in his eye and all I could do was stare blankly straight ahead.

"You're going to love this," he said. "We'll go down first and then Neil will send Clarence."

The side door opened, the pulley mechanism swung out, and Jack pulled me into his chest while he and Neil went through some sort of checklist.

"You're not scared of heights, are you?" Jack asked.

Before I could respond, he held me tight and we jumped out into the air. I burrowed my face as deep as I could into his chest and let out a sustained scream. His jacket, the sound of air swishing by us, and the rotor blades muffled it.

Jack directed Neil through his helmet headset and told him where to put us down.

As we got lower we started spinning and Jack said, "Hold tight, we'll be down in a sec."

What the hell did he think I was going to do? Cut loose and waft around like Tinker Bell?

Later I was forced to admit to myself that we landed softly and safely, but when Jack unhooked my harness, all I could think of was to start punching and kicking him.

WHOMP!

"You couldn't ask me if I wanted to jump out of a plane? If I was okay with being lowered into the jungle with nothing to protect me but you and a giant Schnauzer?"

So I was exaggerating a little, but he had scared the shit out of me. It didn't help that Clarence was now coming down on a rope, looking the epitome of cool, calm, and collected.

"One, it's a helicopter. Two, this is not the jun-

gle, and three, you don't think I can protect you?"
Jack asked with a mock hurt look and hands placed
over his heart.

"I'm just saying," I said.

Jack directed Neil and waited to grab Clarence.

"Come on," he said after unharnessing his dog.
"I'll show you what you would have missed if I'd
asked if you wanted to jump and you'd said 'no.'"

It was hard to accept that we were just about thirty
minutes out of Los Angeles. As far as you could see
in any direction was an amazing panorama of plant
life that I could now experience, up close; pine,
oak, and sycamore trees, California-looking sage
and cactus scrub. Then there was the cacophony
of animal and bird sounds that played like a perfectly orchestrated piece. Red-tailed hawks soared
overhead, and it was clear from the waste piles
scattered around, that deer, rabbits, and coyotes
roamed freely.

*How do you find Mel Tormé in the forest? Follow the
scat.*

For the next while, Jack led me through his wild
kingdom, pointing out fruits and vegetables growing. I'd never seen a wild radish. He loved finding
snakes and other reptiles (such a guy thing), and
he identified all kinds of fowl. When we got to the
creek and I saw ducks, I got a pang of guilt for not
bringing Bardot. This was Bardot heaven.

Once we crossed the creek, which was swollen
and running rapidly from the recent rain, Jack led
me up a hillside to a flattop boulder. I hadn't realized that we had been climbing in elevation, but in

this perfect spot we were high enough to see the ocean.

Why was cynical me wondering who else he had taken up here?

"Sydney tells me the team is about ten minutes away from us, so we've got time for a quick snack," Jack said, opening his backpack. Out came a baguette, cut up slices of apple, paté, and cheese.

We were famished and tucked in while lazing back on the rock. Clarence got water and apples and looked contented.

Now was the time and I caught him up on the case, the surveillance video the cops were working on, and the fact that I was still a suspect. (I left out the Römertopf oven part.)

"I can't believe this. How can they still think that you are the murderer?" Jack asked, incredulous.

"I know, right?"

"Let's toast to finding the killer and moving on to better things," he said, producing a split of French Aix-en-Provence Rosé.

Gets me every time.

"Okay, quid pro quo, weren't you also going to ask your detective friend about Ray," I said, taking a filled glass from him. That pack seemed to be bottomless.

"My friend Mark is part of a K-9 team and assisted from the ground on the possible bust in Playa del Rey, just on the other side of the jetty separating the Marina. He is one of my graduates. The dogs found about fifteen pounds of marijuana hidden in bags between the rocks and caught a guy above it who claimed to be fishing and knew nothing about the weed. Only problem was he had no rod, no bait, nothing, so they took him in for questioning. He claimed to have used a handline and had gotten fed up and threw it in the water. Totally lame, but they had nothing to keep him. Seems the guy works for Ray."

"Was his name Zeke?"

"Something like that, Halsey. If you see him or Ray, run the other way. The cops seem to think that the drugs are coming in from Mexico, and while they have a tight security net around the bigger ships, the small ones still seem to sneak in every now and again. Mark and his dog and I are going to do some recon over the next two days."

"Sounds like a perfect time for Bardot and I to get our tracking feet wet," I joked.

He looked at me, actually considering it.

"I'm kidding, do I look that dumb?"

We both sipped our wine.

"So, in the spirit of getting to know one another, tell me three things you have never done but would like to," he said.

"You want to play 'Bucket List'?"

"We're too young for that, let's just call it a 'To Do List.' "

I looked at him and immediately started filtering thoughts. I could feel my wall going up, even though he was doing everything right.

"Okay, I'll go first. I have never showered under a waterfall." He waited for me to take a turn.

"Er, I have never had a cronut." (Which was actually a lie.)

He did not look happy with my contribution, and I could see that he was thinking about how to make this game more intimate.

"I have never made love on a mountain top."

Ruh-roh. Not happening. I need clean sheets and semi-darkness for that sort of thing.

"This is silly."

He gave me a look.

"Okay, I have never been on a vacation with a group of close friends."

"That shouldn't even count, that is easily fixed!" He sat up, showing his frustration.

I shrugged my shoulders.

He took a breath, looked at me reclining on the rock, and calmed himself. He leaned back down toward me. "And my third, I have never, but I really want to, know someone so completely that words are unnecessary."

Ruh-roh.

After a pause, I began, "I have never been in—"

Clarence jumped to his feet and paced between us.

"You got something, boy?" Jack asked him.

"Got what?" I asked, wondering if he had a rabbit hanging limp out of his mouth.

"He smells the K-9 team even though they are still about fifty feet away. We've got to clear out," Jack explained. "But you're not off the hook, we'll get back to this."

"Oh joy!" Gotta love sarcasm.

He was busy packing up but I could see that I'd hurt him.

"But seriously," I said, softening my tone, "this is

fantastic and so very thoughtful of you, Mr. Jack Thornton."

"Wow, I recognize that we are starting over but 'Mr. Jack Thornton'? Sooo formal."

"Honey pie? Babe? Any of those work?" I asked, trying to get the sarcasm out of my voice. Jack didn't know how to react. He slumped and scratched his beard.

Why do I always do this?

Chapter 19

"STOP THE CAR," I screamed and didn't actually wait for Jack to do so. "PEGGY!"

As we wound our way to Rose Avenue, I could see that the night sky was lit up. I wondered if maybe something just crashed at the Santa Monica airport. When we turned onto Rose and I smelled the smoke, I felt my stomach drop.

The scene was surreal. Neighbors in pajamas were using garden hoses to douse what they could. Firefighters were running through their maneuvers and seemed thankfully to be gaining on the fire. I searched the crowd, looking desperately for my friends, and amid the smoke spotted Sally with Peggy, who was breathing through an oxygen mask administered by the EMTs.

"My God, Peggy, are you okay?"

"She will be," replied Sally, "just keep breathing in and out, Peggy."

I got down on the ground and cradled her in my arms. She kept trying to say something to me through the mask, but all I heard were muffled sounds.

If these are her dying words, I'd better hear them.

"Sally, where are the others?" I asked, distracting her long enough to lift the mask off Peggy.

"What, honey, what are you trying to say," I said, caressing her back.

She gasped for breath and managed to get out, "You better have lots of wine at your house, mine's a little hard to get to."

I had gotten Peggy's mask back on just before Sally returned with Cassie and Aimee. They joined us on the lawn and we had a group Wine Club hug. The color was coming back to Peggy's cheeks, a good sign. While the others were fussing over her, I took a moment to survey the damage to her house. It was hard to see much; there was still so much smoke. The living room window in the front was shattered, but it was hard to tell if that was from the fire or the firefighters trying to get in or something else.

"Mrs. Blake, I'm Captain Sparks," said the mustachioed, helmeted and sooty fireman.

His name is Sparks? Really?

"Oh, just call me Peggy like everybody else."

Peggy was breathing fairly well on her own now. "Sparky" joined our little hugging circle on the grass, much to Cassie's delight.

"Peggy, you are one lucky lady," he continued. "The fire is out, and while it will take a while for the smoke to dissipate, and you'll have to replace some windows and carpeting, the rest of the house is fine. Thanks mainly to your neighbors' quick responses."

I looked back again, the smoke was starting to clear and I could see pretty much everyone from Rose Avenue taking a breather. They were holding garden hoses, water buckets, even Supersoaker water guns belonging to dads with kids. And towering above them was Jack, helping wherever a gentle giant was needed.

I saw Cassie's husband Carl talking on his cell phone while walking around the house carrying an enormous measuring tape. Sally's husband, Joe, who had somehow managed to change into his customary cords and tweed jacket, was assisting him. Joe is a retired philosophy professor from UCLA, and if Sally is patrician then Joe is erudite. Throw in Sally's practicality versus Joe's metaphysical nature and you've got one hell of a marriage.

The rest of the people were starting to clean up while others who had stayed home during the initial emergency arrived with freshly baked cookies, drinks, and moist towels.

"My guys are coming by with the new glass, I just gave them the measurements, and I got Danny on his way to inspect your walls, ducts, and any other areas the soot might have settled into. As soon as the fire inspectors are done doing their thing, Joe and I will go around and open all the doors and windows and place security tape around the perimeter of the house," Carl rattled this off to Peggy and the rest of us in a clipped, take charge voice.

Cassie was beaming.

"And what have I told you about firing your gun in the house, Peggy," he said, pointing a finger at her.

I gasped and looked to the girls for clarification.

"He's just kidding," said Cassie, giving him a big kiss.

Sally helped Peggy to her feet.

"Or was it the crack pipe again, toots?" said Carl, grinning and heading back to the scene.

"Peggy, I have a spare room, a loving, if hyper dog, and some great wine," I said. "Everybody come on back to my place."

Most of us sat on the rug in my living room around my large square coffee table. I have always had a relaxed, cottage style home decor, opting for natural woods and solid fabrics accented with fun, decorative pillows.

This time I had swapped out the more formal, East Coast pinstripes and chintzes for hibiscus, seashells, and nautical flags. I like mixing a Georgian silver tea set on a shelf with Malibu tiles and sea glass. I'm a sucker for vintage sports equipment, like wooden tennis racquets and fly-fishing poles. Capping it all off is my collection of antique oars, which started when I rowed crew in college.

I'd made a run to Whole Foods earlier that day just in case I'd arrived home hungry and depressed from my date with Jack.

What? This is the way things have been going.

On such an occasion nothing beats simple Italian peasant delicacies: prosciutto, Parmigiano-

Reggiano, black truffle oil and a nice, crusty bread. I also got a little wine; a sublime Pinot Bianco, a Gamay, and I couldn't pass up the Sangiovese and Trebbiano Toscano.

Peggy looked totally relaxed after having taken a shower and changed into some of my comfy sweats. She was sipping her wine, lounging on one of the sofas with—guess who—snuggled next to her. Amazing how dogs know when someone needs TLC. . . .

Aimee soon joined us; she'd left Kimberly to close up the Chill Out and rushed back when she heard news of the fire.

For a few moments, we all sat silently consuming and imbibing. And feeding off the comfort of being together.

"I'm telling you, we should never have started snooping around Musso or Ray and their business," said Aimee. "Whatever they're up to is none of our concern, and after tonight, well, we've just got to drop this," she pleaded.

"What are you saying, you think he had something to do with the fire? It wasn't a faulty wire or something?" asked Cassie in disbelief.

"We'll know soon enough when we get the results from Captain Sparky the Bear and his fire inspectors," Sally said matter-of-factly.

"I can't for the life of me understand what Musso would have against Peggy, I'm the most likely target. Did I tell you that I caught him snooping in the window of my office the other day?"

"*What?*" asked Peggy.

"I sure hope the fire was an accident, sad as it is, Peggy," Aimee said, moving up on the sofa next to her and Bardot. "I just think we should drop this whole thing, leave Ray, Ali and Zeke, and Musso alone. I know you need to be cleared, Halsey, but—" Aimee dissolved into tears.

I sighed. She had a point. Someone or ones was trying to scare us off. But that meant that we were getting close, so we can't back away now, can we?

Cassie joined them on the sofa and put an arm around Aimee. Bardot thought that this was the perfect opportunity to roll onto her back and air out her hoohaw.

Chapter 20

My research on Tala was really just a bridge to nowhere. I knew time was running out on her visa, that she was originally from Kiev, and that her last listed place of employment was something called the Orchid Tree Agency. I growled at how much time I'd spent getting just to here. The sound woke Bardot up from a deep sleep and instead of securing the perimeter, she thought this was a sing-along and wagged her tail and howled. I played along and for a few moments we had our own "Dueling Banjos" going.

Of course, just at that moment Sally and Peggy walked in.

"Bardot, for the last time, be quiet! Hi, ladies," I said, trying to be convincing and failing.

"You busy or have a few minutes?" asked Sally.

I looked at Peggy and she did not look like her usual rosy self.

"Of course I have all the time in the world for you, have a seat," I said, steering them to the conference table and looking from Peggy to Sally with a questioning expression.

"The fire inspectors' report came back," Sally began.

"Oh-kay," I replied, starting to get nervous.

"They say that the fire was started by a burning candle left unattended," Sally continued.

"They think I'm a goddamned lush," spat Peggy. "They think I passed out and let the house burn down!"

"Now, the insurance company is giving her some pushback even though the damage was not extensive," Sally said.

"And here's the kicker, I don't own anything but flameless candles. Got a set from my daughter last Christmas, no mess, no fuss. And I hate those damn frou-frou scented things anyway," Peggy groused.

"But the inspectors said they found residue from an actual wax candle?" I asked. Peggy and Sally nodded.

"Peggy, can you tell me what you were doing just before the fire broke out?"

"Yes, like I told all of them, I hadn't gone to bed yet, even though it was close to midnight. I'd gotten it into my head that I needed to clean out my spice cabinet and was in the kitchen going through them. Good thing too, I had caraway seeds going back to the '60s."

"Is this a regular bedtime ritual? Because I'll pick you up and bring you back if you would tackle my linen closet," I said, handing Peggy a coconut water from my office fridge.

"She's a putterer," said Sally, pouring some sort

of vitamin powder into a water bottle she had grabbed.

"Very funny, you two. Shall I go on?"

I nodded and clasped my hands together as if in prayer.

"Things happened very quickly. I heard glass breaking in the living room, there was a 'swoosh' sound, which must have been the fire spreading, and then the house started filling with smoke. I grabbed some photo albums from the dining room shelf and ran out the kitchen door."

"Let me get the sequence straight. Are you sure this is the order in which things happened: first you heard glass breaking, then a 'swoosh' sound, then smoke?"

"Like I just said, Halsey."

Peggy was sitting up now, sensing that I was about to throw out the "lush" theory.

"How fast did these things happen?" Sally was beginning to catch my drift.

"Oh, pretty quick, I'd say one or two minutes . . . those bozo fire inspectors weren't listening to me," Peggy realized.

"Seems not, glass wouldn't break *before* a fire started unless someone broke the window from the outside. And, if a lit candle fell over, there is no way that a fire would break out that quickly and cause so much smoke," I said.

"I don't own any goddamned real candles," Peggy shouted.

"Of course you don't, dear, so someone must have tossed one in along with an accelerant. That would account for the swooshing sound. Something like ethyl alcohol, which smells like and could be confused with a drink being spilled," added nurse Sally.

"Only if you don't know your ass from your elbow," Peggy said, climbing back up onto her horse.

"I'm assuming that you don't know anyone who's mad enough at you to torch your place, and this seems more like a warning shot or your house would have been burned down to the foundation," I said.

"Which means that someone wants to shut you up, Peggy," Sally said.

"Ray and/or Inez, maybe?" I said. "You said they saw you catch them together in front of Rosa's house. Could also have been Musso," I went on. "Peggy, you said you would watch him some nights loading the cars on the truck. Maybe he saw you."

"I don't care if he did, he's now made this personal."

"That's my point," I told Peggy. "First Aimee, now you, I think you all should stop investigating and leave this to me. I've got Jack as my wingman."

"Really? I figured him more as a breast man," Sally said. "In either case, we are not going to abandon you in your quest for the truth!"

My computer pinged, alerting me that the automated search I'd set in motion for the Orchid Tree Agency was complete. I moved over to the screen to take a look.

"Well this adds a new layer of intrigue to the equation," I said.

Peggy and Sally joined me.

"It would seem that dear Tala was a mail-order bride."

"She's married to Musso?" Peggy asked.

"Let me set up another search; I'll check wedding records in both the Ukraine and the US."

That afternoon I called an emergency Wine Club at my office. This was a work session, so everyone was seated around the conference table and I limited us to two bottles of wine.

I brought everyone up to speed, including the fact that my search hadn't returned any marriage documents for Tala and Musso or for Tala and anyone. I'd also seen that she was supposed to be living in Texas.

"Well that explains the visa," said Peggy. It was great to see her back to full confidence.

"What do you mean?" Aimee asked.

"She may have come over here thinking she was going to be a bride, but whoever sent for her must have gotten cold feet and let her loose."

"She was jilted, no wonder she's such a bitch," Cassie added.

"The important thing is to determine if she had a motive for killing Rosa. She certainly had opportunity." I walked up to some charts I'd taped to the wall.

Having done countless websites, I created a blank project flow chart and put it up on the wall to be filled in.

"I'm going to write down the names of every suspect and then let's fill in the evidence underneath each person," I informed them. "Since we were just talking about her, let's start with Tala."

We worked at this for about an hour and ended up with the following:

TALA

- bitter, rejected mail-order bride
- pushes Musso to make lots of money to buy her things
- probably knows that Rosa and Musso once had a romance
- getting rid of Rosa brings Musso's attention back to her
- her visa is running out and she needs to get Musso to marry her

RAY

- two-bit drug dealer, lost house to Rosa
- cops zeroing in on him, suspect he's getting shipments in the Marina
- Rosa's will was being changed to cut him out
- killing Rosa was a way to get the house and money before the new will is finalized
- he's having an affair with Inez who knows everything that's going on in the neighborhood; she could have tipped Ray off about the will

MUSSO

- leasing cars to movie shoots off the books
- lives with demanding Tala who pressures him to make more money and for marriage
- trying to keep really low profile, no debts, and no records
- once had a romance with Rosa and wanted to marry her

INEZ

- having an affair with Ray
- seems to be struggling to make ends meet, relies on recycling
- but refused job offer from Aimee
- how can she afford to live?

"This is all circumstantial, we still don't have anything concrete to take to the cops," Peggy concluded. "I think that we need to divide and conquer, everyone take a suspect and tail them until we get some real evidence."

I started to wonder if Peggy had worked for the FBI in her younger life, and vowed to pick up the research I'd started on her again. This time as an ally rather than a suspect, she was clearly on my side.

"Good idea, Peggy," I said, retaking the floor. "How about you take Ray; Sally, take Musso; Cassie, you have Inez; and I'll tackle Tala. It will be a pleasure," I said, smiling.

"I really wish I could help, you guys, but I just can't be gone from the yogurt shop for any amount of time." Aimee had a hangdog expression on her face. "And this all still really scares me."

"You *can* help, Aimee. You have a ringside seat to watch what Ray and his guys are up to," I said. "You can let Peggy and Cassie know when they appear to be getting ready to move."

"I can do that." Her mood lifted immediately.

"I'll probably get Marisol to help me, she'll be following me anyway."

At that we all looked at each other not knowing whether to high five, fist pump, or hug. We ended up toasting with our glasses in their various states of fullness.

I was so hepped up that night from the potential progress we were making that I couldn't sleep. I figured that I'd download the photos from Carl's camera so that I could make sure that I got it back to her before he came home from his golf trip.

I popped the SD card into my reader and let it start up. I figured that I'd work backward from the last photo taken and download and erase everything along the way. I have to admit that Cassie is not a bad photographer. There were a lot of the ones she took at the Marina that would work great for my presentation to the Coast Guard.

When I'd erased the last one, I saw a bunch that must have been taken one day when she and Peggy followed Musso. Most were mundane, him driving to the Post Office, to get gas, stopping at

In-N-Out. It was when he arrived back on Rose Avenue that it got interesting. He must have parked at home and then walked because the next shot of him was taken in front of Rosa's house. I felt my pulse quicken. There were several of him just standing there. I downloaded one and erased the rest. There was one last burst of shots, about five in a row that Cassie must have taken while holding down the shutter. She must not have been really looking because in these we see Ray approaching and he and Musso talking. Cassie surely would have told me if she'd witnessed that.

I stopped and sat back to gather my thoughts. Had they arranged to meet? Aimee had said that she'd seen Musso and Ray's guys talk a few times, perhaps he knew Ray as well. Maybe they had killed her together. But why?

I had a headache and very few answers. I erased the photos and the disc was back to Carl's last batch. I was about to eject the disc when I looked at the photo on my screen. It was a shot of Rosa's front window, she was inside wearing only a bra and panties.

Dear God.

I waited until eight a.m., hoping that it was not too early to call Sally. She said she'd been up since six, her normal routine and would be right over with fruit and yogurt. I put on the kettle.

I don't know why but I had a sheepish, guilty expression on my face when I opened the door.

"Oh my, you look like you've seen Marley's ghost

with his pants down," Sally said, checking me over carefully. I could see her mentally doing a checklist of my pallor, pupils, and overall demeanor.

"It's not me, it's what I've found. I've been up all night, I really don't know how to deal with this."

I set up my laptop on the breakfast table and hooked up the SD reader.

"This is from Carl's camera. Cassie borrowed it to help me and take photos in the Marina for my Coast Guard presentation. I promised to download them and return the camera so Carl wouldn't know we'd used it."

"Sounds reasonable to me; you need to eat something, dear, you're looking a little green around the gills."

"It's just a cold. Cassie and I sat out too long at the café in the Marina."

I cued up the reader to the photo of Rosa in her bra.

"Holy Jesus on a skateboard!" Sally whelped.

"I know, are you okay? Do you need some wine?" *I know I do.*

"Is this the only one? Are there more?"

"I haven't looked, I was too much in shock."

We spent the next half hour viewing hundreds of photos of the houses on Rose Avenue. There were definitely more of Rosa's place than anyone else's, but thankfully only two more of her half dressed. After we'd run through all of them we both took a deep breath.

"What do you make of this? You must know Carl pretty well, you've been next door neighbors for what, thirty years?"

"At least, and I would never have pegged him for doing something like this, whatever this is."

"It is strange that he seems to be spying on a bunch of people since he has photos of their houses. Could he just be a passive perv?"

"Like a peeping Carl? Just so hard for me to imagine. But I do know that we should keep this to ourselves for now. Cassie would not be able to handle it, especially since they are having some money problems."

"Really? She sure doesn't let on."

"He tries to gloss over it to her, after all, when they married he had the money and she had the looks. But he has money troubles, business is down and he does a good job of hiding it because he doesn't want to worry her."

I wonder what else he's hiding. . . .

Chapter 21

My cold had not really gotten better and I was going to have to sit out my first Halloween on Rose Avenue.

I was disappointed. I was finally in a house and had a chance to hand out candy to the kids. Also Sally and Joe had invited me to a really cool sounding party a few blocks over at a house that was totally transformed for the holiday.

I'd driven by it the night before. They had built a facade that covered the entire front of the house, depicting a Transylvanian castle overlooking a gothic graveyard. Coffins opened and closed with hydraulics, bats flew by overhead on fish line invisible at night, and on the roof they had set up an entire "mad scientist" scene with brains in jars and electrical currents and sparks running through a tin skull cap on the "patient." Lights flashed that made you look from one corner to the other, which I was pretty sure could be seen from space.

I have an acute sense of occasion, the day of the

Super Bowl or the World Series I am passionate
about one of the teams, even if I've never really
followed them. I'm the person who wears my "I
Voted" sticker until it falls off. I wear green for St.
Patrick's, red for Valentine's, and black for 9/11.
Missing Halloween did not make Halsey a happy
camper.

I was also home alone. Jack had convinced me
to let him take Bardot for the second time on the
recon he was doing with his detective friend in the
Marina. He'd said that the night before they'd
tracked and chased a guy for about an hour before
he'd finally eluded them. He was pretty sure that it
was Ray. He also thought it was best to work with
Bardot alone on this and get her used to scent
tracking without my distraction.

"No argument here, although I'm not sure that I
appreciate being called a 'distraction,' " I'd told him.

I'd worked hard to train my dog to behave even
if she is selective about showing it. But he promised
to take me out to dinner on Saturday, so I figured
I'd let them have their fun.

The girls had warned me that if I didn't want to
be bothered by the trick or treaters, I should have
as few lights on as possible and hang a sign on the
door saying SORRY, NO CANDY, SEE YOU NEXT YEAR.

Apparently Rose Avenue was a popular Halloween destination for people coming from all
over Los Angeles. Many of the houses were really
decked out, and someone had spread a vicious
rumor that we gave out better candy. Plus, I'd
heard that we were talked about on the local radio
stations.

Sure enough, even before it got dark, a swarm of cars appeared out of nowhere and squeezed into every available spot, often partially blocking driveways. I peeked out my living room window, making sure that the only illumination came from my TV.

Like every other year I was watching *The Exorcist* with the sound on low. How great is that movie? I love it so much that the theme song is my ring-tone. Ellen Burstyn's lounging pajamas alone are worth the price of admission. And dear little Linda Blair had curses I use to this day if someone cuts me off on the road.

I'd thrown on my trusty tank top and some sweats and was curled up on the sofa watching the rest of the movie. It felt awfully big without Bardot spooning next to me. I crunched up a pillow and settled in. Not that I missed my ex, but these are the kind of nights when I miss snuggling. Bardot filled that void and I didn't have to listen to any annoying banter. I was probably just missing my dog.

At some point I dozed off.

I was woken up a couple of hours later by the guttural, piercing scream of an animal. It took me a moment to orient myself to where I was. The TV was no longer on and it was black as pitch in my house.

SPLASH! Something was thrashing in my pool. I sat up and turned on the table lamp. Nothing. I tried the TV remote, same result. The power was out.

Where the heck did I put the flashlight?

The pool water went silent and I heard the gate to my backyard close.

Shit.

I went out but couldn't see anything in the back either. I could hear faint sounds of kids chiming "trick or treat" from the street. I guess a blackout is no reason to halt the quest for sweet confections.

I could smell something a bit rancid and metallic, which gave me a stomach drop reflex. To dispel the feeling, I tried to chalk it up to my regular night visitor, the skunk. I ran back inside to dig around in the hall closet for a light and jammed my shin right into the edge of the coffee table at full speed. The area with the least amount of skin hit the area on the table with the least bit of resistance.

"Aaahhh," I screamed and fell to the floor.

At that moment someone started pounding at my front door. Then the door shook as if someone was trying to open it. I quickly pushed myself up from the floor and hit my head on the end table I must have fallen under.

"Nooooo," I whined, falling back down on my face again.

I took deep breaths to try and dull the pain and crawled across the living room floor to the front window. For a second I thought about going for the phone and calling 9-1-1, but I didn't want to bother them if this was just some Halloween prank. My head was throbbing and I felt dizzy and nauseous.

I made my way to the window, pulled myself up to my knees, and looked out. Rose Avenue does not have streetlights, but I could see from people's porch lights that much of the crowd had dispersed. This time of night was taken up by teenagers barely in costume, pimply boys with arms draped around pimply girls. Was free candy that much of an attraction for date night?

Wait. Porch lights. My neighbors have power!

I looked left and right on my side of the block to see if their lights were on. They were and that's when I saw him. I couldn't make out his face but it is hard to miss those chrome rims. He got into his truck and drove away.

I dropped the drape and crawled over to my phone and called Sally.

"Hold that on your head and let me look into your eyes," said Sally. She shone a light into my eyes and looked concerned.

"Should we take her to emergency?" asked Peggy, icing my shin with a bag of frozen peas.

"On Halloween? Every emergency room will be a zoo, she'll get better care here," said Sally decidedly. "Joe is coming over to see about getting your power back on," she said to me. "He's going to wake Carl and bring him along, for moral support he claims. Truth is, he really doesn't know the first thing about electricity. But he means well." She smiled.

That's when I remembered. "I need to borrow your flashlight, something happened in my pool," I said, staggering up off the sofa.

Once standing, I was hit with a tsunami of dizziness and would have fallen over if Peggy hadn't caught me.

"You aren't going anywhere, missy," ordered Sally. "You've got a concussion, you need to be still. If not, you're going to end up with a serious case of CRS."

She saw the fear in my eyes.

"Can't Remember Shit." Sally smiled at me.

"But I heard an animal cry and splashing, we need to make sure it got out," I pleaded.

"We can wait until Joe and Carl get the power up," said Peggy.

Sally found enough candles to make my house feel cozy again, even though I felt violated and was sure that I would never be able to erase the mental image of that slimy drug dealer.

"Well, it was easy enough to fix," said Joe after the lights came back on. He and Carl had announced themselves from outside and gone directly through the back gate. I noticed that Joe had taken the time to change into his trademark professorial garb. Carl was barefoot and only wearing shorts, making them quite a pair. It wouldn't surprise me if he and Cassie slept naked, although that wouldn't stop her from having a wardrobe full of sleeping ensembles.

"Someone or something flipped all the circuit breakers," Carl announced. "You okay, toots, you don't look so good."

"It was a someone," I said, "and I know who."

At my insistence Sally and Joe helped me out to

the pool. It was still too dark to see much, so I hobbled over to the pool light switch. "It's quiet now, maybe it was some kind of prank, this is Halloween," I said, turning on the light.

We stared silently as we registered the grotesque scene before us.

The water was streaked in crimson red. Whatever had turned the pool this color left a track all the way to the back fence. This must have been the animal I heard unleash such a plaintive wail.

"What the heck." Carl sucked in a breath as he surveyed the scene.

I felt the ground go soft, my knees gave way and I went down.

When I came to I was in my bed and it took several blinks for my eyes to focus. I could make out sunlight breaking through my window and then heard a thumping sound either coming from inside my head or from my bed.

Do I need an exorcism now?

The thumping got louder and faster and I smelled a familiar breath. Slowly and painfully I turned my head sideways and was about two inches away from Bardot wagging her tail and looking hopeful that it was time to play. I heard fingers snap and Bardot put her head down quietly. I turned to look in the direction of the sound.

Again I blinked and the people standing or sitting on my bed slowly came into view. I saw Jack and assumed that he was the one controlling Bardot. There was Sally, Cassie, Peggy, and Aimee all staring at me with concern. I blinked again to make sure that they were real, and when I saw that

Cassie was wearing a leopard print jumpsuit with a black patent leather belt, I knew that I wasn't dreaming. I could not make that shit up.

"'Toto, we're home! And this is my room—and you're all here,'" I said, not knowing how the hell I pulled that out of my brain.

"How's your head?" Sally asked, shining a pen-light into my eyes. "Your pupils look much better."

"What happened; what are you all doing here?" I asked in a scratchy voice.

"Oh God, she's lost her memory," Cassie said and then looked at Jack. "Good news for you, you've got a clean slate."

"I do not have amnesia. I remember the power going out, hitting my shin, Sally and Peggy coming over, and—oh God."

"We've got that all cleaned up, honey, your pool is back to normal and Augie alerted Animal Control to be on the lookout," Aimee gently explained.

"Augie was here?"

"It's probably nothing, he took a water sample to test, but he thinks that this is just very realistic-looking fake blood. Maybe you should just rest, you look awfully tired, honey," said Peggy.

"You fainted when we turned the lights on in the pool," Sally said. "We got you into bed and I gave you something to sleep. Seeing that carnage would be a shock to anyone let alone someone with a concussion."

"I came back with Bardot just before midnight," Jack softly said, kneeling by the edge of my bed and holding my hand. "Don't worry, babe, I am going to take care of you."

"Awwwww," cooed Cassie.

"What did Augie say?" I asked.

"Unfortunately, he found nothing concrete to follow up on. Figured that this was the work of some sadistic kids. We told him that you said you saw Ray but there's no proof and on Halloween he said anyone could have done this," Aimee explained.

"Anyone didn't do it, that shit Ray did it," I croaked.

"I'll call Augie and update him on our work in the Marina; I told you that we're pretty sure we were tracking Ray the other night. This might be his way of doing payback," Jack said, stroking my hair.

"Payback's a female dog," Sally said.

Add my name to the list this was another warning to stop our sleuthing, I thought. Three down, two to go. So who's next, Sally or Cassie?

True to his word Jack stayed by my side for the next two days. He fed me, comforted me, and bathed me. It was totally innocent, and the warm bubble bath and salts he put in the water took the sting away from the pain in my shin. Bardot helped wherever she could, which mostly consisted of following me everywhere I hobbled and trying to retrieve my toes from under the bubbles in the bath. On the third day, Jack had to get back to work.

"You sure you're going to be okay?" he asked, getting up from the breakfast table.

I had made a lovely frittata for us with smoked ham, Gruyère, and caramelized onions. It was the first thing that I had cooked for Jack, and I wanted him to know that I was also the goddess of gastronomy. I was starting to feel very comfortable sharing my home with him, and not just because I was injured. And, I was stupidly fighting it.

"I want you to check in with me every couple of hours," he said, grabbing his keys and phone.

Where have I heard that before?

"I checked that the gate is locked, and early this morning, I installed a camera above it that will let me see what's going on remotely," he added proudly.

"I'm not helpless, Jack. I need to get back to my life. I can take care of myself, always have, and always will."

I was steaming at his presumption and couldn't control myself. I could see the sting my words had and regretted that I hadn't applied a filter. I quickly tried to backpedal.

"Look, everyone is on high alert here, the detectives, the people who come to work on this street every day, and the neighbors; if I change my life, then they've won, Jack," I said, standing up and wrapping my arms around his waist.

"Just don't get too complacent," he said, pulling away. "I recognize that you don't need anyone, you've made that perfectly clear. But you see that the person who killed Rosa cares nothing about a life, human or animal. There is something bigger at stake, and if you get between this guy and his business, then you could be the next one found floating facedown in the pool."

He half-heartedly kissed me, gave a warm pet to Bardot, and headed out the door.

Ouch.

When I heard his truck start up, I went out back to fetch the ladder and take that damn camera down. Yes, I was scared, and yes, I felt like my whole life had been violated, but I needed to feel in control of *something*.

Chapter 22

Things had finally calmed down, and I was out with Bardot who, after her night training sessions with Jack, now walked crouched low to the ground with her head moving side to side to pick up scents. My heart sank as I saw a notice for a missing cat stapled to the utility pole on the corner. Even though Augie confirmed that the blood in my pool was fake, my stomach still turned to acid just remembering that horrible night.

Bardot's "hunt" walk was better than her pulling but I still tightened my grip on the leash, not sure what she would do if she smelled the right smell. Whatever that was. I never did hear what had happened at the Marina that second night, and the way things were left with Jack, I may never know.

On the return, we hit the other side of the street to give Bardot some fresh pee markings to sniff. Halfway up the block, I saw Peggy planting some impatiens around a tree in the yard.

"Well, there's my favorite dog," she said.

At that, Bardot abandoned the scent and darted toward Peggy, pulling me along for the ride.

As they began their lovefest, I cast a glance up to Rosa's house. The sight made me shiver.

"What's the matter, honey? Come on, let's sit on the front steps."

"Just looking at her house brings back such horrible thoughts. I feel that I owe Rosa and should be the one to find her killer."

It was quiet on Rose Avenue, the few cars that passed were minivans shuttling toddlers to playdates or on errands with their moms. I never thought that I would cheer for it, but the skies were displaying real clouds today, more than just the marine layer, which burns off around noon. The change made me think of home and I suddenly had a mental image of eating grilled cheese sandwiches and tomato soup with my mom while watching the soaps.

Peggy patted my knee with one hand and scratched Bardot's ears with the other.

"You're experiencing classic survivor's guilt; we're going to get him, sweetheart, don't you worry."

"I hope so, this is not how I pictured my new life to be," I said.

"You're still glad to be here, aren't you? Didn't sound like you left anything of value back in New York City."

"Believe me I didn't. Just wasted time and a misspent youth."

"This isn't like you, Halsey, what happened to that wise-cracking, taking names, screw them all, beautiful woman who moved to Rose Avenue?"

I laughed and gave her a hug.

"That's better," she said. "And you sure caught that fellow Jack's eye."

I just looked around and said nothing.

"What? You don't think he's cute? If I were even ten years younger . . ."

"He's cute alright. I just don't know why guys always feel that they have to protect me. Sure, it starts as caring, but the next thing you know, you're not allowed to cut your hair, they tell you what to wear, and constantly track your whereabouts. No thank you. Bardot and the Rose Avenue Wine Club are enough for me," I said, working up into a full lather.

"Halsey, you must have figured out by now that the best way to get a man to stop doing something is to tell him how good he is at it. When the challenge is gone they move on to the next thing. And it really doesn't matter what it is. Why sometimes they take it to extremes. Don't you know what the last words of a male idiot are?"

I shook my head.

"Hey, watch this!"

I laughed, but what she said kind of made my eyes sting. Behind them, my brain was working overtime, trying to decide which mental drawer to file this in.

"Thanks, Peggy," I managed to get out. "You are very wise about all of this, I don't mean just understanding men; you seem to know a lot about how to work this case. It's almost like you've been through something like this before."

Sure, I'm baiting her, so sue me.

"You are very astute, Halsey, although it feels like it was another lifetime ago."

I waited for her to continue.

"There's only so much I can tell you, it all took place in the early '60s. You know Vern served in the Air Force, correct?"

I nodded and Bardot settled in between us. She's a sucker for a good story.

"Well, he was asked to work on a mission that involved Homeland Security and the threat was supposed to be headquartered in the Santa Monica airport. Basically he was assigned to flush out the bad guys."

"Enter Peggy," I prodded.

"Yes, the airport had started allowing business jets to land and take off from there now that WWII and the Korean War were over. The Air Force had called in the CIA, who called me when they discovered a shipment of Russian weapons hidden aboard an aircraft they were servicing."

"You worked for the *CIA*? You are my hero!"

She chuckled.

"It was for less than a year, and it was only surveillance. They gave me a special compact mirror and some other gadgets. I was never told if I'd helped or not, but I sure learned a lot."

"Wow. And you'll help me with Rosa's case?"

She gave me a hug and nodded with a wink.

Bardot gave her a kiss and we went our way.

When I got in the house I called my mom. It was a Mom kind of day.

* * *

I padded into the kitchen to make myself a cup of tea and a late breakfast. I like a healthy meal of scrambled eggs, paper-thin slices of ham lightly grilled, and some sort of fruit with a splash of lemon and agave nectar.

I'm not bragging, this is a recent development. In New York it was bacon, a fried egg, and cheese on a buttered bagel bought at the deli by the subway entrance. There was a line every morning, the people behind the counter worked at the pace of a veteran dealer in Vegas, and if you weren't ready to shout an order out the second it was your turn, the crowd behind would swallow you up like quicksand. And you'd better call it a "BE&C" because nobody has time for all those words. I tried to picture Cassie placing a morning deli order, and figured that it would go something like this:

"Hieee, I'm Cassie. This bacon egg thingy, are those fresh eggs, like from a farm, fresh? And I'd like a whole-wheat bagel, and could you scrape out the dough inside the crust and add a sprinkling of chia seeds instead of butter? And what kind of soy bacon do you have?"

At that point I picture the line picking her up and passing her back out the door like she was crowd surfing at a rock concert.

No, I don't miss any of that. The rushed atmosphere took all the joy out of eating. And I enjoy eating. Growing up, the family dinner was sacrosanct. It started with the preparation; both my parents are great cooks and have their specialties. I started learning and participating almost as soon as I could stand.

I took my tea and plate into the breakfast nook that looks out onto Rose Avenue. This was a nice change; normally at this time of day I am in the office in the back and feeling a bit isolated. I let a bite of creamy egg melt in my mouth and glanced out the window.

Is that Inez? What the heck is she doing?

She was standing in the street at my curb with a broom in one hand and a kitchen knife in the other. She was doing a lot more looking around than sweeping, but I realized that she was cleaning up the dirt and scraping off the debris on the street in front of my house.

I threw on an oversized shirt, poured Inez some orange juice, grabbed my tea, and went out to her.

"Are you cleaning up my filthy curbside? Thank you," I said, handing her the glass.

She was definitely surprised to see me.

"It's no problem, I was here anyway for the recyclables," she said, waving her knife and sipping her juice.

My regular garbage bin was open, I guess that was where she was depositing her sweepings. I looked down at the latest pile, it was an odd collection of debris. Lots of little shards of glass along with some mailing envelopes that I could see had my address on them.

"Isn't it a little early in the day for the bottles," I asked, taking a seat on the curb and patting the spot next to me. "Most people haven't put their cans out yet."

She sat with a sigh.

"Thanks for the juice, it's delicious. I'll be back

for another round later tonight, but I really need the money so I thought I'd get what I could now."

That grabbed my stomach, I'd been poor when I first started out, but never that desperate.

"You have kids?" I really was concerned.

"Two, they are with my mother during the day, but she hasn't been feeling well lately. They think it might be cancer."

"Oh no. Where's the father, if you don't mind me asking?"

"Split a long time ago, left me to raise them."

"Hang on a minute, I'll be right back."

I put down my tea and went into the house. This must be what Marisol was doing that night I saw her hand over bags to Inez.

I returned with some cash and a few T-shirts and sweaters. She was back to sweeping and the curb was now clear.

"Here, take these and here's some money for food. I will go through my clothes and get you a proper donation. How old are your kids?"

"You are too kind, you don't have to do this Miss Hall. If I work hard, we get by."

She had reddish-brown hair that she kept in a net and pretty deep-set eyes. All in all a pleasant face.

"What about Ray, can he help you at all?"

"Who? I don't know any Ray."

She started to shut down and got busy putting her belongings back into her cart.

"I'm sorry, I'd heard that you and Rosa's brother were dating. I must have gotten that wrong."

"You did. Thanks for the juice. And everything."

She handed me back my glass and quickly moved on.

I couldn't help but wonder if Ray had some sort of hold on her and the kids, she was so quick to deny even knowing him.

I'd have to talk to Agent Peggy about this.

Chapter 23

I walked out of my meeting buoyed by the results. When I reached the boardwalk, I did a little fist pump and jump, this was going to keep me busy for at least the next eight months. I thought that this called for a celebration but this time Cassie was otherwise engaged. Just on the off chance that he was free for the next couple of hours, I called Jack. Maybe this was the way to get back into his good graces while showing him how well I take care of myself.

"What are you doing?" I asked when he answered on the first ring.

We agreed to meet at a kind of dive bar in Playa that he said he'd been going to since he got the surfing bug when he was barely an adult.

The Turtle Roll Tavern is nestled at the fairly remote end of Playa del Rey, it is mostly a locals' hangout. This sleepy beach community runs parallel along the Pacific on the Westside of Los Angeles, and the area was once a surfing Mecca. The beach at the northernmost end of Playa del Rey is still known as "Toes Beach" or just "Toes" by the local surfing community, a name born from the Hang Ten surfing stance. Jetties built to prevent beach erosion have since quieted the waters and surfers now hang at the famed El Porto Beach where an underwater canyon creates some "sick sets."

It is a real good old dive bar with red vinyl padded stools, a brass foot rail under the bar, and enough risqué nautical kitsch to make a sailor blush.

It was just past noon, but once inside the shaded windows was a healthy-sized crowd of bikers, Hawaiian-shirted surfer bums, and blue-collar workers in Dickie's. It could just as well have been midnight.

Jack was already seated and blending into this boozy biosphere. He was clearly glad to see me and I hoped that we could just move forward and not rehash our last scene. He explained that Turtle Roll Tavern had all the basic food groups: pool, bartenders with heavy hands, and live jazz jams most nights of the week.

Our booth had the best view of the stuffed blue marlin hanging on the wall sporting Christmas lights, which I am sure are a year round fixture. While I took in the fish, along with the collection of mounted shark jaws, I noticed that the bare-chested mermaid statue behind the bar had transfixed Jack.

"You know her?" I asked, laughing.

"Vaguely, I know her dog better."

He funny.

We ordered beers even though I don't really

like beer, but I was celebrating and it seemed like the right thing to do in a place like this. I didn't see anyone else eating but I was starving and craving an Italian chopped salad. Something about the mixed textures of garbanzo beans, mozzarella, and salami all doused in a tangy, garlic dressing gets me every time. When Jack was on his second pint, I grew impatient to order.

"Is there a menu I can look at?" I asked, waving to the bartender.

He directed me to a chalkboard at the side of the bar. It looked like it hadn't been changed in years.

TODAY'S GRUB

Meatball Sub

Our Famous ¼ lb. Hot Dog

Nachos

Pretzels with Spicy Mustard Dipping Sauce

Corn Nut Beef Tacos

Crap, I was either going to need a Wine Club this afternoon and pass on lunch, or have to call this what it will be. A cleanse.

I opted for what I hoped was the least carcinogenic.

The door to the tavern opened, spilling a pointed shard of light into the room. It was enough for me to recognize the two guys who had walked in. I quickly threw on my sunglasses and grabbed Jack's Dodgers cap off his head and put it on mine. I also sunk down in the booth, hoping that I wouldn't be seen.

"What gives, babe? Though I must admit that you look pretty cute in my hat."

"Zeke and Ali Baba just walked in. I don't want them to know that I'm here."

"Okay, there were only a couple words in that sentence that I actually understood."

I explained it to him in a whisper but it took him a while to understand and be sure that I wasn't just messing with him.

"They don't know me, right? Never seen me? I'll go over and get chummy and see what I can pull out of them."

"I'm not sure—"

Too late, the amber-eyed redwood had moseyed on up to the bar next to the Jamaicans. All I could do was watch surreptitiously from under my/his cap.

When I next looked over, Jack and Ali Baba were laughing and slapping each other's backs. Even Zeke had let down his guard a little bit. I hoped that Jack was getting more than just ganja jokes from them.

The bartender came by with our lunch and asked if I wanted him to bring Jack's to the bar. I told him "no," hoping that Jack's hunger would get the better of him and he'd wrap up the interview.

The tavern door opened again but was quickly shut from the outside. Seconds later, Zeke's phone rang. He didn't say anything but as soon as he hung up he tossed some cash on the bar, grabbed Ali Baba by the sleeve, and dragged him out. This time the door took longer to close, which gave me enough time to see Ray waiting outside. I could swear that I saw steam coming out of his ears.

When Jack sat back down, he devoured his meatball sub. I have learned, being around him enough now, that when a big man needs to eat he will think of nothing else. I nibbled on my hot dog desperately trying to convince myself that this tasted much worse than a salad.

It didn't.

When Jack had finished and worked systematically to remove all the sauce and cheese from his beard, he was ready to talk.

"I couldn't get them to name their boss; I think when I told them I was looking for a kilo they figured that they could sell this one direct and cut out Ray."

"Ray was here, he started to walk into the bar, must have seen you and quickly shut the door."

"Ah, that explains the phone call and sudden bugging out. I wonder if he just recognizes me from tracking him with the K-9 unit or if he knows that we are together?"

"I'm going to guess both; I told you he's the one who defiled my pool, I'm sure of it. He was trying to scare us off."

"Did he see you here?"

I shook my head.

"Well, whatever he tells his two assistants, I doubt

that it will stop basic greed. Especially that Ali Baba one."

"So how'd you leave it with them?"

"Seems that they have a fairly big shipment coming in sometime in the next few weeks. When it arrives, they are supposed to call me and tell me where to meet them."

"Whenever that is, Bardot and I are coming with you. And you'd better bring your K-9 friends."

"You going to eat the rest of that hot dog?" he asked, reaching for it.

"Yes!" I said, pushing his hand away and putting his hat back on his head. "I may even have another."

On my way back home, I got a call from Augie.

"Hey, how goes it?" I asked. Nothing was going to dampen my mood today.

"You sound chipper, much better than last time," he replied.

"What are you, the Halsey whisperer?" I said, laughing.

"Has my aunt filled you in on the latest, or shall I give you an update?"

"So Marisol hears news before I do? Remember, I'm the one who found the body!"

"Ah, now I know I'm talking to feisty Halsey. So here's what we've got: Rosa did in fact file her amended will, although Ray is contesting it. He claims that in the last couple of months before she died she'd gone back to using drugs and wasn't thinking clearly. Even though it's widely known that she gave all that up in her teens."

"Meaning Marisol told you that."

"Among others. Also, Musso's girlfriend Tala? She has only a few weeks left on her visa. She's got to leave the country by then and reapply."

I thought about the photos I saw of Musso and Ray talking and wondered if they were going to share the profits on the shipment that's coming in soon. With that and his car leasing earnings, they might be going on a nice long vacation.

"You still there?"

"I'm here, just thinking. Remember, if Ray is contesting the will, then Inez is part of it. I told you they are partners in crime."

"I remember. A couple more items, we are having a devil of a time finding anything on that film production company, let alone tying it to Musso. You might have better luck doing so. As far as the ongoing investigation at the Marina involving Ray, I'm told they are making progress. All of that is being handled by the DEA, we are no longer involved and you are strictly off limits. Even if your friend Jack is still helping out. Understood?"

I nodded.

"I can't hear you."

"I understand. What about that surveillance video you were sent from an anonymous neighbor, have your guys been able to pull anything useful?" I was trying to hide my anger, I've just never liked being told I can't do something.

"They've had to put it aside for the moment, there was an incident at the airport that takes priority."

"Can you send it to me? I'll see what I can do. And, Augie?"

"Yes?"

"Thanks."

When I pulled into my drive, I saw Cassie and Sally waiting outside with several bottles of wine.

"Congratulations!" they chimed when I got out of my car.

"What? News travels faster here than a New York rat with a slice of pizza."

"Jack called me, he's so proud of you, child." He and Sally had hit it off from the moment they met.

"He's a keeper." Cassie beamed.

"Well, come on in so I can unburden you of those heavy bottles."

We sat out back to watch the sunset and with the amount of wine we were consuming, I was glad that I'd been a pig and eaten that second hot dog. Although Bardot would not stop licking my hands and it was getting embarrassing.

"I have to ask you, Cassie, I noticed when I downloaded the photos from Carl's camera that you and Peggy had done some recon on Musso."

Sally squirmed until she heard which direction I was going with the photos.

"Yes, but we got nowhere, and I had to cut it short because Peggy won't let you eat or drink in her car. Where's the fun in that?"

"Actually you did get something interesting in the last set of shots."

"I did?"

"You'd set the camera on 'burst,' so you probably didn't even notice that you were still shooting. You got Musso on the sidewalk outside of Rosa's house."

"I know, he was just standing there looking all down in the mouth."

"He always looks like that," Sally said.

"But in the last three shots it showed Ray come out of the house and the two of them talking."

"Wow, I didn't see any of that. So they were in cahoots?"

"Chips out of the same stump, sounds like."

Where does Sally come up with these salads of words?

"Did you find anything else on the camera that was interesting? Carl is positively anal about me not going near it, to the point where I start to wonder."

I looked at Sally and she took over.

"You might as well know, honey, we're sure it's probably nothing."

I tried to be subtle in the way I watched Cassie as Sally told her about the photo Carl had taken of the front of Rosa's house.

"At first glance all you see is the big picture window where she always kept a bowl of flowers on the table inside. But then we looked closer and we could see Rosa standing in the living room," Sally explained.

"He takes photos like that all the time," Cassie said, almost annoyed.

"But in this one Rosa was only wearing a bra and panties, like I said, it's surely nothing."

When Sally was done, I noticed that Cassie was sitting stone still, but nodding slightly. We all have different ways of dealing with bad news and in Cassie's case it was to turn off all human emotion.

I poured her some more wine.

"Listen, Cassie, if there's one thing that I've learned since I moved here, it's that nothing on Rose Avenue is at all what it seems."

Chapter 24

The winter holiday season had officially started and I couldn't help myself, I missed being home, Mom's German cookies and Dad's robust wine cellar. He planned all year for his cold weather sommelier selections.

Maybe most of all, I kept thinking about New York City at this time of year, it is just so magical. I would always reserve a day to take in all the beautiful department store windows, lit up and decorated as if the designers expected Mr. DeMille to show up at any moment and film them in Technicolor. I'd, of course, end up buying something at each stop, and if I exerted enough self-control, half would be Christmas presents for others.

As I sat in my office at the computer, I realized that I was starting to take this place and its beautiful weather for granted, much the way I had done with the wonders of New York City.

I'd put on Joni's Mitchell's "Big Yellow Taxi" and resolved to live more in the moment. Which meant getting down to work for the Coast Guard. Right after I check my emails. There was one from Augie with a video file attached.

I'd better open a window, my resolve wants out.

The surveillance video he sent me was indeed too grainy to make out anything but the most rudimentary shapes and shadows. This was going to take some time.

About an hour and a half later after I'd run a number of enhancement processes and manual conversions, it was only slightly better. This was going to require higher tech software and hardware to really get a clear set of images.

Time to call in Peggy.

It turns out that I was right when I suspected that she was not nearly the neo-Luddite that she had pretended to be. And luckily she had a friend from the old days whose son worked in forensics at the CIA. I forwarded her the file, but kept working on it myself a bit longer. I'm stubborn that way.

I noticed that Augie had just forwarded me the email he'd received for my "anonymous" neighbor rather than attach it to a new one. I decided to track down the IP address for the original sender. Just for shiggles. In a few simple steps I had it. I stared at the string of numbers for a couple of minutes wondering where I'd seen that sequence before.

Finally it hit.

These were the same numbers that came up when I ran my search on Musso's security cameras. The video had come from Musso. Or Tala.

So either they were both in the clear or one was trying to accuse the other.

* * *

Since this would be the last Wine Club before Thanksgiving, we opted for an Oaked Chardonnay with its fuller mouth feel and flavors of vanilla and spices. In this case we were pouring a Sonoma Benziger. It was held at Cassie's, and Carl kicked things off by singing a fabulous rendition of "Autumn in New York" before leaving for drinks with the guys. This time I brought the amuse-bouche, a port-soaked pear tart with a Saga bleu cheese crust. Sweet and savory. No one has ever been kicked out of bed for that. I also couldn't wait to tell them about my video discovery, leaving out Peggy's role in deciphering it.

"This is the lead we've been waiting for," Peggy said upon hearing that the surveillance video originated from Musso's house.

"So that means that the murderer could be one of the people in that house, but which *one?*" Cassie was hoping that Sally and I would not mention Carl's photos of Rosa.

"Or neither," I proposed.

"It's one of them, I'm sure of it," Cassie said and I wondered what she knew that made her so positive.

After toasts and a go around of what we were making for T-Day, we got down to business. I'd also filled everyone in on what we'd learned at the bar in the Marina.

"We need a big calendar so that we can get all the dates straight, there are some key milestones coming up," ever-practical Peggy said.

"There's one in Carl's office," Cassie said while setting down a tray of sage butter fried pumpkin ravioli. "But I never go in there it's icky."

"I'll get it," I said reluctantly. I was the closest but it was hard to resist not grabbing a few of these savory pillows to take with me. But if I knew Cassie, she had plenty more.

Carl's office was a typical man cave. It had a flat screen mounted TV on the wall, a vintage pinball machine in one corner, and a neon Bud sign over a small bar. Taking up the least amount of space was his desk, computer, and chair. It clearly looked like Cassie had banished these items to this one room as a trade-off if Carl wanted to keep them. There was a stuffed Jackalope, typical Carl humor, that sat on a large cloth. I'm guessing that the fabric is used to cover up the mythical monster whenever Cassie enters into the room.

Nowhere did I see a large calendar. I was about to give up when I spotted a couple of boxes sitting atop a grid. No wonder I was having trouble. I lifted one box up and the lid popped off revealing a ream of letters printed with Carl's hardware store logo. When I looked more closely (he shouldn't have left them out if he didn't want anyone reading them), I saw a short paragraph of text followed by a photo of a house. I saw that this one had Rosa's place pictured on the letter. It read:

Dear Homeowner,
Your neighbor Carl here. Wish you

could make some upgrades to your house but don't want to spend the money on a contractor and laborers? Schultz Hardware is here to help! For the next 6 months if you buy your materials at one of our stores, we will help you with the renovations for a flat fee of just $100 a day. No matter how many people are needed for the job. You can't find a better deal anywhere!

It went on from there, citing the specific improvements that Rosa's home needed. As I flipped through, I saw that each one was addressed to a different person in the neighborhood. So this is why he carried his camera everywhere and had all those shots on his SD card. The one of Rosa half-dressed must have just been a fluke. I sighed with relief. He was just trying to generate more business and didn't want to worry Cassie.

I grabbed the calendar and put everything else back in its place. On the way back to the living room, I saw that Cassie was in the kitchen and, as predicted, was refilling a tray with succulent raviolis. I scooted in to grab one and to give her the good news. As expected, her bespoke kitchen had everything I'd ever dreamed of. Including a large set of Messermeister knives.

"That's great, thank you," Cassie said, looking totally flustered.

"So you can stop worrying, okay?"

"Okay," she answered only somewhat convincingly.

I tucked her response into the back of my mind.

"So, given that we know about when the drug shipment arrives, and when Tala will be deported, it looks like everything's going to come to a head sometime Christmas week," Sally said, standing back to survey the filled in boxes of the calendar.

"Perfect, that's exactly when Marcie is coming with the grandkids." Peggy was not happy.

"Well, hopefully we'll have handed off enough evidence to Augie by then so that we can just relax and enjoy the holidays," I soothed.

That seemed to make sense to everyone and they fell silent and tended to their wine.

"Now what?" asked Aimee, picking delicately at her slice of tart. Normally she wolfs down her food but she was still trying to shed some weight before the onslaught of Christmas confections. "I still think that we should leave this to the cops, they must realize by now that you're not the murderer, Halsey. What if it is not any of those four, what if someone else had a bigger motive for Rosa needing to be dead?"

"That's crazy," said Cassie.

"But Aimee, I think we've made some great progress," I said, looking at the running notes I'd been taking since the murder. "Once again, I believe that Musso and/or Tala are at the top of the list. I am leaning toward Tala, and here's why:

- She was a mail-order bride summoned by a sugar daddy in Arizona
- When he rejected her, she found Musso, a softie dressed all in black
- No doubt she knows about his illegal business and is probably blackmailing him
- Her visa problems would be solved if she could get him to marry her
- But Tala found out that he has resisted because he's in love with Rosa."

"I'm still taking a real close look at Ray, especially now that we know Rosa's will had been filed before her death, cutting him out any inheritance," Peggy said. "Maybe Rosa was using the will change to force Ray into giving up his drug dealings, but it backfired and he killed her instead?"

"You think that Inez is in on this with him?" Sally asked. She was still hoping that Ray was innocent.

"She may be just going along for the ride," I said. "She's got two kids and a sickly old mother. I don't see how she'd have time for murder."

"She has *what?*" Peggy asked and was quickly interrupted.

Before I could reply the two sequestered Chihuahuas came bolting down the stairs. We were all stunned and I saw Cassie turn fire engine red.

"TA-DAH! I want you to meet the two newest members of our family, Van Cleef and Arpels," Cassie said, quickly composing herself.

Each sported bejeweled collars and orange nail polish just in time for Thanksgiving.

"Aren't they just darling?" Cassie asked, gushing. "I'm going to give them the best money can buy!"

"Well, butter my butt and call me a biscuit!" Sally said.

Chapter 25

After Thanksgiving, which I'd enjoyed with Sally and Joe and her friends, I got hit with a serious case of loneliness. Jack had gone home for the holiday and most everyone on Rose Avenue was busy with relatives.

I'd decided to throw myself into making my home as festive as possible and that afternoon I set some time aside to hang Christmas lights outside. Marisol, obviously spying on me, came out and pretended to pick weeds out of the cracked asphalt in her driveway with BBQ tongs.

I have several lovely, big birch trees in front of my house and I wanted to string tiny white lights as high up as possible. My six-foot ladder didn't quite allow me to reach my target top branch, so I ignored the ominous warning label and stepped on the very top platform. All was going well, but I really wanted to extend the lights to the very end of the branch. The shift in weight made the ladder, which wasn't on level ground anyway, teeter and fall over. Quickly, I wrapped my arms around a limb, scraping my flesh on the rough bark but saving me from more serious damage. So there I dangled, for all passersby on Rose Avenue to see, wearing a lopsided Santa's hat.

Marisol was there in a flash.

Have I ever actually seen her put one foot in front of the other?

While she uprighted the ladder I had a chance to survey the neighborhood from a totally new perspective. For example, I could now see over the fence in front of Sally and Joe's house across the street.

"Hey, I thought this is the weekend that Sally and Joe were taking a two-day trip to the wineries in Paso Robles for his birthday?" I asked.

"Yeah it is, took his golf clubs too," said Marisol as she quickly placed the ladder on level ground and climbed up to see what I was looking at.

"Then why is their front door open," I asked, giving her an imploring look as I hung from the branch.

"I dunno, but I saw them leave. Lots of strange things going on here lately."

Marisol was now perched comfortably on the ladder's top rung, taking in the view. I wanted her to elaborate on the strange things but had a more pressing matter at the moment.

"A little help here?"

If I win the lottery, I'm buying her a cherry picker. With a mini fridge.

She finally got the hint, climbed down, and

dragged the ladder over to me. "I'm going to call the cops."

Oh no, not again.

The self-appointed "Mayor of Rose Avenue" was on a mission. I finished connecting my lights and plugged them into a timer connected to an outside outlet. This time I was staying completely out of any open doors on my street.

Marisol returned with a cushion from one of her kitchen chairs. She dragged the ladder over by my front steps where I was now recovering from my near death experience, and climbed on up, using the cushion to buffer her bony butt on the hard wood.

I guess she's planning on setting a spell.

Not long after, the show began. From both ends of the street patrol cars appeared, I counted at least five. No sirens, no flashing lights. As the officers got out, they shouldered their rifles. Marisol recognized Augie and waved to him.

I hoped there was nothing wrong at their house but started thinking that all this police activity, with guns drawn, might flush out a murderer or two.

Augie didn't seem to wonder or question why his aunt was sitting atop a ladder as she calmly explained the situation.

"I am just hanging Christmas lights, that is all," I said.

Now to me, he looked askance. I guess it was okay to perch on a makeshift crow's nest but something entirely different to be wearing a Santa hat in the middle of the day.

I heard a car start and saw Tala pulling out of her drive in a Porsche Cayenne. She was in such a rush that she hadn't adjusted the seat and looked very awkward trying to reach the pedals and the steering wheel at the same time.

I saw Marisol watching her as well.

Meanwhile across the street two pairs of cops pointing guns had formed a perimeter and were closing in on the house. Augie crossed the street to join them.

"What's going on?" I asked, feeling like an idiot for asking this crazy old woman for a play-by-play, but I couldn't see over the fence.

"They're going up the front steps, and lining up on either side of the front door. Now, they're going in!"

Well, at that moment I guess I crossed over to the dark side because I climbed up onto the porch railing using the vertical support post to pull me up. I needed to see for myself. Also, I figured if shots were fired from inside the house I could stand sideways and be protected by the whitewashed wood I was clinging to.

We watched in silence as they disappeared inside the house. After about five minutes, they started coming out. Augie came back to give us his report.

"There's no sign of a break-in, although I did see a bowl of tiny zucchinis with flowers that were chopped into little pieces. That seemed a bit odd."

"Squash blossoms, Joe's favorite!" I exclaimed.

"You said they went on vacation? Is it possible they just forgot to shut their door?"

I saw Marisol shrug her shoulders.

"Well, we've closed the door but it is still unlocked. If you have their number, I suggest you
contact them and let them know."

"I've got a key, I'll lock it," Marisol said. "Don't
forget Sunday dinner, we're meeting at Sizzler's."

He returned to the cars, and we watched as one
by one they all drove off in different directions.

Godspeed, Officers.

Rose Avenue had been returned to its harmo-
nious self.

Marisol back-stepped down the ladder as I
hopped off the railing. We watched them go, and
although we were happy that nothing had happened to Sally and Joe's house, we did feel a little
let down. That was when Marisol started laughing
nonstop.

*This woman really is about as crazy as an inflatable
ashtray.*

Finally I couldn't take it any longer. "What's so
funny?"

She calmed down a bit and caught her breath.

"Did you see how fast that bitch raced out of
here? I thought that she was going to slide off her
seat and run right into one of them cop cars!"

That started another spate of guffaws, to which I
joined in.

*Crazy like a fox. Wait, she didn't orchestrate this
whole—Naaah.*

I grabbed my cell, gave Sally a call, and told her
about her door being open and the strange bowl
of eviscerated squash blossoms.

"Impossible, Joe always double checks," she said
when I told her what had happened. "We almost

didn't go, Joe couldn't find the golf shoes that match his plus fours. But then Cassie came over and literally packed us into the car."

"Cassie?"

"Well, I guess I'm the next one on the list to be given a warning, but this is so very creepy and so damn personal. Ah well, we're glad we went, we're having a great time. Thanks so much for watching over us."

I guess that Sally and Cassie are closer friends than I realized.

I looked over at Marisol who had given up any pretense of doing anything but spying.

"So come on, you live next door and I know you like to spy, er, keep tabs on the neighborhood, what can you tell me about exotic Tala."

"I seen and hear things, those two fighting all the time. She does all the yelling, he usually ends up storming out and going for a drive."

"What does she say when she's yelling?"

"Stuff about how he doesn't deserve her, some other guy paid good money to have her come here. How if he didn't do this and that, she'd go to the cops. Tell them all about his car business and that he kidnapped her."

"You get all that through the walls?"

"They going to leave their windows open then I guess they want me to hear what they're saying."

"What does he do?"

"Not much, but I can tell that he's miserable."

"Did you ever see her with Rosa? Maybe talking on the sidewalk?"

"HAH!"

"What's hah?" I asked, backing away a bit. She was getting a crazed look in her eyes.

"Ooh, they had a knock down, drag out fight one day. Sounded like two hyenas were singing the National Anthem."

"What happened?"

"Musso finally ran out and dragged Tala home. She was screaming at Rosa all the way into the house."

"Have you told Augie about this?"

"I forgot, I'll tell him on Sunday, before the family dinner."

"He'll want to know, this gives Tala motive. I guess Musso and Rosa once had a thing?"

"He loved her; they were going to get married but she called it off. Broke his damn heart."

"How do you know all this?" I asked, but she had once again disappeared.

The next day started with a beautiful winter's morning, perfect for a drive up into Malibu. The sky was an ice crisp blue and the Santa Ana winds calmed the ocean water to a glass-like surface.

As I headed north on PCH, I had to smile at the passing scenery. In some ways it was life as normal. Gardeners' trucks were making the rounds, bikers were getting in their fifty uphill miles, and the Reel Inn seafood restaurant's sign, which displays a different fish pun each day, was asking *What If Cod Were One of Us?*

The people of Malibu had managed to work the holidays into the fabric of beach living. The palm trees were adorned with giant Christmas ornaments, forced-air inflated Santas dressed in swim trunks and sunglasses were waving at the passing vehicles, and many of the luxury cars were loaded up with both a surf board and a pine tree tied to the roof.

When I was in New York, if we saw images like this, we'd laughed at Californians' air-headed simplicity and questionable taste. And harbor a secret desire to be transported there.

We turned off the highway and headed up a canyon road. Bardot's nose was receiving tidal waves of scents, and she was squealing and fidgeting with excitement.

"Yes, we are going to visit Uncle Jack," I said to her. At the mention of his name, she sat down quietly in the back.

Good to know . . .

Yes, after my outburst with Peggy, I'd done some soul searching and had given her crazy-sounding advice some thought. I decided to take the morning off so that we could surprise him. This time *I* was bringing lunch, and I was excited to see Bardot in action after all his training.

I had gone on the CARA website and saw that there was going to be a training session led by Mr. Jack Thornton. I did a run to the market, threw together a picnic, and Bardot and I headed out. I didn't even stress about what I was wearing. . . .

Okay, you know me better than that by now. After about fifteen minutes of closet trial and error, I chose a denim "boyfriend" shirt with a camisole underneath, white jeans, and Keds sneakers. I was going for an all American girl look.

God, it was beautiful up here. If money were no

object, the best way to experience Southern California would be to have a house on the beach, one in the mountains, another in the Hollywood Hills, and a perched expanse on the Palos Verdes peninsula. I'd heard that there are wild peacocks roaming all over Palos Verdes. They've been running free since the 1920s. While beautiful at a distance, the noise and mess they create has spawned a cottage industry of all sorts of creature deterrents. My favorite is called "Terror Eyes" and I am thinking of carrying some around with me, just because.

These gems are inflatable two-foot balls with brightly colored 3D holographs of roving eyes that seem to follow you around. For under thirty dollars, you can scare the crap out of anything within one thousand square feet. Hours of fun for the entire family.

We turned into the CARA staging area where I saw the rescue dog teams gearing up. I put the car in park and lowered the windows. It was seventy degrees, even up here. It wasn't hard to pick out Jack, he towered over everyone and the sun reflected off of his shiny pate. He was having an animated conversation with a woman and her German shepherd. I could see her react to something he said and give him a light punch in the arm and laugh. He laughed as well and threw an arm around her shoulder.

That's Jodi, I remember her from the last time.

I was surprised at my reaction. I felt heat rise up from my fingertips to my ears. It was fueled by both embarrassment and jealousy. All I knew was that I had to sneak out of there without him notic-

ing me. I started the car. As I was about to put it in
gear, Bardot saw Jack and jumped out the window.

"Shit, shit, shit," I whispered, pounding my fist
on the steering wheel. I watched her run up to Jack
and do her usual "sit and wait for a command."

"Bardot, what are you doing here?" he said, looking around for me.

Since I was busted, there was nothing left to do
but get out of the car. He walked toward me with
Bardot dutifully at his side.

"Hey, I didn't know you guys were working up
here today. It's such a beautiful morning that Bardot and I decided to go for a hike," I explained,
trying to sell it with a smile.

*Why do I keep thinking I can fool an animal behav-
iorist?*

"Really? Your car is running, did you change your
mind?"

He caught me casting a quick glance toward
Jodi, who was watching the entire exchange.

"Just cooling off the car," I said, heading back
to it.

Sooo lame.

He cocked his head and gave me a look and a
smile. "Well, I'm glad you're here, it's a perfect
time for me to show you what Bardot can do."

"Perfect time? I'm not so sure," I said, watching
Jodi and her dog approach.

"What, why?"

He got his answer as Jodi and her dog joined us.
I didn't know if they had any relationship besides
CARA, but I knew damn well that Jodi was trying
to protect what she had and go for more.

"Hi, I'm Jodi," she said in a booming "outside voice," extending her hand.

I shook it and introduced myself.

"And I see you've met Bardot."

My dog was sitting perfectly still and smiling. I gave her a squinting glare when no one else was looking. She was so damn enjoying this.

"We're pretty much going on a hike as well, Jodi and Macy and a couple of others, why don't you join us," said Jack, rubbing his fingers through the side of his beard. A "tell" that he was uncomfortable.

I looked past them to the other teams and they clearly had other plans and were already setting off into the woods. I was about to say something snide, *moi?* When I heard Peggy's words replay in my head.

"The best way to get a man to stop doing something is to tell him how good he is at it."

"You guys go. Jodi, you'll have a blast, Jack knows lots of special spots in there. Hope you brought a picnic," I said, giving her my best smile, which I learned from Bardot. Wide mouth, creating side dimples.

Jodi was at first surprised but then beamed at the thought that I would not be raining on her parade.

Jack's beard was now starting to show a bald spot.

"But you should come, don't you want to see what Bardot can do?"

"You look so hardcore, I was planning more of a 'hike-walk,' " I said, looking down at my Keds.

"We'll go slow, this isn't a trial, it's just for fun."
He smiled and Jodi didn't.

"And whatever's in that backpack smells delicious," he said, cocking his head to the back seat
of my car. "Bring that too."

So off we went.

"Today we are doing things a little differently,"
Jack said to the group. "There is no source tracking
scent that we can provide the dogs. The scenario is
that a small plane has gone down in the woods and
we have to search for any traces of human life."

Right about now I wished my human life could
be untraceable.

"The test subject today is carrying some reward
toys that we have worked with in the past. He is out
there in the woods and is instructed not to show
them until the dog who finds him has performed
the 'stay-and-bark' task. You all remember what
that is, right? The dogs have to bark ten times."

"Perfect-o," said Jodi. "Macy and I practiced this
all last week."

*Well, pin a rose on you. I'm even starting to hate her
dog now.*

When we walked further along the path and the
trees got thicker and closer together, Jack told us
to unleash our dogs. When I bent down to get Bardot's clasp unattached from her collar, she thought
we were playing "Doggie WWF," a little game I made
up for living room rug fun.

I know, I need to grow up and this proves it because she put her paws on my shoulders and flipped
me over onto the ground. Trying to get up and get
control of her just exacerbated the situation. She

did a perfect pounce on my back with her front paws and I can tell you that, no, not all wrestling is faked. With deep humiliation and leaves and God knows what else in my clothes and hair, it wasn't until I laid facedown, counted to ten and slammed my hand on the ground that she let up. When I looked up, she was sitting triumphantly by Jodi's side.

Et tu?

To Jack's credit he did pretty well at stifling his laughter. The other teams looked at me like I'd just stripped naked and taken a mud bath.

Jack helped me up and tried to brush as much forest floor detritus off me as he could.

"Also, there is a little extra snag in today's challenge," Jack continued with a twinkle in his eye that I swear Jodi wanted to lick. "Between us and the 'missing person' is a hill and moving runoff from the basin up above, courtesy of the recent rains. It has formed a creek about ten feet wide. The dogs will have to pick up the scent in spite of these obstacles."

The next thing I knew, I was trying to keep up in my Keds as everyone took off. They had the benefit of boots with rubber cleats. About the third time the treacle-like terrain pulled my sneaker from my heel and my foot landed with force on the hard outer canvas, I gave up and took my shoes off entirely. At least in socks I could use my toes for traction. I happened to have a couple elastic hair bands in my pocket, so I used them to anchor the socks to my ankles.

As I got closer to the pack, I could now see that

Bardot was leading the charge. The hell with everything else, my dog was making me proud. Jack waited for me at the base of the hill.

"Shoes not working out, huh?" He grabbed my hand and pulled me along.

"They're fine, I just want to be more 'one with nature.' "

We both laughed as we reached the top.

Sure enough there was the raging water below. It had the dogs totally confused.

"Come on, Macy, use your advanced sense of smell. You can do it, girl!" Jodi was sniffing with her, as if that would help.

The dogs seemed to be working as a team now, if one smelled something and went in a certain direction the others did so as well. Kind of like a school of sardines in the ocean.

Except for Bardot. For once she was still with her nose extended high over her shoulders. Her throat muscles expanded and contracted with each intake of air.

Oh well, we'll always have Rose Avenue.

All of a sudden she bolted up and raced down the hill. The other dogs took a minute to register this and then tore after her. She was on a direct path to the creek.

Oh no.

I looked at Jack and saw that he was thinking the same thing.

"Jack, please tell me she knows that this is not a pool she can dive into. That it's not deep. She knows that, right?" I could barely get the words out I was running so fast.

"I'm sure she does," Jack said while kicking up his pace to another gear.

Bardot was about five feet from the creek now and was not slowing up. She runs like this at home toward the pool and then points her body down, excited for the first dive of the day.

"Jack, she's not stopping," I shouted.

"Neither am I," he yelled over his shoulder between giving commands to Bardot.

As she reached the water's edge, I didn't know whether to look or not. I let out a silent scream that would have had Edvard Munch reaching for a canvas and watched in terror.

Remember the homerun scene from the movie The Natural?

With grace Bardot lifted herself six feet into the air and in a perfect arc cleared the water with room to spare. She landed and just kept on going.

Moments later we heard it: "Woof, woof, woof, woof, woof, woof, woof, woof, woof . . . woof!"

I screamed for joy and jumped up on Jack who pulled me into him. The other dogs had now crossed the creek on foot and were headed toward Bardot. Jodi just stood and watched, crestfallen. I felt a little sorry for her, this was such an important part of her life.

"You know dogs learn by example. If you ever want to bring Macy over for a pool date with Bardot, we'd be delighted."

Now Jodi was out of her comfort zone.

"Gee, thanks," she mustered in a soft-spoken voice.

Just then my cell phone rang. It was Aimee. I stepped away to talk to her.

"Halsey, how soon can you get here? There's someone on the roof again and Kimberly's gone for the day. I'm scared that more rats will be coming down, but I want to catch them in the act."

"Crap, I'm in Malibu, twenty minutes if the traffic gods are with me. What about your Jamaican boys, can't they help you?"

"I tried calling them but no one answered. Same with Peggy and Sally, I guess I could try Cassie."

"It may be better not to. I'm on my way and if you think you're in danger, call 9-1-1. Promise?"

"Okay, but hurry."

I came back to everyone and explained, "I've got to run my friend needs help right away. Come, Bardot," I shouted to her.

She came running, all proud and puffy, her rescue toy hanging out of her mouth. Her tail was wagging furiously and she wasn't even out of breath.

"What's going on, is everything okay?" Jack asked softly. "I'll walk you back to your car."

"Yes, everything's fine, that was Aimee, she thinks someone is on her roof again and she really wants to catch them. She's still stinging from those rats in her shop."

In a turn of the tables, Jack was now working to keep up with me. Never get between a woman and her mission, right?

"So whoever's up there could also be the murderer?"

"Yes, listen I gotta boogie or we won't have anything."

"This is too dangerous, I'm coming with you," he said, opening the back door of my car for Bardot to jump in.

"You'll do no such thing, we'll be fine. I'll call you as soon as I know anything. Go back and talk to your team, I bet they could use some words of encouragement right about now."

I tried to keep my smile under four hundred watts.

Chapter 26

Even in the strip mall the Christmas spirit had started to take hold. That is to say that the Taquería now displayed a FELIZ NAVIDAD banner in multi-colored, shiny paper letters across their window, along with a picture of burritos standing upright on little legs in green pointed shoes and sporting elf ears. You had to wonder what the sots who wandered out of the liquor store at two a.m. swigging Everclear thought about it all.

I sat parked at the curb across the street, hoping to see who was on Aimee's roof. It was dark by the time I'd arrived and most of the shops were closed and their storefronts unlit. Bardot was passed out in the back, helped by some of her favorite music, Andrea Bocelli singing "Caro Gesu Bambino." His dulcet tenor voice always put her in a trance-like state.

I could make out the shadow of someone moving above the Chill Out but really couldn't see any more detail. I grabbed my flashlight from Dad's backpack, got out, and gently closed the car door. I didn't want to announce my arrival.

Aimee opened the door for me the second I reached it. I gave her a reassuring hug.

"Have you called the police?" I asked in a whisper.

Interesting, unlike any other emotion, I noticed that when Aimee gets scared her face drains completely of color.

"No, so far thank God, they haven't done anything for me to report. Plus, as soon as they heard the sirens I'd bet they'd split and we would never know who did this horrible thing to me."

"I'm going out to take a look, if I'm not back in ten minutes, call the cops."

"Halsey, I don't know, something could happen to you. Maybe we should forget the whole thing."

"We've got to put a stop to this, you know that, Aimee. Besides, maybe this is just the work of pranksters, it would be pretty harmless, then, wouldn't it?"

"I guess."

"Ten minutes, mark your watch."

I slipped out quietly and went around the side of the building to the shed that housed the patio tables and chairs. Right away I saw a ladder leaning against it, and thought that I should just wait for whomever to come down. I got my flashlight ready to shine on their face and set up the camera on my phone. Pretty straightforward and once accomplished I'd run like hell.

The only problem was that no one was coming down and after six minutes I was afraid that I

wouldn't make my deadline before Aimee called
in for reinforcements. Whatever they were doing
up there took time, something I didn't have. I
started to sneak back to Aimee when my foot hit
something hard and I heard the tinkling sound of
a rolling bottle.

I froze.

When the noise finally stopped there was complete silence. I started to think that maybe the person on the roof got spooked and went down
another way. After eight minutes I decided that it
was do or die, so I climbed the ladder and crept up
the building wall to the roof. Once again my rock
climbing class didn't fail me.

When I felt the edge of the roof, I slowly inched
my head up, all I wanted was one look at a face. Instead I saw a shoe coming toward my face.

And that was the last thing I saw.

Chapter 27

A soft beeping sound woke me just enough to try and take in my surroundings. I was indoors because it was very quiet and comfortably cool.

"Well, hello, beautiful."

I blinked several times and Jack came into focus. Afraid to move my head, I let my eyes wander back and forth to try and figure out where I was. It was dark and very little was registering, except that I was lying in a bed. And I could see Jack's beautiful, smiling face inches away from mine.

"I can't really see, where am I?"

"You're in the hospital, darlin'. And don't worry about your eyesight the doctors are keeping it very dark in here so you don't overstimulate your brain. You might also have some double vision but they said that's normal. You've had a pretty serious head injury."

I won't lie, I got about half of that. But I understood "don't worry" and "normal," so I figured that I was ahead of the game. Thankfully my mind was not a blank, but I tried to restrict the flow of memories of what had happened, to go easy on my head.

My eyes went wide.

"Bardot? I left her in the car!"

"Shhh, she's fine. I tried to pass her off as a service dog so I could bring her in here, but she found a spare IV pole, discovered that it rolls, and went tearing down the hallway with it."

I laughed and then regretted it. My hand went to my neck to try and understand why my throat hurt so much.

"You've been through the wringer, babe, besides the head wound, when you fell you hit your neck on a ladder rung. Here, sip some juice, it'll make your throat feel better."

He raised a cup with a straw to my mouth.

"I didn't fall, I was pushed," I managed to squeak out.

"The cops are waiting to hear all about that, just as soon as you are well enough."

He smoothed my hair and stroked my cheek.

"Why do they need to talk to me? Didn't they catch who did this?"

"I'm afraid not, the roof was empty when they got there, and they found very little evidence to give them any clues."

"What the hell," I tried to shout, but sounded more like I was talking through a paper cup and string phone line.

He gently put his arms around me. "Relax, you need to stay quiet. You don't need to think about anything but rest right now."

The door to my room opened, and two cops popped their heads in.

"Everything okay?" asked the nurse. "I think it's time for you to go, all of you, she needs to rest."

"I need to find out whose shoe connected with my head!" That was a little better.

"Can you describe the shoe?" one of the cops asked.

"That's it, OUT!"

The nurse called for a sedative to be brought in.

"Sweetie, I'm going to go, but I'll be back first thing in the morning. I've postponed my trip home until after Christmas and when you are completely better. Maybe you and Bardot will come with me. I love you."

He kissed me gently on the lips and slipped out as the orderly entered my room. He handed the nurse a syringe.

Wait; did he just use the L *word?*

The sleeping potion entered my IV before I had a chance to savor this.

"Okay, I'd like to review everything we have for Halsey," Jack said, addressing the Wine Club. It was late, and no wine was being served.

Jack had dialed in my Skype account while the group assembled around the computer monitor in my office.

"Yay," they all cheered upon seeing my face appear on the screen.

"How are you feeling?" Peggy asked.

"I'm getting better although I suffered a major trauma to my head," I answered.

"She should recover fully but she needs to take everything really slowly or she could get swelling on her brain, and that would be very dangerous," added retired nurse Sally.

"Thank the Lord," said Cassie who had found religion in the midst of this terrible ordeal. She was wearing a white blouse under a black cardigan with the top button closed. A silver cross on a beaded chain was draped above it. However, the red leggings seemed a little off topic.

"Aimee, the last thing I remember is getting to the top of the ladder and being kicked in the head. What happened after that?"

"I found you splayed out on the roof of the shed. I remembered thinking how lucky you were that you didn't fall all the way down, but then I saw all the blood on your head and I retched. It was horrible."

"You saved her life, Aimee, that is what you need to remember now," Peggy advised.

"I had to stay behind and provide the cops with access and answer any questions. The ambulance I called came right away and took you to St. John's. Jack and the girls met you there."

"Thank you so much, Aimee," I said, a little shocked at how serious this was.

"What did the cops say?" Cassie asked.

"They came in the shop after they were done on the roof, and I offered them some yogurt and coffee, even sandwiches, but they said no. You would think they would be hungry being out all night and climbing around."

I remembered that Aimee rambled when she was nervous.

"The cops, Aimee, what did the cops find?" Jack gently tried to steer her back on course.

"Well, they weren't regular cops, their jackets said DEA on them. They said that when dispatch heard the location of the crime, they were told to investigate. They asked about the guys who run that vacuum shop. I know they didn't do this, Halsey."

I took a sip of water.

"Maybe you should rest, Halsey, we can pick this up again tomorrow," Sally said.

"No, no, please go on, Aimee."

"I told them about Ali Baba and Zeke, and they wanted to know if I'd seen them earlier in the day. I realized that I haven't seen them for a week or so. I thought about it more and I guess they've been closed since the fifteenth.

Aimee dropped to a chair; she appeared as though she was trying to piece things together in her mind.

"They said that they talked to the landlord that night, and he said that he hasn't been able to reach them and they are late on their rent. He told them he came by a few days ago and changed the locks. I'm just worried sick."

"I'm sure they're just fine, Aimee, I'll confirm with my friend Mark who works with the DEA," Jack said.

"Have we heard anything about what was found on the roof, Jack or Aimee?" Peggy was all business.

"Unfortunately they found very little," Aimee replied. "Some fibers and some other samples were bagged and sent to the lab; they said that unless Halsey saw who pushed her, we're probably out of luck."

"Halsey, I don't want you taxing your brain, you'll have plenty of time later, good Lord willing, and the creek don't rise," of course Sally said.

Aimee said that she brought the DEA up to speed on Rosa's murder and all that ensued involving Ray, Ali Baba, and Zeke, even Musso and Inez. Some of the information they already knew. She asked a lot of questions back but got few answers except to learn that they were closing in on this drug ring. The lead officer gave Aimee his card and told her to call him at any time if she saw something. He stressed "anytime."

"As I locked up and was finally heading home, I heard someone call 'Miss Aimee.' It was Ali Baba. He said that he didn't know about or have anything to do with the accident."

"This was no accident!" I felt my blood begin to boil.

"I'm sorry, assault and battery. Ali said that he wanted to explain why they left and say goodbye.

He said that Ray and Zeke are relying on this next big drug shipment and are nervous. He said that with all this heat going on Ray wants them to be totally on the down low. He said that he will just be in the background and will then go back home."

"I'm going to call Mark right now, and I am going to speak to Ali Baba, he seems to be the loose link in this drug chain. Maybe I can convince him to turn informant," Jack said, heading into another room.

Aimee applauded.

"Now, let's run through everything we have. Peggy, you're up first," I said.

Peggy assumed the floor. "I have visual aids," she began, "and a bit of a confession."

That got everyone's attention.

"Let's start with 'show,' and then I'll 'tell.' On my iPad I have the video file that was sent anonymously to the cops. It shows someone going in and out of Rosa's house. The time and date stamp indicate that it was shot the day she was killed."

They all gathered around and stared like they were watching a baby being born.

"When the cops got this it was so grainy that you could only barely make out a human form. I have a friend in forensics and I gave him a shot at enhancement."

"Forensics, is that like the study of sick people in Europe?" Cassie asked.

No one answered, there was nowhere to go with that.

"Now, take a look at this version, it's still blurry but tell me what you see." Peggy ran the video twice before she let them speak.

"That's definitely a woman," Sally replied.

"But who? You really can't tell from this," Aimee said, frustrated.

"It's got to be either Tala or Inez, don't you think?" Jack had returned and was tugging at his beard.

"Maybe Tala needed to exercise her revenge for Musso before she left the country. After all, she must have been hoping that he'd marry her so she could stay here for good," Sally reasoned.

"But he was still stuck on Rosa," said Marisol, stepping up in her role as Mayor of Rose Avenue. Her second in command, Bardot, was sleeping at her side.

"How coldhearted," teary Aimee sighed.

"Let's not dismiss Inez so easily. If Ray didn't know that he'd been cut out of the will, then maybe she got tired of waiting to move into that house," Peggy said, closing her tablet.

"You said there was a 'tell' part Peggy, so please, spill it!" said probing Aimee.

"Yeah, and how is it that you have a friend in forensic science?" Jack asked.

Peggy smiled. It was time for her CIA story.

"I knew it!" said Sally. "At that time I remember that you became awfully evasive about how you spent your days. I wondered what extracurricular activities you were engaging in."

Peggy feigned shock.

"So they may have had accomplices, but it looks

like we can narrow down Rosa's killer to these two women," I summed up.

"And we lose one of them in a week and a half," said Sister Cassie, looking at the large calendar from Carl's office.

"She's already packed her suitcases and hidden some of Musso's cash in the padding of her bras. I always knew those boobs were fake," Marisol enlightened us.

We all looked at her and wondered the same thing: *"How does she know all this?"*

"That's good, Marisol," I said, "you keep tracking Tala and let us all know the second it looks like they are ready to leave. I'll try hard to remember details of who I saw on the roof."

"And Marisol, tell Augie all about this, maybe he can go back over the evidence at Rosa's house and tie something to her," Peggy instructed.

Now that she knew Peggy was a secret agent she took everything Peggy said as a direct command and she saluted.

"Aimee, you work with Sally and keep feeding the DEA with as much info as you can. If Inez is our killer, then the best thing would be for the DEA to catch them taking a shipment. From there they can extract the murder charge. Maybe for both of them, it's hard to believe that Ray knew nothing about that," I concluded.

Sally cringed but nodded.

Jack looked at Peggy and Cassie.

"You two will need to help Halsey when she gets home, that is vital to her overall recovery and for anything she might remember about the night on the roof. She needs a lot of TLC and no stress, understand, Bardot?"

Bardot rolled on her back and played dead.

"I'm also giving my friend another crack at enhancing the video, he has some more tricks up his sleeve," Peggy said.

Once again Marisol saluted her.

Chapter 28

It felt so good to be home, there is just nothing about a hospital that says, "this is nice, maybe I'll stay for a while." I had just settled into my favorite sofa when the doorbell rang. Bardot ignored it and wouldn't leave my side. She must really have missed me.

Jack went to the door.

I heard him open it but was too weak to get up and see whom it was.

"This is not a good time, Detectives. She just got home and she needs her rest."

"We know, we just came from the hospital. The doctor who discharged her told us she'd be fine to answer some questions as long as we didn't take too long."

He didn't wait for permission and walked in followed by his partner. Just as Jack was closing the door, he felt some resistance and Marisol pushed her way in as well. He tried again to shut it but Augie held it open and stepped in.

Augie introduced himself to the detectives and explained that he was working a murder case that I was also involved in.

The detective and his partner looked at me with renewed interest.

"Hello, Ms. Hall, I understand that you are feeling better."

"I was."

The detective explained to the group that since this crime was committed in their jurisdiction they had to follow up, at least initially. Without stepping on Augie's toes.

"How many more questions you gotta ask before you figure this out? That bitch next door to me had to have pushed her."

"What are you doing here?" the detective asked Marisol as she settled herself on the sofa with Bardot and me.

"I'm her home nurse," she replied.

It was then that everyone noticed that she was wearing a white button-down nurse's dress and matching white clogs.

"We need to talk to Ms. Hall alone."

"Not going to happen," Marisol said, crossing her arms. "My nephew and I are here to find out who killed poor Rosa."

Augie winced.

"Ms. Hall, can you tell us what happened? Please start with why you were at the strip mall in the first place."

"My friend Aimee owns the Chill Out yogurt shop there. She'd called to say that she thought there was someone walking around on her roof.

She's gun-shy because some weeks ago someone sent rats down the vent to destroy her shop."

"Who could blame her," Marisol said while petting Bardot, who was lying somewhat obscenely supine.

"Was this investigated? What was the conclusion?"

"The patrol cops found little to no evidence and theorized that this was a prank done by the kids from the school next door."

"And you and this Aimee were not satisfied with that explanation?"

"No," I replied. "This had to have been done in the middle of the night because the rats were discovered before seven the next morning."

"We believe that this was some kind of warning because the girls were doing some sleuthing of their own into Rosa's murder," Jack explained.

"Let me pick up from here," Augie said and proceeded to bring the detectives up to speed.

"At this point have you been able to narrow down the field of suspects at all?" the detective asked Augie.

"I think I can help you with that, Detective," said Peggy, walking in with her iPad.

"Sure can," said Sally, who was followed in by Cassie and Aimee.

Peggy showed the cops and me the enhanced video that she'd played for the group the other day.

"Wow, so it was a woman who killed Rosa, and tried to kill me!"

"What do you remember about that night on the roof?" Augie asked me gently.

I went through the sequence of events.

"And the shoe, can you describe it, Ms. Hall?"

"It was too dark to really see, and everything happened so fast."

"Take your time, just let the thoughts come to you."

Everyone gathered around me reminiscent of my initiation Wine Club.

"The shoe was dark, but not black. A deep brown or red maybe."

Marisol stopped petting Bardot and listened intently to me.

"What about the size?"

"If it was a man's, it was probably on the small side. If it was a woman's, then she had a really strong kick. I wish I could tell you more, but that's all I remember."

I was getting tired.

"If someone tried to kill Halsey once, then you can be sure that they'll try to again," said Peggy. "They obviously think that we know something, which we do."

"You think that I have to worry about my *life*?"

"Calm down, honey, I'll be here," Jack said. "You'd better put a unit on her house, or I'll pull together my own protection squad."

It was clear that Jack wasn't kidding.

"We can do that. Please understand that we are here to protect you. I think that when we get the forensics results we'll turn them over to your team,

Augie. It seems clear that this incident is tied to the murder."

"Happened to run into Tala this morning, so I asked how things were going," Cassie said. "Since I live further down the street she didn't seem to think that she had anything to hide. I asked her if she and Musso were planning on taking a vacation anytime soon. She laughed and said, 'why when it is so beautiful here?'"

"She's so full of it her eyes are brown," announced Sally.

"Anybody else starving?" asked Jack, standing up to stretch.

"I've got a mushroom lasagna I took out of the freezer this morning," said Cassie.

"I've had beef burgundy in the slow cooker all day. I could boil up some egg noodles to go with," offered Peggy. "Marisol, want to help me get it ready?"

She nodded but seemed a little preoccupied. It struck me as odd since she'd just been given the opportunity to snoop in a whole new house.

"We'll be back in a bit," Peggy said.

I wonder what the proportion of burgundy is going to be to beef.

"And I've got fresh veggies for a salad, and I'll crust some goat cheese in chopped hazelnuts and bake it," said Sally.

"I need to relieve Kimberly so she can take her dinner break, but I can be back with frozen yogurt in a couple of hours. Are you sure you're up for all this company, Halsey?"

"After being in a dark, quiet room and trying to live off of broth, Jell-O, and cottage cheese, I am so ready for a party with you guys. I know I have wine but I'm not sure what is left in the fridge."

"I got you eggs, milk, berries, and a New York cheesecake," Jack said.

"I'm keepin' him," I proudly announced.

The party went well into the night. This was actually the first time that we had all gotten together with spouses, boyfriends, etc. Even Tom popped in after he got off his shift at the hospital.

Having all these great people around helped me forget the whole murder business and that someone was out there, no doubt planning their next attack on me. I nestled into Jack's arms on some floor pillows, noticing that after all the delicious food, wine, and dessert everyone was sitting in some form of repose. And at the center of us all was Bardot, snoring happily with her head resting on the big stuffed Santa Claus that Jack had bought for her.

As I started to doze off, I couldn't help but think that this was the calm before the storm, . . .

Chapter 29

It was December and, believe it or not, Jack and I were going to the beach. This was to be our little holiday party. He was going to be busy over Christmas with all the new puppies that Santa put under the trees and I had meetings and deliverables for work, so this seemed to be our best opportunity to be together.

Still being fairly new to California, I had not really explored the beaches beyond Venice and Santa Monica. As is Jack's way, where we were going was a "surprise."

"Normally you are not allowed to have dogs on this beach, but since it is so off-season there will be no one there to enforce that."

"I'm a little worried, Bardot has never been in the ocean. I'm afraid that she'll get so excited that she'll swim all the way to Hawaii."

"It's cool, Clarence will be with her and they'll stick together. Worst case, I'll go in and bring her back."

"Better you than me, I read in the paper that the water temp is only fifty-nine degrees!"

"Are you becoming a West Coast wimp?"

"I never liked the cold, I guess I was meant to live here all along."

"Does that mean you're going to stay here for a while?"

"Hah, I have no choice. I owe too much money to leave."

Not the response he was hoping for. After that we rode in silence up the coast.

El Matador State Beach is at the northern end of Malibu and is one of the most spectacular locations in the country. Like anything worth having, it is a little tough to find and a trek to get down to.

Off PCH, you pull into a small area marked only by a brown wooden sign. In the summer, you have to get there pretty early if you want to park or you'll be left trying to find a space on the highway. In December we were one of four cars.

The parking area completely misleads you to the beauty below. Just like a caterpillar reveals nothing of the butterfly it will become. The surface is made up of dirt and pebbles, the surrounding brush is moldy and unkempt, and at the head of the trail down the cliff stands a port-o-potty. There is no way to put lipstick on that pig.

When you start down the 150-foot bluff via an old wooden staircase half buried in the sand, you quickly see what all the fuss is about.

From atop, you get the full vista of this rugged

shoreline with pocket beaches nestled between
the corrugated cliffside. The sand is almost white
compared to the muddier-looking beaches further
south. Just offshore, the often-powerful waves had
created craggy rocks with worn through caves and
sea stacks.

Once down on the beach, you can walk along
the beach pockets until you find your own private
little slice of paradise.

"I'm breathless," I said as we made our descent.

"You want to stop and rest a minute?"

I laughed. "No, I'm just astounded by this
beauty."

The dogs had taken off and raced down the cliff
as if they were in the Iditarod. The ocean was flat,
which made me a little less worried about Bardot
drifting off to sea. Jack, my sand Sherpa, refused to
let me carry anything but my beach bag so I could
get down easily and enjoy the view doing so. He,
on the other hand, was loaded up with a backpack,
an umbrella, two beach chairs, and a cooler, which
he carried on his head. Somehow this beast of burden still managed to move spryly down the steps.

When we reached the shore, Bardot came racing toward us. She was already wet and full of sand.
Clarence was right on her heels in the same condition. I'd never seen him so happy and frolicsome.

Bardot and I have that kind of influence on our
friends.

We found a spot and set up camp. In addition to
the chairs, Jack had brought a soft beach blanket,

which he anchored down on each corner with rocks he had picked up. Bardot watched with fascination and as soon as he was done, jumped on it and rolled on her back and did enough serpentine undulations to twist the blanket into a soggy mess. Once satisfied, she hopped up and joined Clarence who was waiting so they could go back in the water.

"You can't take us anywhere, I'm afraid."

"I could have stopped her but today is about freedom and enjoying just being," he said, channeling his new age spirit. "Besides, I also brought a bunch of towels," which he produced from the seemingly bottomless backpack.

"Cheers," I said, clinking plastic cups which were filled with my new special agave lime margarita potion.

"Happy holidays," he said, taking a sip and then kissing me with sweet, limey lips.

It was a lingering kiss. A really nice kiss.

"So what's home like?" I asked after we came up for air.

"Well, I'm a small town mountain boy, grew up about an hour outside of Denver. I've got a sister, Jill, and my wonderful mom, Mary Beth."

"Jack and Jill? Really?"

"That's the Thornton humor."

"I think it's cute. You haven't mentioned your dad. . . ."

He nodded and scratched at the side of his beard. Not a good sign.

"John, that was my dad's name, was a forest ranger specializing in search and rescue. Basically, he found lost people, gave them medical treatment if they needed it, and managed their evacuation from the area."

"Rescuing runs in the family." I was treading carefully, Jack was speaking of his dad in the past tense and his demeanor was almost fetal.

He nodded slowly and continued.

"On June 3, he headed out early in the morning. It was the first sunny day after a week of heavy rains. He knew that the campers and hikers would be anxious to get out there. I was told that he came into my room and kissed me before he left. I don't remember that, but when I woke up there was a wrapped package at the foot of my bed. I tore it open. I finally had my own Leatherman knife. It was my tenth birthday."

I shifted over to his towel and he wrapped his arms around me.

"To me it was a regular day. No, it was a special day. Mom had a birthday picnic for me at the creek; my friends and their moms came. While they were grilling burgers and dogs and drinking whiskey sours, we were putting my new knife to work cutting up worms and tadpoles to use for handline fishing. Even Jill was in on it."

He paused for a bit and looked back and forth over the ocean as if he was searching for the next part of the story in the waves.

"My best friend Mitch had just pulled in a catfish. They were pretty small in the creek and terrible eating. We had decided to cut it up and feed it back to the fish. Actually the second part was an afterthought, we just wanted to cut up something."

He smiled, remembering.

"I heard my mother call my name and looked up the bank at her. She was standing straight, tall but shaking and she'd gone as white as new snow. I had no idea what was going on, but I felt my shoulders drop with a heavy weight and I turned cold and started to shiver. When I climbed up to the flat land, I saw two forest rangers had joined her, but neither one was my dad. They had concerned looks on their faces and held their heads low. Some of my mom's friends were crying. At that point I mentally shut down."

For once I kept quiet but shifted so that he could lay his head down on my lap. It was then that I noticed that the two dogs had joined us and were lying in the sand side by side, watching us protectively.

"I didn't utter another word for over six months. Mom took me to see a host of therapists and they said there was nothing wrong with me other than shock and deep despair. I needed time."

"I'm so sorry, honey. What happened?"

"A family of four had gone rafting, attracted by the swelled rapids. They had two kids under the age of sixteen. They either ignored or didn't see the signs warning that this part of the river was only for certified guides and experts. They've since restricted access even to get into that area of the forest."

He looked at the dogs looking at him.

"They capsized about a half mile down their point of entry. Luckily a copter running early morning patrol spotted them and checked to see where my dad was. He got the coordinates and drove over there.

The parents and one of the boys had made it to shore. The father was cut up from the rocks and looked like he had broken a leg from his efforts to try and rescue his other son. Dad radioed for help but knew he couldn't wait if he was to have any chance of saving the boy. He anchored some lines to a tree and waded in.

"Over the roar of the water, the family said they heard faint cries for help. They directed my dad to the area it was coming from. He held onto the line and drifted toward a rocky island in the middle of the river. There he found the boy shivering and clinging on for dear life to a jutting rock. His lips were blue and he wasn't responding to Dad's questions. Dad secured him to the rope and instructed his parents on the riverbank to pull their son in. They had to pull up and against the current.

"With a lot of effort they managed to get him to shore. Once the boy was untied, they tossed the rope back in and Dad grabbed it and started to pull himself in. Just then the rushing water loosened a large boulder, which came crashing down, taking Dad with it. The rope grew taut and then snapped. They found Dad's lifeless body in the calm pool of water at the end of the rapids."

We were both crying and hugging each other.

"From that point on, I was raised by a house full of women; my mother, her sister who never married, my sister, and my gran. I miss my dad every day, but I am grateful for the strong female influence I have in my life."

"And look who you gravitated to," I said, elbowing him in the ribs.

"So I did. I should just let you run things, like the women did when I was growing up."

"I'm sorry, what?"

"I should just let you—" he suddenly caught on. "You heard me."

We looked up to see Bardot racing along the shore with a long strand of seaweed in her mouth. It was airborne and the leaves were flapping like a semaphore. Clarence was following behind.

"I don't know what took you so long, your dog got it right away," I said.

We spent a magical afternoon together. I could see that Jack was both exhausted and relieved that he had shared his family tragedy with me. He seemed at peace.

Which is why I couldn't tell him what Sally and I had planned for later that evening.

Chapter 30

To get into Musso's backyard, we had to jump Marisol's fence. And there was no way in doing that without her involvement. Heck, she'd probably eavesdropped on our conversation anyway and knew exactly what we were up to.

When it was dark enough and while Musso was out delivering cars to another movie shoot, we headed over to Marisol's. She opened the door before we could knock. Sally and I had dressed in black for the occasion, which actually made us more conspicuous. If this had been New York where everyone dresses like mimes that would be different, but in LA black is only worn on a string bikini.

"You sure you want to do this?" Marisol asked as we followed her to the back of her property.

"I don't see how we have a choice, if we don't get evidence on Tala before they leave on Saturday, then she gets away with murder," I said. "Either way, you'll be rid of her as your neighbor."

That made Marisol's eyes light up.

"Hope the door doesn't hit her bony ass on the way out," she said.

The fence was over six feet high and even Sally, being as tall as she is, was going to have trouble scaling it without some help. I spotted a rusty wheelbarrow and dragged it over. It was full of leaves and stagnant water and I hoped that the rats had jumped ship when we arrived. I stepped up into it, drenching my feet in muddy sludge.

"I didn't know he had a pool."

"He never uses it," explained Marisol. "What are you doing up there?"

With that, she pushed on two of the slats and they pivoted up creating a nice entry into his yard.

"Fantastic," Sally exclaimed and crawled through.

"You couldn't have mentioned this earlier?"

"You didn't ask."

Why I oughta . . .

"If we get into any trouble, you call Augie and the cops, okay?"

Marisol nodded and I slipped through the fence.

It took a moment for our eyes to adjust to the dark. Musso characteristically had no outside lights on. The blinds were all drawn on the windows facing the back, which meant that if there was anyone home, they would see us before we saw them. I was starting to think that we should have planned this better.

"Come on, it looks like that window is open a

bit, could be our way in," Sally whispered. "All you need to do is identify the shoes she kicked you with, take a photo, and we're the hell out of here."

In hindsight, we had no reason to assume that Tala had gone with Musso; it was clear that she wanted to distance herself from his illegal doings so she could cleanly blackmail him. I suppose we were just being naively optimistic, but heck, if you imagine the worst and it happens, then you'll have gone through it twice. . . .

"Your phone's on mute, right?"

I nodded.

Sally was about to do the same when hers chimed. She quickly silenced it.

"Phooey, that's an alert I set to remind Joe to take his pills," she explained.

We saw a light go on in the house.

"Time to boogie," I whispered.

"What a nice surprise, I wasn't expecting guests."

Tala caught us halfway between the house and the back fence and we froze. Not because she had such an intimidating presence, but because she had an impressive-looking gun pointed at us.

Tala held the gun to my head and pulled a zip tie from her jeans pocket. She ordered me to cinch Sally's hands behind her back. When she was secured, Tala turned to me to do the same to me. I had the presence of mind to make a fist so that the restraints would be looser.

Her face was about a quarter inch from mine and she wore a sinister grin.

"You might want to think about trying a chemical peel," I suggested.

WHACK!

I saw a blur and then felt a painful sting and neck lash from her slap.

"Holy Easter bunnies."

For that she slapped Sally as well.

While she was looking away, I kicked her arm like a Rockette in the line, she yelped, and as she fell to her knees, the gun popped out of her hands and slid along the coping of the pool. It was slippery from the night mist and the gun dropped into the water.

Tala struggled to her feet and pulled out a handful of zip ties.

"Perfect, now I can add assault and battery to the charge," she sneered. "I'm going to tie you down to the chair and call the cops. Sit here, both of you, I've had enough of your snooping and prying," she said, pointing at a lounge chair.

"We thought we heard someone in your yard, we came to help," I tried.

"Save it for the confessional, Sister Halsey. You and that witch next door have been a thorn in my side for too long. And you, missy," she said, looking at Sally, "should have stayed home minding your own business. I caught you both breaking into my house; my boyfriend works at nights so I have a gun, just for protection. This time when I call the cops there will be no question, I'm pressing charges."

I saw a hand reach in and take the restraints from Tala.

"Don't move a muscle." Musso stepped forward out of the darkness and instructed us. "Go inside," he told Tala.

"But—"

"Go!"

This was really one of the few times that I had seen him up close. His jet-black pageboy length hair rested behind his ears. A high forehead swept into his aquiline nose and compressed lips, giving him a look of constant ennui. Still, this in itself did not make him look evil. From a distance you might mistake him for a dancer or a musician. But close up you notice his eyes, deep set with coal-black pupils surrounded by gold rings. Just like a hawk's. The complete image made me quake inside.

He looked at me for a prolonged period doing, I suspect, the same analysis of my features

"Nice to formally meet you, neighbor. We'll make sure to invite you to our next potluck. By the way, why don't you ever have any trash?"

This is what I do when I'm nervous.

He proceeded to secure us to each other and the chair before returning to the house.

"Who pissed in his Wheaties?" Sally asked. "I think we're in deep shit!"

"They can't kill us in the middle of Rose Avenue, Sally, they'd have to move us, and that would give us a chance to get away," I reassured her, but not with much conviction.

We could hear the arguing coming from the

house. Much as I tried to listen, it was too faint for me to make out what they were saying.

Suddenly I felt something wet on the palm of my hand behind my back. Was I bleeding? I gently turned my head, hoping that my movements would not draw the attention of Musso or Tala.

Bardot! And back in the bushes Marisol could barely be made out. She lifted her head and nodded toward the pool. What was she thinking? Surely they'd hear Bardot. I lightly elbowed Sally, hoping she would look behind her as well.

I saw Tala return, looking pissed and carrying a roll of duct tape. This could not be a good omen, although if they were afraid of us screaming, then our deaths weren't imminent.

Right?

"I have to pee," I tried to stand and announced to Tala. "You need to untie me so I can go to the bathroom." I was going on a hunch that I could talk Musso into letting us go.

"You're not going anywhere," she said, pulling off a strip of tape. "Thanks to you we've got to leave right now," she whispered, looking back to see if Musso was listening. "I had a mani pedi scheduled for tomorrow at The Regal!"

So that is what they were fighting about.

"Listen, I gotta go, let me into the house to use the bathroom," I said as loud as I could.

She tore off a strip and fiercely wrapped the tape around my head and mouth. Thank God I'd left the house with a ponytail or she'd have to pay for extensions until my hair grew back.

"It is very dangerous and a terrible strain if you don't let her relieve a full bladder. She could suffer an infection, you need to let her evacuate," Sally said.

Well, that confused the hell out of her, she wasn't sure if I had pee or find a panic room. She got another piece of tape ready.

"You keep your mouth shut," she yelled in a whisper, exasperated. In her anger and with the dark she had managed to stick the tape to itself, and had to work to peel off another piece.

She uttered a long string of words in Ukrainian that I would love to have had translated.

When she finally had a strip ready, she yanked Sally's head back.

"Please," Sally said softly. "I won't say anything more, and if you restrict my airways you may trigger my COPD, and unless you have a respirator standing by that you are trained to use, you will have quite a mess on your hands. And you do not want to hear one of my asthma attacks. The walls rattle, it's deafening."

She heard a tap on the sliding glass door and saw Musso wave her in. Before she walked away, she grabbed Sally by the throat.

"One sound and I snap your neck."

She was feisty, I'll give her that.

At the back of my hand, I felt what I now knew was a wet nose made damper by an ever-so-quiet dip down to the bottom of the pool. Bardot had retrieved the gun while Sally and I were arguing with Tala. I grabbed the heavy metal instrument and waved Bardot away with my fingers. I heard Marisol faintly call her.

I had never held a gun before, let alone behind my back in the dark. I was not even sure which way was up, and couldn't count on Bardot having passed it off to me in the right position. I carefully juggled it around, praying that I didn't drop it in the process. Faintly in the distance, I could also hear the sounds of police sirens.

God bless Marisol.

In seconds they would hear them too, and who knows what that crazy bitch might do before they bug out?

I visualized what I wanted to do. I couldn't even whisper anything to Sally, restricted by the NASA approved adherent qualities of the tape I now sported. I turned my head slowly and slightly, just enough so she could see my eyes. I blinked three times and gave her a slight nod. God knows if she understood what I meant.

Having now heard the approaching cop cars, Tala came out one last time intending to tape Sally's mouth.

"I'm hoping that this will buy us just a few more minutes to get away cleanly," Tala said. "One false move from either of you and it will be your last."

She backed that statement up by showing us another gun, this one smaller, her purse gun I'm guessing.

Do I see a Hello Kitty graphic on its handle?

I looked at Sally and gave her the three blinks and leaned over toward her. She leaned to her left as well, giving me room to lie prone on my side and point the gun in my tied hands in the general direction of the house. I squeezed what I hoped was the trigger. It jolted my body so violently that we both fell backward as the chair tipped.

Who knows where the shot went, I only hoped that it was enough to convince Tala not to bother with us.

At this point dogs were barking, lights were going on all over the street, and people were screaming. Tala had dropped the tape and was pointing the gun at us.

"Leave them, you idiot! We've got to go," Musso said from the back porch door. "Now!"

I saw him disappear and heard the deep motor of a Mercedes start up.

"Just go and leave us," Sally shouted. "Otherwise you won't get very far!"

This infuriated Tala so much that she leveled the gun at Sally and shot. The small gun made more of a champagne cork pop noise than a bang.

"Mmmmmmmmmm," I screamed through my muzzle.

The last thing I remember hearing were the sirens approaching Rose Avenue and a foot closing in on my face.

Chapter 31

I watched Jack's face cringe. Two hospitals in as many weeks, these places always made him queasy. He'd been in too many—first to visit the kid his dad had saved and then for his own problems. And now I was the cause of his recent return to the land of the sick.

St. John's in Santa Monica is a huge facility, which gave him some distance from the sick, but one of the first things we heard walking in was a "code blue" call over the hospital's speakers. He started to turn and leave.

"I can go see her on my own, Jack, why don't you wait for me in the garden," I said, seeing his obvious distress.

He did a kind of Zen breathing exercise and said, "I'm fine and I want to see Sally."

The good news was that orthopedics shared the same floor as labor and delivery, so once we arrived, we saw more happy people than otherwise. We checked in at the nurses' station and although it was an hour before visitors were allowed, Jack charmed our way into Sally's room.

Her right shoulder was heavily bandaged and she looked pale and in pain. But she brightened somewhat when she saw us.

"You two are a sight for sore eyes," she said, trying to smile.

Jack gave her a kiss on the cheek.

"How're you doing?" I asked, getting mad all over again at Tala.

I noticed that she looked sad; getting shot traumatizes even the most stoic.

"Well, unfortunately the bullet didn't cauterize the bleeding as it often does, so I needed immediate surgery and a transfusion. Then the ortho surgeon performed debridement and sutured up my wound. Because of the clavicle damage they had to go back in and do an ORIF. An internal clavicle fixation," she explained, seeing the confused and petrified look on Jack's face.

"I am so sorry I wasn't there to stop them," Jack apologized.

"How could you have known? We didn't tell anyone and we didn't really have a plan. That was our stupidity and our desperation."

She paused and took a sip of water, still very weak.

"This is all my fault, I should not have roped you into this, Sally. Besides when the cops arrived and saw that I was holding a gun, they pretty much called housekeeping at the California Women's Prison and told them to get my room ready."

"Now, worrying is about as useful as a doggie

door on a submarine, Halsey, we will all set them straight."

"And how about that sexy shiner?" Jack said. "Tala kicked Halsey after she shot you."

Sally winced and I struck a pouty pose.

"Well, that should prove that she was also the one on the roof of Chill Out. She's in custody, isn't she? And Musso?" Sally asked.

Jack started tugging on his beard.

"What?"

"They got away; by the time the cops sorted things out, their plane had taken off."

Jack continued to work on his beard.

"That's why we have extradition, she should be arrested and sent right back here!"

More tugging.

"Out with it, Jack!"

"Well, the only gun they found was in Halsey's hand, so they really don't have any evidence that it was Tala who pulled the trigger."

"See what I mean about being measured for an orange jumpsuit?"

"What about Tala's prints, they must have been found on the weapon? Even if it did end up in the pool."

"Not enough." Jack was sullen.

"Ooh, that makes me twelve kinds of angry."

Jack took a quick look out into the hallway.

"Listen," he lowered his voice. "The cops will be here to question you any minute now. We've got to convince them that you and Halsey did nothing wrong, and erase how bad this looks in their minds now. Tell the truth, of course, but it's important that you seem confident, forceful, and very credible. You up for that?"

"Hell yeah."

She realized that she didn't sound convincing.

Sally rang for the nurse.

"You need something?" Jack quickly asked, turning white.

Sally put her index finger to her lips.

"And Halsey, you need to say nothing, nothing!"

Yeah, good luck with that.

"You okay, Sally?" The nurse responded almost immediately over the speaker.

"I'm fine, Melissa. Listen, Dr. Redding okayed a B12, it would be great if I could get that shot now."

"Umm, I don't see it updated in your chart. . . ."

"Mel, you were there when he said it. I just need a little energy boost. We used to give each other B12 shots all the time when we worked together for Dr. Levin."

There was a pause.

"Gimme five."

Sally smiled and winked at us.

"So you are saying that you two broke into this guy Musso's backyard?"

Detective Marquez and Augie had crammed into her room, making it tight quarters with Jack and myself there and an orderly taking Sally's blood pressure.

There had been a big argument right from the start because they wanted to question Sally alone. Jack and Detective Marquez stood face-to-face, about an inch away from each other. I actually did keep my mouth shut. Finally Sally prevailed.

"Here's the deal, fellas. I didn't sleep well last night and I can see that my blood pressure is high."

The orderly looked at her confused and Sally gave him a slight headshake. He wrote in her chart and left.

"Jack and Halsey calm me down, we've known each other for years, we're practically related."

Jack started to look up and caught himself.

"So either they stay and I'll answer your questions, or you ask them to leave and I ask the nurse for a sedative. Either way is fine by me."

And so the interrogation began.

"What was the question again?"

"You were saying that you two broke into Musso's backyard."

"Very clever, Detective, but I am not going to let you put words in my mouth. I assure you, I can formulate a perfectly proper sentence on my own."

"So how did you end up in Musso's yard," he re-asked, swallowing a whole lot of frustration.

"We were in our neighbor Marisol's backyard, at the far end where she keeps her recycling. Did you know that recycling one aluminum can saves enough energy to run your television for three hours? I sense you're a *Duck Dynasty* fan?"

He ignored the question and stared at her. Augie stopped taking notes and joined in the staring contest.

Sally cleared her throat.

"We had Halsey's dog Bardot with us and while we were saving the planet, Bardot discovered a loose slat in the fence and slipped through into his yard. She must have seen a squirrel. Halsey and I quickly went after her."

"So you weren't spying on Musso and his girlfriend Tala?"

"Puh-lease," I said and got a death stare from Sally.

"Why on earth would we do that?"

Sally went on to recount the facts (pretty much) of what ensued.

"And that's how the cops found me, hands tied, hemorrhaging from my subscapularis where Tala shot me."

"Was anyone else there to witness this?"

"I was! And if you ever find him, Musso." I was about to lose it.

"Yes, we have your statement, Ms. Hall, and we are looking for Musso now, but it seems that he may have left on the plane with Tala under an alias."

"You shouldn't need to wait, this is as clear as day. That asstard bitch shot me and I want her put away for good!"

There's the Sally I love.

"Without more evidence we can't even begin applying for extradition," Augie said sheepishly. "Plus, it's clear that the gun in Halsey's hand was fired, forensics found GSR."

"And with no other witnesses, we are pretty much done," the detective added.

"Are you kidding me?" Jack was on his feet and in the detective's face. Both men on reflex reached for their holsters.

"Jack, calm down," Sally entreated. "You're going to raise your systolic."

Jack didn't move but his breathing was slowing down.

Sally closed her eyes and appeared to be dozing off. When she opened them suddenly, it was clear that she had thought of something.

"Now, you guys listen to me. I saw who shot me and it was Tala. The gun that Halsey had did go off, but that bullet went God knows where. Your people should be looking for it. Marisol may have seen where it went, I take it that you've talked to her?"

They looked confused and Augie hung down his head.

"Who the hell is driving this bus?" I yelled and Jack reeled me into him.

"NO? Marisol's the one who called the cops initially. She had to have given a statement to the first responders, and I'll bet she saw the whole thing." Sally gave me a calming look; I caught her drift and made a mental note to call Marisol.

"I can handle that part; as soon as we leave, I'll go speak with her," Augie said.

"You can't look at the police report? Jesus, one hand doesn't know what the other is doing."

Sally was visibly tired.

"Who's got the bullet they took out of me? Melissa, can you come in for a minute?" she asked after hitting the nurses' call button.

"I don't think we've logged it in, so it should still be here. It is SOP to keep everything as evidence. I'll be right in," Melissa said over the intercom.

"Hi, hon," Sally said when she walked in. "Do you think someone can track down the bullet they removed from me and give it to these fine officers of the law?"

"I'll call down for it."

I smiled at Sally.

"You're going to want to write this down. When you get the bullet, you are going to know if it could have been fired from the gun that has Halsey's prints on it. You're going to find that the bullet I was shot with is too small and had to have come from a different gun."

"That would still not be enough to bring Tala back, but we'll check on it."

"Of course you will. Now if you don't mind waiting outside for your evidence, I'm going to have my nap now," Sally said, dismissing them.

"It may not be enough for Tala, but it'll prove that I didn't shoot anybody." I gave them a steely stare.

Once the door closed behind them, Sally gave us a wink and a hug with her one good arm.

Chapter 32

"So the two of them have just disappeared?" Peggy asked, taking a healthy tug on her wine.

We'd pulled out all the stops for Christmas and were enjoying a Rosenblum Cellars Zinfandel California Désirée Chocolate Dessert Wine. This luscious liquid dessert is meant to be sipped, but try telling that to this crowd.

"They have a manifest from the airline that shows that Tala was onboard a flight from LAX to Honolulu, but nothing after that, and no records for Musso."

We were having the "Secret Santa" Wine Club and Aimee was hosting it. Several weeks prior we had each drawn names to let us know whom we'd be buying a Christmas gift for. It was supposed to be a surprise, but with this group that is nearly impossible. Cassie had consulted me on what to get for Sally, Peggy suddenly got up in one Wine Club and started measuring my torso, and Aimee had let everyone know that she didn't care; she was getting everyone a gift.

"It's really a damn shame," said Sally, pale and a bit fragile. "Even now that we know the bullet I was shot with came from a much smaller gun."

"Well at least it's over with, she sure as heck isn't going to come back here," Aimee said, laying out napkins printed with 'TIS THE SEASON TO DRINK WINE on them.

"It sounds to me like this was a love triangle gone terribly wrong," said Cassie.

"I wouldn't call this all tied up and wrapped with a Christmas bow just yet," Peggy said, looking concerned. "Why on God's green earth would they need to set my house on fire? I've hardly ever talked to them." She punctuated her statement by licking the peppermint frosting off a cupcake.

"People have killed for less," Cassie said.

Aimee walked in carrying a scrumptious-looking platter.

"There's another tray in the kitchen, can somebody grab it?"

Cassie zipped out, as best as she could while wearing green felt elf shoes with the toes curled up.

We had all dressed up for the occasion. Peggy was sporting a hand-knit sweater with a patchwork-quilted square sewn into the center. Quilting was Peggy's specialty and this one did not disappoint. Lest you think it was one of those Granny holiday jobs depicting "Twelve maids a-milking" in the style of Hummel figurines, let me clarify.

Peggy collected the most beautiful fabric swatches

going back sixty years. Damask with gold filaments, crisp linens, brocades, moiré silks, all in the most gorgeous colors and patterns. And she had a great eye for composition. When the event called for Peggy to set aside her fleece and bring out the good stuff, she brought it.

Sally stood tall and regal despite her bandaged shoulder in a Ralph Lauren sweater and pants. She looked like a guest at the Ahwahnee Lodge who had suffered a small skiing mishap.

Aimee had the day off and was finally able to exchange her Chill Out togs for something more festive. She'd chosen a mini dress in traditional red over which she wore a cropped black leather motorcycle jacket.

I'd had to change in the last minute as work was really heating up with the Coast Guard project. I chose brown leggings, ankle boots, and a vintage '50s oversized turquoise and tan sweater that I had gotten at a thrift shop in lower Manhattan. I was going for the '60s Mod look. And did I mention that it was sixty-eight degrees outside?

"Okay, for today's festivities we will be enjoying a sampling of Mexican street food," Aimee proudly announced, laying down a beautiful and intriguing tray of comestibles.

"How Christmassy," said Peggy, clapping her hands with delight. I suspect that I was the only one to pick up on the veiled sarcasm. But then, that's my forte.

"I'm going to need some descriptions on this, but it all looks fabulous," Sally said.

Okay, so it wasn't Swedish meatballs and spiced

nut cheese logs. My knowledge of Mexican food consisted of the guacamole and nachos I ate at one a.m. after a long night of clubs and bars, so I was excited.

"I think that's everything from the back. Yummy," Cassie said, making an entrance. Did I mention the elf shoes? How about the accompanying red and white bolero pants?

"It's called 'street food' because that is what you find when you visit the non-touristy towns, particularly in the Yucatán. Tom and I discovered it when we backpacked down the peninsula all the way to Belize. We carried an inflatable kayak the whole way but only used it once. We were too busy enjoying the open-sided palapas kitchens and the local culture."

Food and all sorts of cuisines were Aimee's métier. She really needs to leave the frozen yogurt gig behind. She could run almost any kind of great restaurant. She just needs a little encouragement and some self-esteem.

"So what have we got?" Sally asked, carefully perusing the array as if she were surveying a mountain panorama for a section to paint.

"These are mini chipotle shrimp tostadas. We've got jicama and mango salsa. That goes with these homemade plantain chips. There are two kinds of guac, small chorizo and apricot tamales, and Cassie has a bunch of sauces and veggies and chips on that tray."

Spontaneously we all stood up and applauded.

Marisol, who had just walked in, thought that she was the one getting such a warm reception.

"And for our imbibing pleasure," I added, having been told in advance about the menu, "I'll be serving a zesty, crisp and bright Albariño from Spain. It should be perfect for this repast as it is ice cold, has notes of grapefruit and pineapple, and will calm the sting from even the spiciest of peppers."

"Damn cops must be really anal retentive," Marisol said, dropping onto the sofa, "after I explained everything to Augie they sent over another officer to write it all down. What kind of food is this?" Marisol asked, trying to disguise her mouth watering.

"How nice of you to join us, Marisol. However did you know that we were having a little gathering?" I asked and got a squinted eye response.

"So now, do they have enough to put Tala away for good?" Cassie asked.

"They think so," Marisol replied, "they just need to get the sign off from the DA."

"That makes me happier than a turtle on an escalator," Sally exclaimed.

"I propose a toast, to getting back to normal and to saying 'sayonara' to the murderer of Rose Avenue." Cassie took off her elf ears and placed them over her heart.

I wondered why I didn't feel better about this and then noticed that Peggy and Marisol were also not displaying exuberance.

"Who wants another glass of wine?" Aimee said to the group.

Hands went up, and Cassie waved with aplomb, as if only one person could be chosen for this fantastic elixir.

* * *

It was well after dark before the holiday Wine Club broke up. Marisol had left before me, saying something about an early dinner with Augie, which of course, got my curiosity up.

As I was passing the ugly, rotting fence of Musso's house, I felt something grab my arm and then a hand go over my mouth.

Not again. Really?

I was dragged up the driveway from behind and lifted into the house. Once the door shut, I was released.

"I hope I didn't hurt you," said a soothing male voice. "Sorry, I don't want to turn the lights on but this may help."

A soft glow emanated from a cell phone and when my eyes adjusted, I recognized Musso. I gasped and tried to recoil toward the door.

"Calm down, Halsey, I mean you no harm," he said, raising his palms up to show he was sincere.

"Why are you still here?" I asked.

"I want to come clean and explain. I think that Tala killed Rosa; I'm the one that sent in the video."

The cell phone light went off, sending us back into blackness. For a second nothing happened and then I heard and smelled a match being struck. Then it touched the wick of a candle and we were bathed in warm, flickering low light. He brushed his long straight hair back and I saw something in his face that I had never seen before. Emotion. It really was a nice face.

"I've seen the video, and even enhanced, it is

hard to make out anything more than the person in it is a woman, what makes you think that it was Tala?"

"She wasn't at home when it was shot but all the cars were still here. And she knew about me and Rosa." He dropped his head in silence.

"Maybe she went for a walk; where is she now?" I asked, slowly looking around and fearing the worst.

"I don't know really. After she shot your friend, I made a deal with her that I would give her enough money to go wherever she wanted, as long as I never saw her again. How is your friend, I heard that she was shot. I didn't know that Tala had her own gun."

"She'll be fine but it'll be a long recovery. Why, what, you seem so much better than her?"

He smiled sheepishly.

"We met at a car show, she was a model. I was swept away for an instant and when I woke up, she was living with me and demanding all sorts of things. I just wanted peace, so when a friend told me about a way to use cars to make some quick money on the side, I took it. I know I shouldn't have, but I couldn't just throw her out on the street. I hoped that after a bit she would just tire of me and move on."

"I take it she didn't."

"Worse, she had snooped enough to know I was into something illegal and she held that over my head. Cost me everything I had."

"So her visa expiring was a gift from the heavens?"

"I had to tell her that I'd go with her, we'd take a long vacation and then decide where to live. Even though I knew that this was my one and only chance to escape her. I will never forget Rosa, and I will never forgive Tala if she killed her. But at least I can turn myself in, set the record straight about everything and go from there."

I nodded. He suddenly looked like a scared little boy sitting cross-legged on the rug.

"I am so sorry that you have had to keep proving your innocence to the cops about the murder. I can't tell you how often I wanted to tell you the truth, but Tala had me on a very short leash."

I wondered if the time I caught him spying on me at my office window was one of those occasions.

"Let me call Augie and have him meet you, he'll be the most understanding. And if you can testify to Rosa's murderer and who actually shot Sally, that should go a long way to getting some leniency."

"Grazie," he said, placing his hands together in prayer.

Is this really over? Can I breathe again?

Chapter 33

It was Burger & Chimay night at the Carbon Beach Club, the delectable terrace restaurant that hangs over the sand of the Malibu Beach Inn. The heat lamps and the mild temperature made it a perfect spot to watch the December sunset.

Both of us were sad that we weren't going home for Christmas, but it just wasn't in the cards this year. Jack and I agreed that we would celebrate the holidays by kicking back and treating ourselves to some really nice meals. This was the first one.

Served on a wooden plank, my mouthwatering gourmet burger was held together by an impressive steak knife speared through the middle. I'd lost about nine pounds from the ordeal of the past few weeks, so I happily ordered mine with bleu cheese, bacon, and extra avocado. I'm not a big beer drinker, but Chimay is an authentic Trappist dark ale brewed by monks who have renounced all the pleasures of normal life to stay in an abbey and live off the land. Slowly poured into an icy stemmed snifter, this copper-colored elixir with a creamy head and fruity apricot aroma had me at "bonjour."

"So—"

"Don't talk, just eat."

My eyes were closed so that I could properly absorb the heavenly combination of fat, starch, red meat, alcohol, and salt air. And I certainly didn't want the soothing sound of breaking waves muffled by idle chitchat. I could sense that Jack was watching me but I didn't give him the benefit of a look. After about five minutes, I opened my eyes and the table for discussion.

"You know you were humming while you were chewing, right?"

"I was not!"

"You certainly were," Jack said, laughing. "And that shiner becomes you, by the way."

"I'm not admitting to anything but this really is perfect, isn't it?"

"Yes. I wasn't sure for a while that we would ever have this."

"Jack, you know that I come off as an easygoing person, but when I get pushed too far look out."

"I do now."

Jack's cell phone went off.

"Excuse me a minute," he said after seeing who the caller was. He walked down the short flight of stairs to the beach.

"Oh crap," I whispered to myself, thinking it was probably the ex-girlfriend again. I wasn't worried about the possibility of them getting back together, our relationship was past that. But Jack has a big problem saying "no," and she could be calling to have him come by and hang a picture on the wall for all I knew. He returned rather quickly, so maybe he'd gotten better at "no."

"I don't like that look on your face," I said, seeing his hard expression.

"That was CARA. I'm so sorry but I've got to go," he said, handing me a bunch of cash. "I need to take the truck, I've got Clarence in the back. Can you have them call you a cab to take you home?"

"Sure, what's happened?"

"They're putting the sting together at the Marina, the DEA needs everyone there now for a briefing. We'll use dogs to track and trap the dealers."

He was already heading out when he turned back.

"Listen," he said, kissing me. "Why don't you go and stay with one of the girls until I can get back? Even going to Marisol's would be safer than being home alone, just until we are sure that this has all blown over."

"I'll be fine," I protested. "Tala, who we now know is the murderer, has left the country and you'll be running down Ray and his people."

"Okay. Also, I spoke to Ali and he agreed to talk to the DEA and make a deal to turn evidence. That should give us a time and a place so we can tie everything up."

"Love you," I said but he was already out of earshot.

* * *

I'd never actually been inside Marisol's house; my experience was limited to what I could see from her doorstep and the time she quickly ushered Sally and me through to the backyard. Something just didn't sit right with me when I got home, so I'd figured Marisol's wacky mind would be a welcome distraction.

Bardot sure knew her way around the house. She was more than comfortable hopping up on Marisol's king-size bed.

"Bardot, get down," I shouted.

"It's okay."

"No it's not. Bardot, you are a guest in this house, where are your manners?"

I suspect that she understood everything we said, which is why she remained standing on the bed with a big smile and lots of tail wags. She loved that Marisol was giving her a free pass.

"Jack called me a few minutes before I came over, he said he's going to be a while. We'll just stay for a bit and then we'll go home. Bardot and I will be fine."

"You don't look 100 percent sure; if it would make you feel better, you can sleep in one of the girls' old rooms."

I'd met a couple of her daughters when they visited for Thanksgiving; they were sweet and fully aware that their mom is a professional snoop.

"If she's bothering you just let me know. I'll tell Ms. Nosy Pants to back off. But just remember, she's got your back, girl," the oldest daughter Martha had told me.

Boy did I know that now. Marisol had gone from

being a thorn in my side to a jewel in my crown. We walked down a hallway lined with photos to the kitchen. I couldn't help but stop to take in a wedding photo. Every bride should be beautiful on her wedding day and Marisol was no exception. And her groom looked handsome and proud, almost regal. We'd never talked about him, so I pulled myself away and followed her into the other room.

"I'm making tea," she said as I sat at the family kitchen table.

Bardot leapt up onto a barstool at the counter. I swear she had springs for legs.

"My family came to America in 1940. I was ten," Marisol began.

"You don't have to—"

"Javier's family, same thing," she continued, ignoring me. "We'd grown up on the same street in Mexico."

The characteristic twinkle had gone out of her eyes.

"We did two big things when we turned eighteen. We became American citizens and we got married."

"I love the wedding photo, such a beautiful couple."

"In 1951 Javier was sent to Korea. He was so proud to be fighting for America, he wore that damn uniform even before he needed to."

"Had you started a family by then?"

"We had a one-year-old and twin baby girls."

We moved to the living room to drink our tea.

The TV, which was constantly on, had the sound muted.

"He got shot one week before he was coming home."

I gasped.

"He had a bullet in his spine and them doctors said it was too dangerous to operate. He came home in a goddamn wheelchair."

"Marisol, I'm so sorry."

"They said he was an American hero, but that didn't buy us shit once he was discharged."

"Didn't the service pay a pension or something?"

"Barely," she said with a dry laugh. "But he couldn't work, he couldn't play with his girls, we couldn't—"

She was tearing up and I thought I was going to lose it.

"One day he said he was going to lunch with a friend who came by and picked him up. Another guy back from Korea. I'd never seen him or heard about him before. When they drove off, I had one of them bad feelings."

On the television was some kind of game show. Two people in arm and kneepads were fighting each other atop a slippery platform with giant Q-Tips. I tried my best to block that out.

"He never came back."

She finally took a sip of her tea, relieved to have told me her story. She really did think of me as another daughter.

I moved onto the sofa and held her in my arms. Even Bardot recognized the sadness of the situation and gently licked her hand. My attention was drawn to the TV as a box with a black-and-white picture appeared in the top right corner of the screen.

"Ah-ha!" she said, jumping up and scaring me.

"*What?*"

"Shhh, somebody's at Musso's house."

I looked at the screen and sure enough we were watching someone enter the house.

"Why you little sneaker!"

"I didn't do this, my godson did. He just wants me to be safe. Now, where's that damn remote?"

"You know how to work all this stuff?" She seemed to be more of an abacus and cave drawing gal.

"I'm still learning. Alex, that's my godson, is teaching me. Don't tell Augie, I have a feeling we shouldn't have been in Musso's house putting up cameras."

Ya think?

She located a small device and pointed and clicked it at the television. The whole picture changed to the interior of the house.

"You've had the whole house wired?"

I made a mental note to check my house inside and out for cameras.

"Just recently. We thought that the house was empty, this was just in case someone came back." She was grinning. It was hysterical to see this little old lady in a housedress running such an intricate espionage mission.

I looked closely at the screen. A light was turned on in the living room.

"That's Musso," I said.

"Someone else is coming through the door!" I swear that was a squeal.

My stomach sank and I felt my heart go into overdrive. Please let it not be Tala.

"That's Augie, I wonder what he's doing in there?" Marisol asked.

I let out a deep breath and sat her down to explain. When I'd finished it was Marisol's turn to tell me her thoughts. She admitted to hating Tala with a passion, she'd be happy if she stayed gone or was hauled off to prison somewhere.

"But? I sense a 'but.' "

"But I don't think that she could have killed Rosa," Marisol said sheepishly, looking down at her shoes.

"Why, what makes you so sure?"

"Well, you know how I like to keep any eye out, just in case anything happens on Rose Avenue?"

"I know that you have eyes like a hawk, both in front and in back of your head which you use to spy on us. I'm pretty sure that you have the whole street bugged for sound and visuals. And I suspect that somewhere under your house there is a safe room filled with computers operated by the women of the Bletchley Circle."

She looked at me smug and slightly confused.

"*Well?*" I asked, getting frustrated.

"Well, that day I saw Tala quietly shut the front door to her house and walk up and wait in front of your house. Then a car pulled up and she got in. There was a guy driving."

"So? She could still have come back and killed

Rosa, and maybe this guy helped her. Maybe he was her new mark in case Musso didn't work out?"

"Not possible because I followed them in my car. They drove up to the Palisades to a house. When they got out they were all kissing and flirting on their way inside. Made me sick. They played 'hide the salami' for almost two hours."

Now I felt sick on so many levels.

"Crap," I said after I'd sufficiently recovered. "Well, we know it wasn't Musso, so I guess that Rosa's brother Ray must have done it. So sad."

We both knew that we were close to solving this, and that hopefully Jack and the DEA are right now catching the killer. We agreed to call Augie together in the morning.

This day had been exhausting and I couldn't wait to crawl into bed, curl up with a dog, and slip into blissful slumber land. When we got inside, I didn't even bother to turn on the light.

Bardot was uncharacteristically silent, sniffing softly into the air and creeping low along the floor. When she got to the hallway, I could just make out that she turned left into the den rather than right toward my room.

I heard a growl and then the loud, reverberating bang of a door slamming. Bardot then growled and barked like a rabid bear and I figured that she was behind the door in the den.

What or who had slammed the door?

"This is the last time that you mess with my business, New York. You should never have come here."

I saw a woman's hand in my face, and more importantly, a knife at my throat.

"You are going to be my insurance ticket out of here, missy. You owe me for ruining my nice little business, I can't go anywhere without the cops on my heels."

A second hand came around and placed a cloth over my nose. As I breathed in I felt my knees give way. Just before I landed I saw her familiar red shoes.

Chapter 34

I felt a chill and then a piercing headache. It was pitch black and my arms ached from being pressed under my body. I tried to sit up and hit my head on something above me. It was enough to make me black out for another minute or two. When I woke, I had that horrible numbing feeling from lack of circulation and tried arching my back and flexing my hands to get the blood flowing. That was when I realized that my hands were tied. All this started to knock something loose in my woozy mind, but I couldn't quite get there.

I could hear talking, although it was faint. I tried to call for help and discovered that my mouth was taped. I quickly stopped as it dawned on me that the voices I heard might be coming from the people that put me in this condition.

"We're on our way, baby," I heard a male voice say.

"More than you know, honey," a woman answered.

"Woohooooo!"

That didn't sound good. I rolled over on one shoulder to give my back a break and tried to think back to the last thing I could remember. I was drawing a total blank. Instead, I decided to try and figure out where I was and how I could get out of this tight, dark space.

The good news was that my head was starting to clear. The bad news was that this meant that I was far more aware of what a lousy situation I was in.

I was still very disoriented, but I got the sense that this thing I was in was outside. I was pretty sure that I heard raindrops pinging off metal. Since I couldn't use my hands to explore my space, I kicked off my shoes and figured I'd try the *My Left Foot* approach.

The floor and top were soft, like they were carpeted. On one side I felt something uneven with holes in it. I was able to grab a piece with my toe and pull. It had some give and stretching ability. I knew this was a clue, but I couldn't sit up or move enough to try and get a look at it. Instead, I closed my eyes and tried to picture what I was feeling. Just then I felt a jerk from below that bounced me off the bottom and back down.

I'm in something that is moving. That thing on the side was an expandable pocket to store things. I was riding in the trunk of a car!

But whose? And where was I going?

I tried to reposition my body to get more comfortable and felt something fall out of my pocket. Thankfully my hands were tied in front, so if I squirmed and crunched just right, I should be able to reach it.

Success! I was wearing sweats that had deep floppy pockets and whoever grabbed me must have missed my cell phone in one of them. I raised it up to my face and noticed that my earbuds were still attached to it. I struggled to put on the headphones and was about to dial 9-1-1 when it occurred to me that I don't know where I am or whom I'm with.

And then I had an idea. In the middle of all the police investigations into my comings and goings, I had figured that I'd try and stay a step ahead, so I downloaded a fully robust police and other law enforcement scanner app. It was so fine-tuned that I was able to zero in on a specific area and choose which service I wanted to monitor. I chose the Beach Police and Marina del Rey, hoping to hear about Jack and his crew. I listened noiselessly through the earbuds.

I waited through reports of the smell of gas leaking at the Marina boat filling station and a possible stolen beach cruiser that the cops were pursuing.

Seaplane N9063M approaching south jetty 100 meters from breakwater, this is pilot Jack Thornton. ETA 2002.

Bingo! Hearing his voice made me feel much safer in spite of my current predicament.

Roger N9063M, are you carrying any passengers?

Unfortunately more than I'd planned, three adult fe-
males and a canine that I am working with in search
and rescue. Issue a BOLO for a fourth female arriving
by car, will be asking about a possible kidnap victim
named Halsey.

Are all the women to be deployed in your mission,
N9063M?

Hell no! They are under strict instructions to remain
aboard the aircraft at all costs. Just the canine and my-
self will be in pursuit.

I could hear talking and boos in the background. And then I heard:

I'm coming with you, tell them! I'm the reason we're
doing this, if I hadn't called by the time you realized
Halsey was gone, she'd be halfway to Mexico!

That was Marisol, have fun trying to stop her
Jack.

The transmission ended, but I could only imagine how the conversation was continuing off the air-
waves. Jack had said he had three women aboard, I
know Marisol was one and guessed that the other
two were Peggy and Cassie. Aimee was probably
working.

And maybe Joe was driving Sally. With her shoulder, she would have trouble boarding a small
plane.

I listened longer and heard Jack in communica-

tion with the Coast Guard in the Marina attempt-
ing to explain the situation.

*I know exactly where they're going to be, Ali Baba, er,
our informant caved and came over to the good guys'
side. I'll read you coordinates.*

I heard Jack say. It was time for me to get out of
this car and into the Marina.

The buzzing sounds of driving and car horns
that I'd been hearing were now gone and replaced
with other ambient noises. It sounded like we were
driving over wood planks; I could hear a bell ringing in the distance, a repetitive crashing noise, and
the sound of the rain which had gotten heavier
and was now accompanied by gusting wind. I
smelled salty sea air.

All of those stimuli brought my brain back to re-
ality. The chloroform that I remembered being
used to knock me out was finally wearing off. When
the car came to a stop, I closed my eyes, afraid of
what was coming next. I heard a woman say, "I'll
get rid of the car and bring the cash, you go ahead
and look for them."

I know that voice.

I heard a chirp and then the trunk door rose
evenly on its hydraulics. I blinked several times to
get my eyes adjusted to the darkness.

"Good, you're awake. I was hoping that I wouldn't
have to carry you. You're my ticket out of here and
the fact that you're mobile makes it much easier."

I could see that we were on the Playa del Rey side of the jetty. I was close to the Marina!

She tied a rope around my waist and gave it about a five-foot lead, then tied the other end around herself and sliced off the extra length with her knife. When I saw a light blink twice just off shore, I knew that I was running out of options.

Chapter 35

"Inez, please, what about your kids? You said your mother is sick, who'll take care of them?" I asked in my best Catholic guilt voice.

"Hah! You believed that crap? Maybe I should take up acting, I had the whole street roped into my story and making donations to the cause."

That thought had dawned on me more than once but I'd pushed it back, ashamed. Now, I felt like an idiot and it was time to go on the offensive.

"But you couldn't sustain it, Inez, could you? Did Rosa catch you depositing drugs? Is that why you killed her?"

"What? I didn't kill her!"

"Yes, you did, you and Ray needed her gone so that you could move into her house and deal out of your own backyard. She wasn't budging, so you decided to take matters into your own hands. Is that another knife from the collection? Just like the one that you used to kill her?"

I knew that it was.

"And those red shoes, last time I saw them they were coming toward my head from the Chill Out's roof."

"The shoes were a gift from Marisol, one of the few donations I liked. I was up there refilling my drug stash. A shipment was late so Zeke had to go out on the street to buy it. We'd let go of our shop so he left it on the yogurt place's roof. We didn't think that anyone would go looking up there twice. But nosy you just couldn't resist."

"And this two-hundred-dollar knife you're holding, was that up on the roof too?"

"Hell no, I found a whole set of them in one of the trash bins on Rose."

"How convenient."

"Listen, Rosa was back on drugs, see, everything was just too much for her. That family got it bad. I'd tried to get Ray to help her, they were really close as kids, but he's just as bad, spends money the minute he gets it. Both their parents had been addicts, it was in their blood. The two of them were ruining my little business."

"What business?"

"The local dealership. I may as well tell you since we'll be in Mexico before you can talk to anyone. I have drugs brought up to me here from my cousin and his friends in Mexico. I pay them with the money I've collected from my customers and then deliver the drugs."

"How?"

"In recycling bottles, all over the neighborhood. They leave the cash in one bottle, I take it and re-fill it with the drugs." She smiled, proud of herself.

"We have that many druggies in Mar Vista?"

"I'm spread out over the Westside. In fact Ray was a customer, that's how I met him. He decided that he wanted in and introduced me to his guys who were great at getting new business."

"Hold on a minute, let me call *Forbes,* they'll want to do a cover story."

"Very funny. The boat's drifting in, as soon as it gets close enough, we're going to wade into it."

I watched the seaplane descend at exactly the place Jack had described. When it stopped skimming the water, I saw Jack drop a small anchor down to the bottom to hold it in place. The water in the marina channel was dead calm. He cut the engine and stood by the door with Bardot on her leash, ready to go. They both jumped down on the plane's pontoon and then ran up the jetty toward the shore.

I felt the tug at my waist as she made a move toward the water.

"Rosa tried everything, changing her will to use as an incentive for Ray to keep supplying her, threatening calling the cops, and just telling the whole neighborhood about us. She really didn't care what happened to her anymore, she'd given up."

"So sad," I said. "I wish she had told her neighbors, they could have helped, something you didn't do."

"You need to exchange those rose-colored glasses for ones with dark lenses and UV protection. The world you're seeing doesn't exist, missy."

"I still don't get why Rosa needed to be gotten rid of."

"You got a hearing problem? I told you I didn't kill her and Ray didn't neither. She got in some-one's way but it wasn't ours."

Despite the unfavorable conditions, a light went on in my head sending energy up and down my damp body.

"Do you remember which house had the bin with the knives in it?"

"The Tudor, and some knives are still there, I only took the one."

Of course.

"Inez, you've got to let me go, I know who killed Rosa."

"No can do, you see all these people swarming? We don't stand a chance of getting away without you."

"Then let me make a phone call, okay?"

She hesitated and weighed her options.

"Make it quick," she said and I reached in my pocket for my cell. It was already wet.

"Hello, Peggy? Listen to me very carefully."

"Okay, I've enjoyed our little chat and games, but fun is fun and now it's over. Get deeper into the water."

We waded in, and I saw that the drug boat had cut its motor and was drifting toward us. It was not easy to walk knee-deep in the water, a strong rip-tide was pulling us over to the jetty. Her cousin's vessel was having similar problems.

"We can't get any closer, Inez, or we won't be able to get out. You got to swim to us," her cousin yelled. "We've already dropped the shipment in the rocks for Ray. Just come closer and toss us the money and we'll disappear."

"We're coming with you. Toss me a rope, we can't keep our balance in this current," Inez called back.

I could hear commands being shouted and saw a spotlight from a Coast Guard boat hanging just outside the breakwater illuminating the jetty. I watched Ray being cuffed and saw that Zeke had also been apprehended.

A spotlight swung over to the boat and us.

"You in the boat, drop anchor, we've got you covered," a voice broadcast from the Coast Guard boat.

"Cut the girl loose, it's too hard to pull you both in the boat," her cousin yelled.

"She's the only way we'll get out of here," Inez said.

The Coast Guard was getting closer.

Inez held the knife up in the air so that everyone could see it. She then grabbed me from behind and held it to my throat.

"Halsey!" I heard Jack call and saw Bardot and him at the base of the jetty where it met the water. Bardot was trying to jump in and he was holding her back.

"Uno, dos, tres," shouted her cousin while engaging the motor.

The boat spun around and the motor just barely missed chopping our heads off. One of the crewmen grabbed a gaff and caught part of the floating rope that was tying us together. The others quickly grabbed onto it and yanked us up onto the boat.

"We'll never be able to outrun the Coast Guard," her cousin said. "Our best chance is to slip back into the marina channel and try and hide around one of the docks. Then if we have to jump ship we'll be close enough to land to escape."

That all sounded good unless you had a sharp blade against your throat.

"Whatever you need to do, do it fast. I'm freezing," Inez screamed back.

When we were rounding the tip of the jetty, two things happened: I saw Bardot go airborne and land onto the deck of the boat. She didn't skip a beat and tore into Inez, forcing her to drop the knife. And I heard a splash and saw Jack swimming toward us.

A Coast Guard vessel appeared and blocked the boat from exiting the marina. It had the momentum and would clearly crush our fishing boat. I struggled furiously with the rope that was tying my hands together so I at least had a chance of swimming to safety.

One of the Mexican crewmen abandoned ship. Inez's cousin turned the rudder as hard as he could, sending us straight for the rocks of the jetty. I felt the boat dip down heavily on the portside, sending me down to the floor. Sliding on the sandpaper-like surface of the deck was enough to fray the rope around my wrists. I quickly got free and dispensed of the one around my waist as well.

Then I saw the reason our boat had almost capsized. Jack had pulled himself up over the gunwale and had overpowered Inez's cousin. The last of the crewmembers jumped off but were picked up moments later by the cops.

That left Inez. I looked over and saw that she was being pinned to the floor by Bardot. I couldn't help myself. I went over and did the knockout count. While down I saw Jack's big shoe step on the rope around her waist.

"Take it all in, Inez, and enjoy because you will be spending a long time in prison," he said.

He then pulled me up and kissed me. Long. In the distance I heard applause and saw Peggy, Aimee, Marisol, and Sally clapping and waving from the jetty.

I fought to push him away and when I did his whole face dropped.

"Jack, Inez didn't kill Rosa, she's a drug dealer but that's it."

"What?"

"We've got to get back to Rose Avenue," I yelled to all of them. "I'll explain on the way," I said to Jack.

"Wow, you're sure about this?" Jack asked.

We were riding in the back of a cop car, having persuaded the driver at the marina that we had a murderer to catch. The girls were also en route in Joe and Sally's car.

"Absolutely, it all fits. She suddenly came into what she believed was a lot of money, her husband showering her with gifts. Not long into their marriage, she sees him spending time at Rosa's house talking to her. She pretends that she hasn't looked at the photos on his camera but acts very stoic when I show her one of Rosa in her bra. And she discovers that the money faucet is in danger of being turned off. And the icing on the cake is that she's left proof that the murder weapon is hers right out on the curb."

We crept onto Rose Avenue without sirens or lights, hoping not to announce our arrival. The car pulled up in front of Peggy's house and Jack, the cop, and Bardot went in. Peggy had told me where she hid the extra key. I stayed behind to retrieve the evidence.

I'd placed the knife set with its wooden block on the coffee table, and we were staring at it when Aimee, Sally and Joe, Marisol, and Peggy walked in. Two of the slots for larger knives were empty. I put the missing knife that we'd taken from Inez and bagged on the table next to the block. Augie was bringing the other one from Rosa's murder evidence collection.

"You sure they're home?" I asked Sally.

"I saw them both milling around a few minutes ago. Carl goes to bed early, maybe she has as well," Sally explained.

"Nonetheless, I think we should go over there; she could be halfway to Atlantis by the time Augie gets here," Peggy said.

"So she'd told you about her senior year college Greek adventure?" I asked. "She told me when we made our photo study of the Marina. I remember thinking to myself, 'who are you and what have you done with Cassie.' "

"She told us all, we were captivated when she first told us the story at Wine Club, as I'm sure you were," Sally said. "But then I had the wine store order a bottle of Gavalas for her birthday, it's from one of Santorini's best wineries. When I gave it to her, she didn't say a thing, she'd clearly never heard of it."

"But she talked about the great wineries on the island, how could she not have known it?" I think I know why. . . .

"Because she never went there. I did a little checking and it seems that she's said she did a lot of things that she really didn't do," Peggy said.

"We thought that she just craved the attention, you know how she likes to be in the spotlight," Aimee said to me.

"Well, this is probably the one occasion when she doesn't want to be the star."

Ironically it was at that moment that Cassie walked into Peggy's house.

"Good evening everybody," she slurred. "Van Cleef, Arpels, and myself thought we'd drop in."

The dogs were dressed in identical silk lounging robes and Cassie wore the kimono I'd seen on the mannequin in her living room.

"Have a seat, Cassie," Peggy said, getting up and locking the front door.

I saw Jack go in the other room presumably to tell Augie that we had Cassie with us.

"We've been wondering about a few things, Cassie, would you mind providing some clarity?" I said.

"Color, cut, carat, and clarity, the four important Cs of diamonds."

"She loco in the cabeza," Marisol whispered to me. That was the first time I'd heard her speak Spanish.

Sure, she'd had a few but something else was going on, maybe pills or some kind of meltdown.

"You want some water, Cassie?" I asked, motioning with my head to Aimee to get some.

"I want some wine!"

"Not tonight, honey, you're going to be asked a lot of questions later and you'll need to think straight," I cautioned.

"Should we get Carl?" Sally asked.

"Hah! Good luck finding him, I couldn't. He's cheating on me again!"

This was getting sloppy.

"This is the night he rehearses with the barbershop quartet, dear. I can see his car pulling in now," Joe said, opening a few slats of Peggy's shutters.

"Cassie, did you really think that Carl was having an affair with Rosa? You saw the photos of every house in the neighborhood and then the flyers," Sally said.

"Yeah well, by then it was too late. I thought that I'd landed in wonderland when I married Carl. I sure worked like hell to get there. But a year and a half later he's running around with the single woman across the street and suddenly I can't buy whatever I wanted. I knew Carl had money, I assumed that he was spending it on that bitch."

I winced at her words. Poor Rosa.

"So did you plan this, Cassie?" I asked.

"No, I went over to tell her to keep the hell away from my husband!" she shouted, scaring the two dogs in her lap.

"But then I saw these sweet, sweet, sweethearts, and I knew that they needed the love and attention only I could provide. She took someone I loved from me and I decided to take something she loved from her. Quid. Pro. QUO!"

Van Cleef and Arpels, or whatever they were called before, jumped off Cassie and ran and hid behind Bardot.

"Honey, have you taken your pills today?"

I gave Sally a questioning look.

"Bipolar."

"So is that when you killed her?" I asked. I had turned on the recorder on my cell and placed it beside her. She hadn't noticed.

"Well, what would you do? You know, that was one of the knives in the set that I'd never used."

"And the fire in Peggy's house?"

"That was me, she was starting to get suspicious of Inez and I wanted to push her further in that direction."

"The rats in my shop?" Aimee asked timidly.

"I figured that you'd pin that on Ray and Inez. I hated leaving a perfectly good bag of weed up there."

"Halloween night, my pool?" I asked.

"It was just fake blood, don't be such a wuss!"

We saw the lights from a couple of police cars as they approached.

"Cassie, I'm going to get Carl now, you just sit quietly and calm," Sally soothed.

"Yes, Daddy; bring my daddy."

"Can I have the Chihuahuas?" Marisol whispered to me.

Epilogue

The mood at Joe and Sally's Christmas party was nothing but festive.

We'd cried and talked out poor Cassie and her problems for hours and hours in the last two days. We'd circled around Carl, who was truly in shock. He decided to go to Arizona to be with his son, and planned to stay for a month. Time heals all wounds. And we'd been assured that Cassie would be getting the help that she needs.

It turned out that Cassie came from a long line of grifters; the gypsy life was in her blood. As was her inherited mental disease. When she met Carl, she tried to put that all behind her, he was the only one she'd married.

I'd had an inkling of something when I first met her. She tried so hard to be sweet and giving, but if that caused the spotlight to move off of her and onto you, she would quickly course correct. Some things I just couldn't explain to myself at the time. Her abrupt departure from Wine Club when Rosa's dogs were mentioned, her knife skills that she exhibited every time she brought food to our meetings.

She rarely let Carl out of her sight and controlled which of his belongings could be set in any room but his sealed off study. Yet with that amount of control, she claimed to not know what was on his camera, even though she was an expert at using it, and she pretended to be oblivious to any financial issues.

Finally, she was the only one who didn't get some kind of warning from the alleged murderer.

At the first Wine Club after her arrest, Peggy suggested after we'd consumed three bottles of a robust Shiraz from Beckman vineyards, that we each tell our favorite Cassie story.

Such a shame, there was so much to love about her.

I was standing near the bar, of course, talking to Joe and Tom when Aimee joined us with news.

"I just talked to Ali Baba, he's back home, he sounds really happy!" Aimee told us.

"Probably thanks to the whacky tabacky," Peggy said, joining us.

"Aw, he's a good guy, I'm so glad Jack was able to talk him into giving up Ray and Inez's big shipment," Sally said. "Joe would you get me one of those kebob thingies that are going around? Sauce on the side please!"

"What's the latest on Musso?" Aimee asked.

"I talked to him and then Augie yesterday. He's got to pay down his tax debt and do some community service, but since he helped with the video that we now know shows Cassie, that may be it," I said.

"Now he's got to heal his broken heart. I guess Rosa was already dipping back into drugs when he asked her to marry him, and she wouldn't even think of putting him through that," Aimee said.

"He's a good guy, and don't think that Tala is in the clear, I still have some friends in certain places," Peggy said, winking.

At the other end of the room, I spotted Marisol and two of her daughters. It was funny to see her acting kind of shy, I guess she is just most comfortable peering from behind drapes or spying with her network of planted nanny cams.

I heard the doorbell and saw Jack walk in. I had hoped that he'd had time to change from dog training; everyone had dressed up for the occasion.

He didn't disappoint.

He had on creamy chocolate cords, a cashmere Glen plaid cardigan over a white shirt, and a green striped bow tie. And dress shoes.

This I had never seen.

"Wow, if I beg you, will you dress up like this all the time?" I asked, kissing him.

"Kinda fun every once in a while. Dinner later? I've got a surprise place in mind."

"You always do."

We heard the clinking of a glass and Sally took the floor.

"Joe and I want to thank you all for coming and wish you the merriest of holidays. We are so blessed to have such lovely friends and we cherish you all. Cheers!"

We raised our glasses, drank, and were about to go back to our conversations when Peggy stepped up to the floor and made an even louder noise with her glass.

"There is one more bit of business to take care of. As many of you know, some of the ladies here partake in what we affectionately call the Rose Avenue Wine Club."

"Yeah." Aimee clapped.

"Well, today we want to welcome our newest member."

Peggy held up a silver miniature flask like the one I'd received upon joining. It was engraved with the words, ROSE AVENUE WINE CLUB.

"Marisol, please come up an accept your membership gift."

Now everyone applauded. I saw Marisol consider a quick dash for the door, but both her daughters grabbed her and escorted her up to receive her gift. She was beet red and my heart was bursting. I thought about how lucky I was to have her as a neighbor, one who saved my life, no less. Then I remembered that I still needed to sweep my house for bugs and hidden cameras that she'd probably planted.

"Gosh, look at all these empty bottles," Sally said, eyeing the counter of her bar.

"Don't worry, tomorrow's trash day," I said.

What the Rose Avenue
Wine Club Drank

2008 **"Quady North Steelhead Run Vineyard"** *Applegate Valley Viognier*

2010 **"Bodegas Montecillo Rioja Reserva"** *Tempranillo from Rioja, Spain*

2012 **"Vina Bujanda Crianza"** *Tempranillo from Rioja, Spain*
Emilio Lustau **"Solera Reserva los Arcos"** *Dry Amontillado Sherry*
Croft **"Ruby Port"** *Red Blend from Portugal*

2015 **"Miraval Rose"** *Rosé from Provence, France*

2014 **"Tiefenbrunner Pinot Bianco"** *Pinot Blanc from Trentino-Alto Adige, Italy*

2013 **"Valle Reale Trebbiano d'Abruzzo"** *from Trentino-Alto Adige, Italy*

2013 *Henry Fessy* **"Chateau des Labourons Fleurie"** *Gamay from Beaujolais, France*

2012 *Rosenblum Cellars Zinfandel California* **"Désirée Chocolate Dessert Wine"**

2010 **"Gavalas Xenoloo"** *Megalochori Santorini, Greece*

2009 *Hughes Cameron* **"Cabernet Sauvignon"** *Napa, Stag Leap District, California*

The Rose Avenue Wine Club
Glossary of Wine Terms

A

AERATION:
The process of letting a wine "breathe" in the open air, or swirling wine in a glass.
RAWC: "I'm not waiting, it'll swirl enough going down my throat."

AFTERTASTE:
The taste or flavors that linger in the mouth after the wine is tasted, spit or swallowed.
RAWC: "That's what *we* do, taste after taste after taste . . ."

ASTRINGENT:
Describes a rough, harsh, puckery feel in the mouth, usually from tannin or high acidity, that red wines (and a few whites) have.
RAWC: "Sounds like the Brie is overripe, just toss it and move on to the English cheddar."

B

BACKBONE: Used to denote those wines that are full-bodied, well-structured, and balanced by a desirable level of acidity.
RAWC: "What you need to live on Rose Avenue."

BIG: Describes wines with massive flavors that fill your tongue and mouth.

RAWC: "The contribution we make to recycling each week."

C

CHEWY TANNINS: Wine with this characteristic dries out the mouth interior so that you "chew" the tannins out of your mouth.
RAWC: "Sally's bowling name."

CRISP: Used to describe a simple white wine.
RAWC: "Better buy extra; these wines go down easy."

D

DECANTATION: Pouring of wine into a decanter to separate the sediment from the wine.
RAWC: "What's a little dirt among friends?"

DENSE: Bold red wines with a multitude of flavors and characteristics.
RAWC: "Time to break out the stinky cheeses."

E

EARTHY: Wine with aromas and flavor of earth, such as forest floor or mushrooms.
RAWC: "Manly."

F

FAT: A wine with massive taste that may overwhelm.
RAWC: "*Who?* Oh you mean the wine."

FLAMBOYANT: Wine with an abundance of fruit.
RAWC: "If you've got it, flaunt it."

FOOD FRIENDLY: Wine that tastes best when drunk with food.
RAWC: "This is why we've got two hands, right?"

H

HARD: Tannic tasting without charm or smoothness.
RAWC: "Keep it for another week, it will mellow with age."

HINT OF . . . : Often not so subtle flavor profile.
RAWC: "Sometimes you need to drink several glasses to find the hint."

L

LIVELY: Used to describe a young wine with fruity acidity.
RAWC: "Our discussions about murder and murderers."

LONG: Describes a quality wine with excellent flavors that linger in the mouth.
RAWC: "The length of Marisol's spying capabilities."

M

MELLOW: Wine properly aged to soften and smooth drinking.
RAWC: "Not in our lexicon!"

N

NOBLE: A clearly superior wine in all respects.
RAWC: "We like to pronounce it 'no bull' as in what's required at Wine Club."

O

OAKED: Wine flavors and aromas outside the grapes that are imparted by the oak wine barrels they are stored in.
RAWC: "Is that Eau de Oaked fragrance you're wearing?"

OPULENT: Wines that are rich, smooth, and bold.
RAWC: "I'd rather be rich, smooth, and bold than poor, crusty, and mealy mouthed."

P

PIQUANT: Pleasing fruit flavor and tangy acid balanced wine.
RAWC: "Piquant? Of course you can."

PLONK: An inexpensive bottle of wine.
RAWC: "The cheap stuff. Serve it last."

R

RICH: French term for a very sweet wine.
RAWC: "I hope somebody brought the dark chocolate."

S

SILKY: Refers to red wines that are creamy and velvety.

RAWC: "I could drink this all day." "You are."

SPLIT: A wine bottle that holds one-fourth of a typical bottle.
RAWC: "Want to split a couple of bottles of wine?"

T

TANNIC: Refers to red wines that haven't aged enough and are harsh tasting.
RAWC: "You know what would make this wine better? Fruit. Sangria time."

TART: Young wines that are overly acidic and tannic.
RAWC: "Makes your lips pucker, but not in a good way."

TASTING FLIGHT: A selection of wines presented for sampling only.
RAWC: "Where's he going with my wine? I wasn't finished."

U

UNCTUOUS: Wines layered with rich, lush, and soft fruity flavors.
RAWC: "I'm unctuous to open another bottle."

Acknowledgments

To my agent, Sharon Belcastro, and the exceedingly talented Ella Marie Shupe. Thank you for shepherding me to a path that welcomes humorous mystery. Thanks to John Scognamiglio and all the great people at Kensington Publishing. It has been a delight.

And to my wonderfully encouraging friends Diane, Grace, Mark, Joellen, Aimee, Dorine, Sue and Lee, Dana, Christina, Pat, Nancy, Linda, Ofelia, and Betty. I owe each of you a bottle of fine wine.

Oh and Bardot, there'll be an extra bone in your bowl tonight.

Please turn the page for an
exciting sneak peek of the next
Rose Avenue Wine Club mystery

**MURDER
MOST
FERMENTED**

Coming soon wherever
print and e-books are sold!

Chapter 1

"DIRT?"

I said to my yellow Lab, Bardot, while we were trudging up the hill.

"For my birthday they got me *dirt?*"

As the incline sharpened so did the weight of the wagon I was pulling behind me, loaded with shovels and claws and other garden accoutrements that had been included with this oh-so-thoughtful, gift.

Nothing about this early morning trip was pleasant until I had an idea. Slowly and without her noticing, I tied the end of Bardot's leash to the handle of the wagon. She couldn't have cared less because the promise of open space and critters filled her with excitement from her nose to her caudal vertebrae.

I prepared myself and took in some deep breaths from my diaphragm.

"SQUIRREL!" I yelled and then lowered myself

into the wagon like a Luge racer starting down the track.

We reached the top in no time but here was the problem, Bardot hadn't found the squirrel yet. Which meant that we kept on going. She veered right and ran to the only thing better than a squirrel, people. To her excitement, she'd found not just adults but a team of four- and five-year-old little leaguers. When she stopped to be adored, I had two choices: do nothing and be convicted of manslaughter, or do a self-imposed wipeout to stop the momentum of the wagon. I chose the latter and was dumped out onto the dirt road. A bright yellow kneeling pad with a smiling frog on it landed appropriately across my face. The group, assured that I was okay when I sat up, quickly went back to the Bardot lovefest.

Oh, she's working it all right.

This might be a good point to stop and bring you up to speed.

I am Halsey, which is actually a truncated moniker for Annie Elizabeth Hall, the name on my birth certificate. You can see why I needed a nickname shortly after being weaned. My parents were not playing some kind of cruel joke on me. They just weren't big Woody Allen fans. After that, they did a pretty good job of raising me.

I have my own company writing code and designing websites; a job that allowed me to pack up my toys and move to a Los Angeles beach community after my marriage and life in New York City went up in smoke. That was just over a year ago and boy, have things changed.

You've met Bardot, she's an American Field Lab versus an English Lab; she's smaller, much leaner, and built with a Ferrari engine. She is hardwired to run through caustically thorny brambles and crash into pond ice to retrieve whatever form of fowl you have shot out of the sky. Since I am not a hunter, and the only ice that can be found three miles from the beach is crushed in a margarita, she has developed other skills. The highlight? She can dive underwater. Deep underwater. Try twelve feet underwater. Which actually saved my life once. But that's a story for later.

Now to the "they," I refer to the ones who celebrated the anniversary of my birth with a gift of dirt. I am proud to be part of this coterie of oenophiles who call themselves the "Rose Avenue Wine Club," because well, we all live on Rose Avenue and we all enjoy a touch of the grape. Our members range in age from thirty-two to eighty-seven and are an all-female cast of characters that imbibe shamelessly and say whatever comes to mind. Everyone has a story and last year the group created a new one through crime and murder that now binds us together for life.

More on that later.

I'm not really being fair when I call my gift "dirt." I don't want to appear ungrateful, it really was very thoughtful on many levels and ties me more deeply to my new life in Mar Vista, California.

At the top and Eastside of Rose Avenue sits a hill that in the 1930s and '40s was home to truck farms, producing vegetables to take to market. A particularly rich area for agriculture, Mar Vista historically played host to fields and fields of lima beans giving rise to the title, "Lima Bean Belt of the Nation."

The open land is still preserved today despite continuous offers from drooling developers, and is home to a local little league and a community garden offering six acres of fifteen-by-fifteen-foot plots of incredibly rich soil that seems to defy even the least adept of horticulturists.

My gift is making more and more sense.

I am told that, like any apartment in New York that has running water, people wait for the owners of these plots to die in order to pounce on the coveted patches of soil. That makes my share, which was not the result of a recent death but the final settlement of a probate, all the more special.

When it was time for the young boys of summer to take to the field and when most of the gardeners had dispersed, I righted my wagon, gathered the last modicum of dignity I possessed and consulted my map for the plot's location. I had skinned knees and elbows making this thirty-something look more like an over-grown middle grader.

The shade provided welcome relief as I plopped down beside my garden to be. I was pleasantly surprised to find that the soil had been turned over; with the drought I had fully expected to see a dry crust from a long time of neglect. I wasn't planning to accomplish much today, this was basically a scouting mission to give me enough to do some substantive online research. You see my plan was to grow grapes.

"Someday this will all be 'Halsey Vineyards,' Bardot."

She looked around wondering if any of the words in that sentence were euphemisms for "critter." My chore for the day was to start to aerate the soil to get it ready to accept and nurture the vines. This wasn't going to happen overnight, but at least I'd feel like I'd accomplished *something*.

I chose the shovel with the more tapered head and went to work. The goal was to loosen as much of the old soil as possible. Grapevine root systems like to run deep. This got Bardot curious, she'd never seen me do this kind of activity before. With each toss of the dirt she peered into the hole, hoping for anything that moved.

Sure enough, after working a section for a bit, I hit something more than dirt. Something that made a clanging sound when the shovel made contact with it.

Great, I've probably hit a main pipe and killed the water for the entire hill.

I looked around to see if anyone could offer guidance, but I was alone. I dropped the shovel and bent down for a closer look. As I cleared a square of soil around the object, I was able to determine that it was a rusted metal box. With a little more digging and some help from Bardot, I managed to loosen it enough to get my fingers underneath and lift it to the surface. It had been painted red at one time and after tilting it toward and away from the sun I was able to make out writing that said LA UNION CIGARS.

Cool. I have just the spot for this antique in my office.

When I placed it in the wagon, I could feel something inside shifting. Once again I looked around, this time hoping that nobody was in viewing distance.

I used a small knife and delicately worked on the seal between the lid and the main box. It looked very old and may be worth something, so I didn't want to damage the box anymore if I could help it. Like wrestling with opening a pickle jar, I finally heard the sound of air escaping and the lid popped up.

Inside I saw a piece of blue velvet fabric cut to fit snugly in the box. I carefully lifted it and placed it on the wagon. Beneath was a yellowed folded document. It had printed type on it as well as pen and ink handwriting. It all looked very official. When I opened it, I saw the words "DEED" and below the name "Anderson Rose" and the date, "April 16, 1902."

I didn't want to risk exposing it to the elements, so I folded it back up and returned it to the box, facedown. On the back was written *Transfer of mineral rights.* I hadn't a clue what all this meant but my heart was racing. As I moved the box, I once again felt the weight of contents moving. It clearly wasn't coming from that light piece of paper. I noticed that the deed and the fabric only took up a small portion of the depth of the box, so there was something under the bottom piece of velvet. Carefully, I lifted the deed up, sandwiched between the two protective pieces of fabric. Underneath was what looked like a men's gold signet pinky ring and it bore a strange looking engraved crest and embellishment.

Cool.

When I looked up, I saw that Bardot was embracing her green paw and had been working feverishly on the far corner of the plot.

I need to nip this in the bud.

"Bardot, no more." She looked at me with a big grin on her muddy face, and promptly went back to digging. I figured "just this once" and secured all the contents of my find back into the cigar tin. I had a fun project, now dirt *is* good.

I heard Bardot give off a high-pitched whine and noted that her digging had stopped. She was crouching and backing away from the hole.

Then I spotted it, a still partially fleshy, liver-spotted hand that seemed to be reaching out from the grave.

Crap. Here we go again.

Connect with

Us

Visit us online at
KensingtonBooks.com
to read more from your favorite authors, see books
by series, view reading group guides, and more.

Join us on social media

for sneak peeks, chances to win books and prize packs,
and to share your thoughts with other readers.

facebook.com/kensingtonpublishing
twitter.com/kensingtonbooks

Tell us what you think!

To share your thoughts, submit a review,
or sign up for our eNewsletters, please visit:
KensingtonBooks.com/TellUs.